RESPECT

JOSEPH BENTIVEGNA

outskirts
press

To Eric Garner:

"Every time you see me, you want to mess with me. I'm tired of it. It stops today. Why would you...? Everyone standing here will tell you I didn't do nothing. I did not sell nothing. Because every time you see me, you want to harass me. You want to stop me selling cigarettes. I'm minding my business, officer, I'm minding my business. Please just leave me alone. I told you the last time, please just leave me alone."

"I can't breathe! I can't breathe! I can't breathe! I can't breathe! I can't breathe! I can't breathe! I can't breathe! I can't breathe! I can't breathe! I can't breathe! I can't breathe! I can't breathe!"

The officer, Daniel Panteleo, whose chokehold killed Mr. Garner was never indicted by either a grand jury or by the Obama administration. He remains on the New York City police force.

Acknowledgements

*Thank you to my wonderful agent,
Dr. Maxine Thompson. The comments of Mr. Ernest Pierson,
Attorney Anthony Bentivegna and Dr. Samuel Seltzer
were invaluable.*

CHAPTER 1

Cord Campbell glared at the radar gun protruding through the window of the police car. He instinctively slammed on the brakes. The domino effect of the other cars doing the same created a sea of red lights.

"Easy," Cord's father, Herman, said as his torso was propelled toward the glove compartment. "Lucky I'm wearing this seatbelt." He adjusted the seatbelt that had jerked him back into position in the passenger seat.

"Sorry, Dad. Speeding tickets on the Merritt Parkway are a main source of income for this state. I have to be careful."

"You're going at the same speed as the other cars." He did a sweep of the surrounding cars with his index finger.

"Yes, but I'm still ten miles per hour over the speed limit," Cord said. "If that cop decides to pull someone over to meet his quota, which one of us so-called speeders will he pick?"

Herman looked around again at all the vehicles he'd just pointed out. He laughed. "I taught you well, son. You have a point." It hadn't taken him long to figure out that all the other drivers, unlike him and his son, were of the Caucasian persuasion.

Cord looked in his rearview mirror and was relieved to see the police car remain stationary with no flashing blue and red lights. He turned his attention back to the road in front of him. Suddenly, a sea of red lights appeared again, warning him of the slowing traffic. He slammed his fist on the steering wheel. His left foot quickly shifted to the clutch as he down-shifted his Lexus IS250 into second gear. The police car was now a distant past, so why in the world was traffic slowing down again?

Herman shuffled in the front seat. The hip surgery had not worked as well as advertised. A two-month recovery his doctor had told him. But six months later, significant pain persisted, and he could barely climb stairs. After a month of pleading, Cord had finally convinced his parents to come to Connecticut and stay at his house until he had completely recovered.

"Calm down," Herman said, flinching and grabbing his hip.

"Sorry, Dad." Cord was genuinely apologetic, but still aggravated with the slow flow of traffic. "But look at this." He pointed straight ahead and then let his arm drop to his middle console like dead weight. "Construction! Really?" He shook his head. "This is why I never drive. These cops and construction guys drive me nuts."

The slowed traffic, which was just a few miles per hour from being at a standstill, was caused by the cars being forced into a single lane. But no one was near any of the orange cones or Jersey barriers that bottlenecked the narrow two-lane highway. The unionized construction workers, who were supposed to be adding to the scenery by planting trees, were sitting on the side of the road, probably laughing it up and watching real-time porn on their tablets. And this was what tax dollars at work looked like? It was a sight Cord could have done without.

The Hegamon corporate jet had just delivered his beloved parents to Westchester County Airport. Cord would have dispatched a limo to pick them up and deliver them to his Greenfield Hills estate where his wife of twenty-seven years, Clara, was preparing a feast; but his mother, Betsy, frowned upon such behavior. A son should pick up his parents at the airport, even if he was the chairman of one of the most successful hedge funds on the planet. And Cord agreed. After all, she had scrubbed the floors and cleaned the toilets of the landed gentry of Charleston to pay for his MIT education.

When he made his fortune, he bought his parents a Southern colonial with gabled roofs, a colonnade that rose to the second floor, and a long Magnolia tree-lined driveway. The house reminded him of the houses his mother had cleaned during his youth. He had no idea of the indignities she had suffered until he obtained his driver's license and would go to these houses to pick her up when she was finished working. The mere fact that some of these houses had statues lining the driveways of black figures holding lanterns, caricaturized by huge lips and obsequious smiles, should have been enough of a clue for what he was about to encounter.

He recalled knocking on one door where a rude lady answered. She smirked at him and said, "She'll be right out." She then slammed the door in his face. Even behind the closed door he heard the lady screeching at his mother. "You can't possibly think you're about to leave now. That toilet bowl is still filthy. What am I paying you for?"

The next words Cord heard made him want to go through that door.

"Get your lazy, fat, black butt out here and sweep the veranda again. You people have no sense of cleanliness."

Something inside Cord told him this woman's disrespectful display was on purpose. Her mission was not only to humiliate his mother in front of her boy, but to also humiliate Cord. Black folks had to be kept in their place . . . right?

Had Cord not been raised better, he most certainly would have gone through that door and laid hands on that woman . . . and not in a spiritual manner, but in a manner in which a teenage boy didn't know any better. But he'd known better. So he briskly wiped the tears of anger from his eyes and waited for his mother to appear through the doorway; just like a good Negro boy was expected to do.

Now Cord wanted his mother to hire white people to clean her house. He wanted to have her inspect their work, making snide comments if the top of the toilet bowl wasn't clean or if there was dust under the Persian rugs. He wanted to put statues of white people holding lanterns along the brick driveway leading up to the spacious portico. But she would have no part of it. As a lifetime member of the Morris Brown Church, she upbraided her son for forgetting his Bible:

"Vengeance is mine; I will repay, says the Lord," Romans 12:19.

_____

The traffic came to a complete stop. Cord was actually pleased with this development. It would allow him to program his GPS, which failed to respond when the car was moving, to take an alternative route. He pushed the memory button, and the address of his house appeared. The traffic had started to crawl, but he remained motionless as he chose his preferred route, which was a collection of side streets that would avoid the highway altogether. An obnoxious honk from the driver behind him broke his concentration; but then he proceeded to complete the program.

"Please proceed to the highlighted route and the Route Guidance System will guide you," the GPS device said in its globally recognized annoying voice.

Cord tapped the gas pedal.

"Please take exit forty-one in one-point-two miles, on the right."

Cord now began to creep along with the traffic.

"Where are you going?" Herman asked.

"Alternate route. This thing is the best invention since the TV remote." He nodded toward the screen that displayed a map.

"You mean that thing tells you where to go?"

"Yes, Dad."

"How much did it put you back?"

"You don't want to know," Cord said, recalling the $4,300 extra he had paid to have the option. Herman was one of those guys who still took soda cans to the store to redeem five cents. If Cord shared with him the actual financial setback, it would be his father's heart that was in trouble instead of just his hip.

"I still think a map is better. You can still get them for free if you know which gas station to go to. And a map keeps you out of the wrong neighborhoods."

Cord laughed. "There are no wrong neighborhoods . . . unless we go to Bridgeport." Bridgeport was the poorest city in affluent Fairfield County.

"I mean, a neighborhood where we don't belong. That thing won't tell you if you're going to get shot."

Cord smiled at his father. "This is Connecticut, not South Carolina."

***

His father did not share his mirth. "You remember the time when you and your pals took your prom dates to that nice restaurant on the wrong side of town?" He let out a reminiscent *tsk* as he shook his head. "Me and Denise's dad had to come down there and prevent you from being arrested."

"I ordered my steak rare, and they deliberately overcooked it. I had a right to complain. I even offered to pay for a new steak. I had the money." Cord remembered the incident all right; just as well as he remembered his mother's rude boss.

"That was the problem, Cord. You flashed all your cash in front of their faces. Made those white waiters feel low. They don't like to see our kind pulling out wads of cash. You weren't thinking, son. And that's why they called the cops."

Cord smiled. "We're living in civilization now. When Clara and I walk into a restaurant, I get the best table, and they love it when I leave a big tip."

"That's your problem. You like to show off."

"People in this area like to show off a little. It's not a crime."

"Are you sure?" He let out a harrumph. "Well, how about the time in college when that store in Boston accused you of shoplifting? All you had to do was be polite and respectful and there would have been no problem. But, no, you had to show off."

"I wasn't shoplifting."

"I knew that, and you knew that. But then, why did you have to go back there the next day with a wad of cash you made gambling and try to buy everything in the store?"

"It wasn't gambling. I made it on oil futures."

"Sounded like gambling to me, and it sure sounded like gambling to the cop that almost cuffed you if your buddy Joe hadn't saved your sorry ass."

His mother shouted from the back seat. "You know I don't like that word."

Both men were surprised that she was wide-eyed and awake. She'd been so quiet that they had each assumed she'd dozed off, the day's travels getting the best of her.

"Sorry, dear," Herman apologized to his wife.

Cord laughed as he recalled the incident his father had just described. He was so insulted that a store along the South Shore of Boston had accused him of shoplifting that he returned the next day, bought every shirt and tie his size, and threw $1,200 on the counter. To top it all off, he told the white proprietor to "keep the change." When the owner refused to allow him the large purchase, Cord protested, resulting in the local cops being called. Only the intervention of his roommate, Joe, a second-generation Sicilian whose family had deep and complicated ties in the area, prevented Cord from being arrested.

"Dad, you were actually proud I did that. You've told that story at every family reunion with a huge smile on your face."

His father did not respond. No need vocalizing the fact that his son had him on that one.

The traffic began to pick up speed before Cord was able to exit the highway and follow the route his GPS had given him. He debated with himself as to whether he should continue on the highway. When he heard the ding of the GPS signaling the approach of the exit and saw the red lights illuminating from the miles of vehicles in front of him, his mind was made up. He concluded the back roads would take him less time. "Right turn ahead."

He wondered if there was a way to program the GPS for a sultrier female voice but kept this thought to himself. His mother would not approve. He shot her a quick glance through the rearview mirror.

She sat in the backseat, engrossed with her iPhone. Unlike his father, his mother embraced modern technology, even at the age of eighty. His mathematical ability had come from her.

After taking the exit, Cord made a right onto Wilton Road as the GPS had instructed.

"Left turn ahead onto Red Coat Road, and then, in two miles, take a right turn."

He made a quick turn onto Red Coat Road. He looked at the GPS and saw that the right turn would be a continuation of Red Coat Road. He snaked along the tree-lined street.

"Make a right turn, ahead."

The road doglegged to the right, but there was also a side street. New England roads made no sense. He made the sharp right turn onto the side street, but, to his annoyance, he noted the street name: Winker Lane. He should have just taken the dogleg, but he decided to continue until he saw a place to turn around. He gazed at the massive colonials recessed from the New England stone walls.

Just as he realized he was approaching a dead end, he heard, "Recalculating. Make a legal U-turn ahead."

He approached a gated estate, pirouetting his Lexus with a masterful three-point turn his father had taught him at fourteen. No one waited until sixteen to learn how to drive in South Carolina.

Just then, unbeknownst to anyone in Cord's car, a small camera, which was ensconced in the crevices of the gates' stone pillars, rotated soundlessly and focused on the license plate of the Lexus, transmitting the random numbers and letters to a server in India housed at a company called Cozy Bed Security. There, the information was scanned into a database. The camera then focused on Cord's face and transferred his image to another server where a snippet of JavaScript code converted the color of his face to the hexadecimal number 3D1F00. Another snippet of JavaScript code created a database of his various facial ratios: the distance between his pupils, the width of his nose and lips, the height of his nose and lips, along with a dozen other parameters. This hexadecimal number and his facial ratios were then inputted into another snippet of code that spit out the hexadecimal number 4B1, which, in computer language, meant "West African descent."

This then resulted in the server executing a subroutine that connected to a SQL database to ascertain if any other of the 1,327 residents of the neighborhood had the facial features that generated a 4B1 hexadecimal number. There was one family comprised of four individuals. Another subroutine ascertained that Cord Campbell was not one of them. The final subroutine placed 4B1 into a three-dimensional database where it correlated with the term "suspicious vehicle." This term, along with a Google map showing Cord's exact location, was relayed to the dashboard computer of a patrol car several streets east of his location. This entire process took approximately 1/100th of a second.

"Due to poor signal strength, the route guidance system is suspended. Street-to-street guidance cannot be provided." Those were the dreaded words heard from the GPS.

"I can't believe I paid over four grand for this piece of . . ." Reminding himself that his mother was in the car, Cord bit his tongue.

But his mother couldn't resist. "You should use the WAZE app. It's more accurate and it's free, but I can't get your father to use it."

"I'll just head back to the Merritt," Cord said. "I can't believe it stopped working."

He made a left turn back onto Red Coat Lane. He started speeding up the street.

"It must be a male thing," his mother commented, "speeding up when you are lost so you can go nowhere faster. We could always ask someone."

Cord was of the opinion that most divorces were caused by the line, "Why don't we ask for directions?" Of course, he kept this opinion to himself.

He tore around a corner and started to accelerate. From out of nowhere, a black-and-white appeared from behind. No siren; just flashing red and blue lights.

"Unbelievable," Cord said as he looked in the rearview mirror. "These guys really have nothing else to do?" He pulled over onto the side of the road.

He heard his father's calm baritone voice say, "Relax, Cord. Both hands on the top of the steering wheel and in plain sight. No sudden movements. Ask permission to move and lower the window." Herman lowered his window too.

Cord pressed the button controlling his window, and it descended silently. Dealing with police officers in South Carolina was a requisite survival skill passed onto to their sons by all black fathers for generations.

Cord watched, this time through his side view mirror, as two officers exited the police car now parked behind him.

The officer wearing a badge that read Jack Fletcher stepped to the driver's side, while the officer with a badge that read Kevin McMahon approached the passenger side of the car. McMahon, the shorter of the two, donned a uniform that was at least two sizes too small, accentuating his muscular frame. Fletcher looked like a professional wrestler, at six feet four with arms the diameter of most men's thighs. Fletcher's uniform was the proper size, except for the tight collar that made his neck appear like a protruding tree trunk. Both men had buzz haircuts and wraparound Carrera sunglasses.

"License and registration, please," Fletcher ordered.

"May I open the glove compartment?" Cord asked.

"Yes, very slowly and only with your right hand. Keep your left hand on the steering wheel."

Cord could not hide the slight tremor in his hand as he opened the glove compartment. After a few seconds, he produced the required documents.

"What is the problem, Officer?" he said, handing Fletcher the documents.

"I'll ask the questions here." Like most police officers, Fletcher was trained to establish dominance quickly in such situations. He also enjoyed doing so. That was apparent by the slight smirk he was making every effort to conceal.

McMahon chimed in, "Speeding. That's the problem."

"How fast?" Cord asked.

"Too fast," Fletcher answered, and then added, "I'll ask the questions here, or didn't you understand me the first time?"

The chairman of Hegemon Capital, with a net worth of $1 billion, was not about to tolerate these indignities, especially in front of his parents. Like the few Homo sapiens who achieved super wealth, he had the smirk of privilege, the smirk of power, the smirk of superiority. And he was all but trying to conceal his smirk.

Thus, Cord continued while affecting a slight British tone in his delivery. "You, gentlemen, could not have recorded my speed. You were not posted in my line of travel, and a moving vehicle from behind cannot accurately estimate the speed of another moving vehicle, even with radar unless both cars are moving at constant velocity."

Such was the value of an MIT education. Fletcher did not appreciate Cord's smirk. Furthermore, Fletcher, who once struggled with simple algebra, was not impressed with Cord's knowledge of physics and was becoming quite annoyed.

"Sir, could you please step out of the car?" Fletcher said.

"For what?" Cord tried to keep calm. He knew that was the purpose behind his father clearing his throat upon his question to the officer.

"I'll ask the questions here." Fletcher's tone was becoming less cordial.

"Do what he says, Cord," his father pleaded. "The man has a gun, and you don't." He reminded his son of the obvious.

"Sir, could you please step out of the car?" Fletcher repeated.

"What did I do wrong? Since when is it a crime to make a wrong turn?"

"Sir, would you please step out of the car? I am not going to ask you again."

Cord's eyes narrowed. "Don't you guys have anything better to do?"

"Son," Cord's mother chimed in, in a both worried and pleading tone.

Fletcher and McMahon heard this line at least three times a day. The answer, of course, was, "Yes." They did have better things to do. They could be golfing, playing poker at Foxwoods, coaching their children's Little League games, having a barbecue in their backyards; anything but trying to keep blacks out of a politically connected posh neighborhood. But this was their assignment, and Fletcher was losing his patience with what his father—a retired police officer—called an "uppity nigger."

"Are you telling me how to do my job?" Fletcher asked with an eyebrow raised.

"I'm not telling you how to do your job," Cord said. "I'm just asking why you stopped me."

"Are you telling me how to do my job?" Fletcher was starting to sound like a broken record.

"What is your job?" Cord decided he'd entertain the officer and pretend to care what he had to say.

"Sir, my job is to patrol this neighborhood and make sure nobody is speeding so that nobody gets hurt. These roads have blind curves. Children are on bicycles, and many residents are jogging."

"So simply answer my question. How fast was I going?"

"Sir, could you please step out of the car?"

"You can't answer my question because you didn't check my speed. You stopped me because I'm black."

"That's not true, sir. We are treating you with the upmost respect."

"Respect? I pay more in taxes in one month than you make in a year. You work for me. You stopped me because I'm black."

"Sir, you get out of that car. Now!" Fletcher's jaws could be seen tightening.

Cord's father now spoke. "Cord. Please," he said in a hushed tone. "Why does everything have to be a fight? Stop insulting the officer. The man is doing his job. Get out of the car, be polite, and we will soon be on our way."

Cord glared at Fletcher. "I live in Greenfield Hills. Your houses look like shacks compared to mine. You racist thugs have no right to stop me because you don't like my complexion."

His father realized his words of advice to his son had fallen on deaf ears as he closed his eyes and shook his head.

At these words, Fletcher no longer cared about controlling the situation. All day he ate shit from the pretentious, obscenely wealthy Fairfield County denizens.

"Listen, you nigger, you get out of this car, and you get out now or I will make you get out." Fletcher thrust his face six inches away from Cord's.

Suddenly, McMahon shrieked, "Video! Video!"

Fletcher looked in horror as Mrs. Campbell had the back of her iPhone facing him; the small clear eye glaring at him.

"Jesus Christ," Fletcher bellowed. "Grab it!" he yelled at McMahon.

McMahon propelled his torso through Herman's open window, displacing the older gentleman's body as his arms shot over the leather seat. He grabbed Mrs. Campbell's wrists as the iPhone tumbled onto the car seat. He pushed himself further, his legs suspending in the air as he groped for the iPhone. He gently cradled it from behind, taking great care not to push any buttons.

"Got it!" McMahon exclaimed. He then pulled his body out of the car.

Everything happened so fast that Cord didn't even have the chance to come to his mother's rescue.

The public perception is that cops feared guns, knives, and the chiseled bodies of physically intimidating thugs. For most cops, this was true. But some cops relished physical confrontation of any type. If one were to come to this conclusion about Fletcher, they'd be correct. He lived for the adrenaline rush. He was a bully as a child, and now, he was a legalized bully as an adult. He could verbally abuse, shoot, and pummel disrespectful citizens with impunity, and then doctor the paperwork to justify his actions. There was a plethora of phony charges—resisting arrest, interfering with an investigation, loitering, being a public nuisance, obstruction of justice—that had such vague definitions that they could be applied even if he found one of the nuns from Mother Teresa's order feeding a beggar.

But there is one thing he feared: a video, especially a video with audio. And once the icon was pushed that placed that video onto the Internet, no amount of verbal and written obfuscation could hide the truth. Videos had cost cops their jobs, their pensions, and put them behind bars. Videos had caused riots. And this video, complete with the verboten n-word, could cost Fletcher his badge.

Fletcher opened the back door of the car and shrieked into Mrs.

Campbell's face. "Did you e-mail the video?"

She stared at the police officer politely, but unintimidated, even as Fletcher's sputum pummeled her face. "No, Officer," she said.

"You better not be lying," he seethed through clinched teeth.

"I don't lie, Officer." There was actually a friendly lilt in her tone.

McMahon looked at the iPhone in terror. He wanted to just place it under the wheel of their patrol car and crush it into an infinite number of plastic, silicon, and metallic bits. But iPhones were also equipped with a GPS. This meant that it could be proven that the iPhone was present at the scene. He carefully fondled the iPhone, staring at the various icons. Thank God, he had the same model himself. He went to the camera app and stopped the video from recording.

"Quick, quick, before it locks. Keep your finger on the front surface," Fletcher said while turning toward him.

"I know what I'm doing," McMahon responded.

He swished his finger on the screen and looked at all the apps Mrs. Campbell had downloaded. Then he made sure that none of the common streaming apps such as Vimeo or the ACLU app was present. The proud civil rights organization claimed credit for the expansion of the rights of Americans for decades, but this app had done more to prevent police abuse than any courtroom activity they had sponsored. This app streamed videos with their audio onto the Internet immediately, rendering bullying and police mendacity impossible to deny. Any cop who tried to lie after this app was activated was soon watching himself in action on YouTube, along with the entire community.

McMahon found the icon to Mrs. Campbell's e-mail account that wasn't password protected. The old lady wasn't a liar after all. She had not e-mailed the video. He also checked for recent text messages. Again, no recent activity. He swished through the app until he found the video. He replayed it. She had caught everything, including the lie about clocking the car's speed and Fletcher's use of the n-word. He then deleted the video. McMahon nodded to Fletcher and pointed to the patrol car.

"You've got what you wanted," yelled Cord. "Give that back to her."

"Shut your goddamn mouth and don't move. Keep your hands on the steering wheel," Fletcher yelled.

The two police officers walked over to their patrol car and began speaking in hushed tones.

Mrs. Campbell said quietly, "I recorded the whole thing, but I think he deleted it."

"You mean you had him calling me a nigger recorded on your phone?" Cord said.

"Yes, but like I said, I think he deleted it."

Cord looked over his shoulder at the cops talking. "Shhh, let's see if we can hear what they're saying." The car fell silent as they all strained to hear the officers' conversation. But they could not hear a word the cops said.

"We have to cover our ass here," Fletcher said to his partner.

"Calling him a nigger may have been less than prudent." McMahon was surprisingly articulate when he wanted to be sarcastic.

"I know. I lost it, but I'm tired of eating these people's shit. But at least he can't prove it. That video is gone. Right?"

"I deleted it. Nothing to worry about."

"Then it's his word against ours," Fletcher said.

"But all he has to do is make the accusation. Then Chief is going to be all over our asses."

Fletcher pondered this for a second. "You're right. But remember why we are here. These goddamn country clubbers want us to keep the niggers out of their neighborhoods so they won't distribute drugs to their spoiled brats. We were informed by the system that this was a suspicious vehicle. We have to search the car for drugs, and then we're covered. Even if Chief gives us a hard time, we can tell him we were following policy. We were doing our job. We were doing what he ordered us to do."

McMahon's lips tightened. "How are you going to get him to sign the form giving us permission to search the car?" He nodded at

Cord's vehicle. "This is not some gangbanger with a record or some gardener we can intimidate. This is a professional guy who knows his rights and who is already pissed. We don't have him on the radar. No speeding. No running a stop sign. No nothing. Not even a broken taillight."

"No. But, we have them for interfering with an investigation."

"How?" McMahon asked.

"She videotaped us."

"That's not illegal," McMahon said as his voice became more irritable and louder.

"But that video had an audio. That is illegal."

"That's pushing it." The slits in McMahon's eyes decreased.

"But they don't know that," Fletcher said in a hushed tone. "And, shhh." He placed his index finger over his lips. "Do you want them to hear us?"

Both men looked at the car they'd pulled over, then continued on with their conversation.

"Let's threaten to arrest the old bitch unless this guy agrees to allow us to search the car," Fletcher suggested. "If I put his mother against the car and start searching her, he'll cave. He'll sign the form. Then we're covered. And I will get him to sign the form."

"How?" McMahon said.

"Just get the release form and leave the rest to me." Fletcher took off back toward Cord's vehicle.

McMahon grabbed a release form, then caught up with Fletcher and handed it to him right before he approached the driver side. "I hope you know what you're doing."

With paper in hand, Fletcher addressed Cord. "Sir, we believe you were in this neighborhood with intent to distribute."

Cord stared at the police officer in bewilderment. "Distribute what?" he said.

"Illicit substances."

"You mean drugs?"

"That is a distinct possibility."

"There are no drugs in this car," Cord said.

"In that case, you should not object to signing this form and allowing us to search." He extended the paper to Cord.

Cord looked down at the paper. "I'm not signing anything." It was clear he was refusing to accept that paper.

"If there are no drugs, you should not object. What are you hiding?"

"How do I know you won't plant anything?"

Fletcher scowled and folded his arms. "Are you questioning my integrity?"

Is this a trick question? Cord thought to himself. "I'm not signing anything."

"In that case, we are going to have to place your mother under arrest."

"For what?" Cord snapped.

"Interfering with an investigation. She videotaped us. That's interfering with an investigation."

"It is not against the law to videotape you."

Fletcher gave Cord a gloating smile. "Technically, you are correct, sir. But your mother was not just videotaping us, she was recording us too. Connecticut is what is called a two-party consent state, meaning you cannot record our words without our consent, which we did not give her. Thus, she was not only interfering with an investigation, she has violated our civil rights."

"This is bullshit!" At this point, Cord was talking to Fletcher like he was some thug on the street. Technically, in Cord's opinion, he was; a thug on the street in uniform with a badge and gun. "You stop me for no other reason than the fact that I am black. You call me a nigger. You grab my mother's iPhone and delete the video that proves you called me a nigger, and now you say my mother violated *your* civil rights? You are a lying, worthless piece of scum."

"This discussion is over," Fletcher snarled. He walked to the back-passenger door that remained open from when he'd opened it earlier. "You are under arrest, ma'am. Please get out of the car."

Cord watched helplessly as his mother exited the car. His father quietly started to cry. Herman had been here before. Mrs.

Campbell's pleading eyes looked at her son while he watched helplessly.

"Place your hands on the trunk, ma'am," Fletcher ordered her.

"What do you mean?" she asked. He wasn't going to search her and handcuff her, was he? That wasn't necessary. She had every intent on obeying him willingly.

"Place your hands on the trunk," Fletcher repeated. He was done answering questions.

She complied as Fletcher reached into his pocket, pulled out a pair of Latex gloves, and put them on his hands. He roughly kicked the woman's feet apart. She buckled and started to fall, but Fletcher roughly grabbed her waist. There could be no physical injury. He padded her legs and her crotch. He then pushed his hands into her buttocks. Finding nothing, he moved to the torso, running his hands under her blouse.

She and her husband took this treatment without complaint; however, her son was another story.

Cord, who had previously refused to get out of the car, now did so on his own volition. "Leave her alone, you worthless piece of shit," he said.

"You shut your mouth and don't move," McMahon bellowed. He was now pointing a forty-five Sig Sauer P220 at Cord's center mass.

Most men would have now had trouble controlling their bladder, but Cord did not. The evolutionary response hidden in the limbic system of his brain made the rapid transition from flight to fight.

"Hands in the air *now*!" McMahon said as Fletcher handled Cord's mother before his eyes.

Cord did not comply. "Fuck you, you arrogant pig. Just shoot me. I refuse to take anymore shit from a worthless piece of white trash like you."

Suddenly, Herman bellowed at his son. "Cord, I'm talking to you. You sign that form and allow them to search this car, and you do it right now. Your mother is being abused, and you're behaving like a four-year-old. You're going to get yourself killed! The man has a gun, and you don't!"

Cord had never disobeyed his father, but was tempted to make an exception. His lip trembled as he pictured himself plummeting at Fletcher and taking a shot in the back from McMahon. But it would have been worth it. Or would it have been? That sad, defeated look in his mother's eyes would be permanent if she had to bury her son. He could never—would never—be the cause of such pain. So on that thought, Cord relented. Bowing his head and raising his hands, he said, "Give me the form."

Fletcher stopped frisking Mrs. Campbell and produced the form and a pen. He had learned never to let a suspect search for a pen. In one case, a perp had produced a gun and almost killed him. He handed them both to Cord, and without reading the form, Cord signed it.

McMahon and Fletcher demanded Herman exit and move away from the car, so he meekly did so.

For the next ten minutes, McMahon kept the gun trained on the passengers he had lined up in front of the car, while Fletcher inspected the vehicle.

Fletcher opened the trunk, which contained nothing but Cord's golf clubs. He ripped up the carpet and looked in the well that housed the spare tire. He turned over the golf bag and let the clubs hit the ground. He shook the empty bag and then unzipped the numerous compartments, heaving the tees, balls, and gloves into the trunk. He then threw the bag into the trunk, threw the clubs on top of it and slammed the trunk shut. With his flashlight, he crawled under the car.

"What do you think you're going to find?" Cord called out.

Fletcher ignored him while he continued his search. He looked under the trunk and under the hood. Nothing suspicious and definitely no drugs. He opened the glove compartment and threw the contents on the floor. After looking under the dashboard and the car seats, he was satisfied. In fact, Fletcher already knew he wasn't going to find anything and was just going through the motions.

Hoping to still have a shred of dignity, Cord screamed, "Do you know who I am? I can buy and sell the two of you, and your white trash families. Do you think you can get away with this?"

"Cord, we are still alive. Let it be," his father stated calmly. "These people like to shoot folks like us for target practice."

Fletcher looked at Cord's license and laughed. "I know who you are. Your name is Cord Campbell." He shoved the license in Cord's face. "You see, it's written right here." He then tossed the license into the car. It landed on the floor with all the other papers. He nodded his head toward his own vehicle and looked at McMahon. "Let's go."

McMahon put away his gun and then returned the iPhone to Mrs. Campbell.

Cord glared at the buffed-up thug. "You haven't heard the last of this."

Fletcher sneered at him. "Oh yes, I have. We tried to take a civil tone with you and got nowhere. If you know what's good for you, you will pretend this never happened."

Cord was about to erupt when he felt his father's arm on his shoulder. "Calm down. It's over. Nobody's hurt, and nobody's in jail."

Fletcher was walking away, but turned abruptly. "Listen to your father." He and his partner then returned to their vehicle and got inside.

Cord and his parents got into his car. There was silence as they all sat, slightly in disbelief at all that had transpired. The longer Cord sat there and thought about things, the angrier he got. Finally, he slammed the car into gear. He looked in the rearview mirror at his mother. "Are you okay, Mom?"

"I'm fine. I have suffered much worse indignities, but I do not approve of your use of foul language. Your father never took the Lord's name in vain or used obscenities, no matter how unpleasant the situation."

"Sorry, Mom, but I can't believe that just happened." He slammed his fists on the steering wheel. "This is Connecticut in the

Joseph Bentivegna

twenty-first century. We even had a black president." Cord pulled back onto the street and drove off . . . slowly. He didn't want to get pulled over for speeding again, especially considering the officers were still parked behind him. They were probably just waiting on him to give them another reason to pull him over, not as if they had reason the first time. But things would probably be even worse this time; worse in the sense that his car could end up getting shot up. He wouldn't put it past those two for trying to claim that he was leaving the scene without permission, igniting a chase with fatal results.

"Doesn't matter, son," Herman drawled. "To these white people, a nigger is always a nigger. That's what I like about the South. At least you know where you stand."

Cord grit his teeth but did his best to quash his anger. As his college roommate used to say, "Don't get mad, get even." And he did not care how much it cost, Cord planned on doing just that—getting even.

CHAPTER 2

"**S**o, how you hitting them?"

"Barry, I am not in the mood for inane, irrelevant chit-chat. Save your refined social skills for new clients."

Barry Hoffman was visibly startled, both eyebrows rising over the pince-nez readers. He stood up from his leather-backed chair and walked over to his bar. His Westport office was quite unostentatious for a lawyer of his stature: a medium-sized maple desk, a beige Berber carpet, and the requisite oak bookcases containing impressive law tomes. But when it came to the bar, Barry did not cut corners. Everything was top-shelf. Life was too short to drink inferior booze.

"Some single-malt scotch?" he said to Cord while lifting a snifter toward his seated client. A mischievous smile crossed his face as he hoped to put an obviously upset Cord in a better mood.

"No, thank you!" Cord spat at him. "Can we just discuss my situation?"

Barry set the glass down on his bar, and his visage became serious. He returned to his chair. Cord had been his client for almost two decades, and he had handled some of his legal issues; everything from the closing on his real estate to disagreements with neighbors and tax assessors. Once there was a fight with a neighbor over the height of a stone wall. Another was with a neighbor who complained about Cord's cigar smoking. And, of course, there was donnybrook with the infinitely greedy town of Fairfield over his property taxes. But he never once recalled Cord making a rude or impertinent comment.

Rather, Cord dealt with his legal battles with good humor. The case about the cigar smoking was Barry's favorite. Like most blacks in overwhelmingly white neighborhoods, Cord bent over backwards to never irritate anyone. But one woman complained when he lit up on his front porch. In an attempt at peacemaking, Cord first stopped smoking on the front porch and retired to the porch that protruded from his attic. She still complained. So, he personally designed a filtration system that prevented any cigar smoke from leaving the attic porch.

The woman continued to complain, arguing that the sight of his smoking was a bad example to her children. At this point, Cord told him, "Barry, I don't care what it costs. You put that whining bitch in her place." Two hundred thousand dollars in legal fees later and some "independent research" into the skeletons held in his neighbor's closet forced the woman to throw in the towel.

But, when Cord had called Barry at his house last night, he had never sounded so upset. He was manic, yelling hysterically about how "America sucks," but refusing to discuss the reason for his outrage.

"My apologies, Cord." Barry cleared his throat.

"I don't want your apologies, not at $625 an hour. Uttering that sentence cost me a whole buck twenty." Cord loved to show off his mathematical acumen, especially when irritated.

"Cord, why are you doing this? If I have offended you in anyway, I'll waive my fee. I canceled another client for you. We've known each other for years, and I consider you a friend . . ."

"Well, as a friend, I am asking for your help." Cord continued. "It's all a scam, this equality bullshit, this diversity crap, this pretense of a colorblind society. It's a big goddamned joke. But you know who the only one's laughing are? *They* are!" He ranted, referencing the white man, of course. "They let me into the Patterson Club because they wanted a house nigger. Every week I get another invitation to be on some board. Same reason. Hell, the deans' wives at these Ivy League schools practically offered to perform fellatio on my son if he would agree to attend their paternalistic, racist institutions. And if you must know, I am hitting them lousy. Golf is another scam." Cord addressed Barry's initial query. "You either suck or you don't, and if you suck, there is nothing you can do about it: lessons, Ping putters, Pro V1 Titleists are all useless. Hell, I just blew $700 on Epic driver so now I can whack the ball twenty yards farther into the woods. I suck. And what's worse is that I'm black, and I suck. Do you know what it's like to be black *and* suck at sports?"

Barry Hoffman was at the point in his legal career where money was not the issue. Even with ten-year treasuries paying 2.90 percent, he made enough cash from interest to cover his living expenses. Any money he made working was just gravy. Unlike most of his clients, Barry had learned the values of his parents who survived the Depression: no debt, no divorce, and no problems. His unostentatious house was long paid for, and his marriage to Eileen was still going strong after thirty-five years. Thus, he had the luxury of choosing his clients and turning away those who annoyed him.

He took off his pince-nez glasses and gazed at his client. Cord Campbell was black—iridescent black. No slave owners raped his great-great-great-grandmother. Perhaps she fought them off. Perhaps his great-great-great-grandfather surreptitiously knifed the thug in the back. But somewhere in Cord's ancestry, the multiple random combinations of DNA culminated in the awkward six-foot bald, bespectacled, black man whose 1530 College Board score—800 in math—resulted in this descendant of slaves, whose father was a garage mechanic, being admitted to MIT.

But as Cord always told him, "Smart people are a dime a dozen; you have to perform."

And perform he did. Hired as a paid intern at Goldman Sachs during college, Cord quickly realized that not only wasn't he suited for the corporate culture, but that the subtle racism was nauseating. What drove him nuts was when his so-called colleagues were amazed that he was smart. "A white brain in a black body," was how one of his colleague's alcohol-loosened tongue put it.

It continued after he graduated and was interviewed for promotion to an analyst position. After two days of brutal discussions into every aspect of his personality, he ended up in the office of some top dog in which the entire interview consisted of one question. "Is 8,099 a prime number?"

He immediately responded, "No, sir."

The guy just looked at him waiting for him to elaborate, but Cord remained silent. He had been told not to leave dead space during interviews; but he didn't know what to say.

Finally, the guy said to him in an annoying tone, "You seem quite sure of your answer."

Cord just smiled weakly and said, "Yes, sir."

More dead time.

The guy looked at him and said, "What is your reasoning?"

"Eight thousand ninety-nine is one less than 8,100, meaning that it can be expressed by the product of 90 minus 1 and 90 plus 1. Therefore, 8,099 is the product of 89 times 91, which when expressed in prime numbers, is 7 times 13 times 89."

The guy just looked at him in amazement, as if he were a monkey who had figured out how to thread a needle. Any white guy who had given the same answer would never have seen that look.

Cord took the job when it was offered. How could he say no to $120,000 a year plus bonus right out of college? Yet, the indignities persisted. When he would figure out an option price quickly in his head during the heat of a trading day, the bewildered looks on all the white faces made him wish he could individually strangle every one of them. But the last straw was when he was invited to join the Goldman Sachs basketball team so that "We can go to the club and kick Chase's butt."

He arrived in his gym shorts and quickly realized he was the lousiest player there. As he missed layups, open jump shots, and allowed faster players to get around him, he could feel the stares of the other players. He knew what they were thinking. *Why did we hire this eight ball if he can't play basketball?*

He soon realized that it was just a matter of time until he lost his temper. Besides, he could make more money on his own. Why should a bunch of racist, macho, pseudo-samurais make a fortune off his sweat equity? So, he started his own hedge fund, from scratch. He quickly turned $50,000 of his own money into $300,000, and the word got out. Soon, he had more clients than he knew what to do with.

Cord was a wizard at analyzing global political and economic trends, and using sophisticated financial instruments—calls, puts, credit default swaps, currency swaps, collateralized debt obligations, and collateralized mortgage obligations, to name a few—to make piles of money. While other analysts preferred to dig into the account ledgers of companies and start-ups, Cord saw this as a sucker's game. He quickly discovered that the CEOs and CFOs of these companies, along with their bevies of accountants, were nothing more than pathological liars. Their only goal was to inflate the price of their stock so that they could exercise their options and buy some palace on Palm Beach, complete with taxpayer-subsidized flood and hurricane insurance. The employees of the rating agencies were even worse. They were just a bunch of toady nebbishes who would put a triple-A rating on junk bonds to finance a surfboard franchise in Alaska, in return for a box seat at the Super Bowl.

But the worst of the worst were the professional politicians. They were the most disgusting and conniving creatures on the planet; buying votes with inanities such as taxpayer guarantees for housing loans that could not possibly be paid back. He loved to watch these blow-dried hacks look into the camera and utter blatant lies so preposterous that it confirmed the famous quote of Hitler's Propaganda Minister Joseph Goebbels: "The bigger the lie, the more people will believe it."

Cord could read a scam a mile away and then figure out a way to make money on it. At the height of the Internet bubble, he took a huge short position on the tech stocks, pocketing hundreds of millions for his clients when the market crashed.

Once when asked to finance an Internet start-up, he commented that not only didn't he like the idea, but that there was no collateral. When one of the principals told him that there was human capital, Cord said, "Does this mean I can sell you as slaves if you default?"

———————

When the housing market tanked, he purchased the packaged collateralized mortgages, knowing full well that the mendacious politicians would bail out the ever-whining home owners who were stupid enough to overpay for a house without even making a down payment; along with the useless bankers who lent them the money. He made a real killing shorting Spanish bonds after he was done laughing at the Spanish prime minister, who said, with a perfectly straight face, that Spanish banks were stable, even though they had locked the doors to protect themselves from irate depositors. He predicted, with great accuracy, that the IMF and central bankers from the Eurozone would bail out Greece, scooping up bonds that paid 17 percent. Even though he was a Republican, he could not bring himself to vote for Trump; but he knew the market would skyrocket when Trump implemented his economic agenda. And he made a bundle.

But his real forte was his ability to make anyone trust him. Maybe it was his nerdy appearance or his quiet but brutal honesty. Whatever the case, this, combined with his analytical ability, sent his Hegemon Hedge fund into the stratosphere. His initial clients were black athletes. Not only did they trust him because he was black, they trusted him because he never patronized them. While the white fund managers sucked up to these guys by reciting their foul shooting percentages or yards per carry, Cord never even discussed their athletic prowess. In fact, it was rumored that Charles Barkley wrote him a check for $15,000,000 after Cord asked him what team he had played for.

Cord never wanted acceptance though. His father had taught him that whites, no matter what they said, were simply genetically programmed to think they were superior because of their skin color. Complaining about this was like complaining to the sun for rising in the east and setting in the west. But at least he wanted respect.

"Cord, you refused to speak on the phone. Just tell me what's eating you. I've never seen you like this," Barry said.

"They called me a nigger. They deleted the video that proved they did so. They pointed a gun at me. They made my mother spread her feet apart and bend over while they searched her, Barry. They ran their gloved hands over her buttocks and down her legs. They patted her waist while she had her hands on the trunk of my car. They did this in front of me and my father, her husband of sixty-one years."

Cord paused, but his body was heaving, his eyes gyrating as Barry pondered what he should do, what he should say.

The veins bulged in Cord's head as he bellowed, "In front of me and my father!"

"What are you talking about, Cord? When? Who?" Barry was truly concerned about what it was that had led his client to this state.

Now Cord was in a full panic attack. His heart was racing, his shoulders rising and falling as he attempted to breathe. Sweat beaded down his forehead and even dripped off his earlobes. His lips darkened, matching the color of his face. He was one of the few people in high-risk finance without a Xanax prescription, and now he wished he had one.

"Cord, I'm calling 911 now!" Barry sounded as if he'd be the next to go in panic attack mode if he didn't do something about his client.

"Please don't. I'm fine. Don't call. Please. I'll behave. I'm sorry, Barry." His breathing gradually improved, and the color returned to his lips.

"Can I have some Scotch, the twenty-one-year-old Balvenie Port Wood? Please, Barry? Neat."

Barry quickly rose, opened the oak cabinet beside his Chagall print, rummaged through his top-shelf collection, and filled a snifter to the brim. He gave it to his longstanding client, spilling some on his new carpet as he rushed to Cord.

Cord did not gulp it as Barry had expected. Rather, he took several sips, savoring the precious liquid as it rolled down his throat. This was definitely better than Xanax, he thought to himself.

Slowly, Cord recounted the incident while Barry kept notes on his laptop; not interrupting until they came to the part of the story about Cord signing the release form.

Barry looked up. "Did I hear you correctly? You signed the form?"

"One of the thugs was groping my mother. The other was pointing a gun at me, and my father was crying. What was I supposed to do?"

Barry silently cursed to himself. The justice system rigorously protected its own at every turn, and once there was a confession or a signed document, no matter how it was obtained, it would be next to impossible to win a case.

Cord read his lawyer's mind. "That wasn't a smart move, was it?"

"It makes things a bit more difficult."

Cord finished his recitation.

Barry asked, "Your mom has the iPhone. I heard you correctly, didn't I?"

"Yes, but Mom said they erased everything."

"Cord, I'm not a technical wizard, but sometimes data can be retrieved. We could have some experts look at it."

"That would be fine, but my mom is pretty sharp. She says it's gone, although she said you can show that something was erased."

"Too bad she didn't have the ACLU app. I had a case of police brutality in Shelton where the cops grabbed the iPhone and destroyed it after whacking around some tattooed biker. They thought they were smart, but the biker had the app. I played it for the cops' lawyer, and they settled."

"Did the cops lose their jobs?"

"No. They never do. Desk duty with full pay."

"Why didn't the biker press charges?"

"He just wanted the money. In fact, he said he deserved to be beaten. I even think the guy provoked the incident to get some money."

"So how much did the cops have to pay?"

Barry laughed. "No. Cops never pay. The taxpayers pay."

"Well, these cops are going to pay. I promise you that. Just tell me how big a retainer you want and let's get started." Cord reached into his jacket and pulled out his checkbook.

Barry held his hands up to halt his client's enthusiasm. "Cord, let's talk about this."

"What's there to talk about? These fascists are not going to get away with this. Over my dead body." Cord continued, "Barry, when there is a moth flying around our house and my wife wants it killed, you know what I do? I get a plastic cup and a piece of cardboard and trap the moth. Then I take it outside. I won't kill it. All these macho guys I work with, they want me to go to some ranch and kill a buffalo. How many buffalo are there even left? I won't go, even though it has cost me some clients . . ."

Cord sat back in his chair and continued. "But you know what I did last night? I got the shotgun I keep in the basement and was about to go down to the police station and kill the first cop I saw. What gives them the right to treat my mother like that? What gives them the right to stop me and search my car because I made a wrong turn?"

Barry did not know what to do. Cases like this were called by his colleagues, "ego cases." It was when someone with monopoly money had his dignity offended and was willing to spend any amount of money to get it restored. When he started his practice, he took some of these cases, only to find that the clients expected him to be at their beck-and-call twenty-four hours a day, and then screamed bloody murder when the slow grinding legal system produced nothing but endless interrogatories, depositions, hearings, and settlement conferences with no closure. He refused all these cases now, except for the cigar-smoking caper with Cord, which he had actually enjoyed. But this was different.

"Cord, let's think about this first. I don't want to take your money."

"You mean you won't help me?"

"That's not what I'm saying. There is no hurry to act here. We can look into things before we act."

Cord had one of the best bullshit meters on the planet. "You

---

won't help me, will you?" he said in a surprisingly civil tone.

"Let's just give it some time. You know, Cord, sometimes, it's just not worth the trouble. Human beings are horrible creatures. I know you're outraged, but there is no physical damage here."

"They called me a nigger."

"And I used to be called 'Jew Boy' and 'Kike' to my face."

"Used to. Does anyone call you that to your face now? Anyone?"

Barry's silence answered the question. He continued to pause while waiting for Cord to comment further. As Cord remained silent, Barry continued. "You know about my aunt Sophie, don't you?"

"Not really."

"I lost her several years ago at the age of eighty-three. She was the only survivor . . . the rest of her family, gassed. The only reason they spared her was that she was adept at sewing Nazi uniforms. She remembered smelling their burning flesh. She still had a number tattooed on her wrist. I offered to pay to have it removed. 'Never,' she said. 'I want the world to see it.' But she never sought revenge. In fact, when there was a settlement with the Swiss banks over the deposits of her dead relatives, she wouldn't even file a claim."

"She said, 'It's too painful to think about. I was lucky. I survived. I came to America. I met a nice man and had a wonderful family. Why jinx it now?'"

Barry looked at his client. "Keep your money for now. Let me make some inquiries. Suing the town or the cops will create a media circus with no winners in the long run. The most you would get would be several million dollars, and given your net worth, it would not be significant."

"I don't want their money."

"So, you don't want me to sue them?" Barry was now more confused than ever regarding the matter. "Then why are you here, if you don't mind my asking?"

"We need to discuss strategy," Cord responded. He stood and began pacing in thought.

"Strategy? Like what? You want them to be fired and stripped of their pensions? Good luck." He blew air between his lips and teeth, causing his lips to blubber. "The police unions negotiate contracts that make that practically impossible. Hell, the cop in Hartford who was forcing women to have sex with him to avoid being arrested was retired on disability with full pension because of PTSD."

"PTSD?"

"Post-traumatic stress disorder, the latest medical scam du jour. Don't get me started." He shook his head in consternation.

"I don't want them fired, and I don't want them to lose their pensions."

A perplexed Barry looked at his client quizzically. "Then what *do* you want?"

Cord paused, looking his lawyer dead in the eyes. Then, with all sincerity, he said, "I want respect."

"Respect? What are you talking about?"

"Respect. R-E-S-P-E-C-T, just like the song says."

Barry simply stared at Cord.

"I want you to get them to walk into my house, give my mother a bouquet of flowers, and apologize. That's what I want, and that's all that I want." He went and sat back down on the chair, lifted the glass to his mouth, and took in the last of his liquor.

"You're not serious?"

"I'm deadly serious."

"How did you come up with that idea?"

"Listen, Barry, they're getting off easy. Once my grandpappy forgot to duff his hat to some fat, white woman. Not intentionally. He just didn't notice her walk into the store. The local sheriff made him kneel in front of her and beg her forgiveness."

"Did he?"

"Of course. The alternative was to be thrown in jail for a few weeks . . . or worse."

"Worse?"

"Beaten, lynched. Who knows? Those Southern rednecks were animals. Still are."

"Did she accept the apology?"

"Yes. But not until she spat on him and called him a worthless nigger."

"Do you really think this is a comparable situation?"

Cord was getting weary of going back and forth with his attorney. He didn't understand why he had to. The man had helped him fight a cigar-smoking case, for Christ's sake. This had to be somewhat higher on the totem pole. "Are you going to help me or not?"

Barry Hoffman had been a lawyer for over thirty-five years. He had learned how to talk without saying anything while he figured out his next move. But now, for the first time in his legal career, his mind was blank. After twenty seconds that seemed like an eternity, he responded. "How do you expect me to negotiate this? You have no concrete proof that any of this happened."

"I don't know. You're the lawyer. Threaten to sue or go to the media and force them to compromise. Put them in a position where they may be fired and lose their pensions. I know you said that's hard to do, but sometimes, just the threat may work. I don't know. But that is what I want. How much of a retainer do you need?"

"I don't want a retainer. Can you let me look into it? I know Driscoll, the Westport police chief. Let me get their side of the story . . . even if it is all lies. Then, we'll be in a position to bargain. Am I being reasonable?"

"Not really, but I trust you."

"I appreciate your trust, but I do have one technical question." Barry paused as he collected his thoughts. "Why did they pull you over?"

"They said I was speeding."

"Did you see them while you were driving around the neighborhood?"

"No."

"So how did they catch you? I know they don't use helicopters for speed traps anymore."

"That's a good point. In fact, I forgot to mention to you that I told the cop there is no way he could prove I was speeding. They did not mention a radar gun. I'm sure if they had one, they would have.

I suspect they all have accurate time readings on radar guns so that it would be difficult to fabricate evidence."

"You would have made a good lawyer, Cord. Do you think someone saw you and reported you?"

"Could be." These are all considerations Cord hadn't bothered to ponder until now. He'd been too outraged.

"But if you never saw the cops before, and no one reported you, and you did nothing wrong, how did they know to stop you? It makes no sense," Barry said, shaking his head, but at the same time intrigued. He loved puzzles. Maybe he would take this case on.

"I have no idea, Barry. All I know is that I was driving along, and they came up behind me, lights flashing."

"Cord, a quick recap to prevent future misunderstanding. No retainer and no bill for this meeting. Nothing. Let me talk to the Westport police chief. I'll get back to you in a few days."

"I understand, but I insist on paying."

"Absolutely not." His tone was adamant.

Cord was visibly irritated. Both men knew that to exchange cash implied a promise for Barry to do something. By refusing to accept payment, he was in a position to refuse to help.

"That's fine, Barry. But don't think I don't know what you're doing. You're hoping I'll calm down. It ain't happenin'." The veins in his head began to bulge again.

"Don't do anything foolish."

Cord did not respond but rose and extended his hand. The two men shook hands and Cord left for his office in Greenwich. Not another word was spoken.

CHAPTER 3

Barry Hoffman sauntered into the office of the Westport Police Chief Ray Driscoll. Public servants had good benefits but lousy working conditions. His metallic desk appeared to be a relic from the Coolidge administration. The brown carpet, just dark enough to conceal any coffee stains, was torn, and the window overlooking Myrtle Avenue had not been cleaned during the current millennium.

Chief Driscoll, who had announced his retirement six months ago, did not look any better. His hanging jowls, bulging abdomen, and rheumy eyes displayed the ill health of a man battered by decades of daily stress. Barry suspected he single-handedly kept the pharmaceutical industry afloat. Barry, on the other hand, looked like life had dealt him a good hand. At the advice of his internist, he no longer jogged but remained fit due to his ability to perform the most important exercise: the push away from the table. A scraggly mop of gray hair, a remnant from the sixties, sat atop a round tanned face and deceptively welcoming brownish eyes that belied a fierce competitiveness.

Barry pointed to the Jets coffee mug on Chief Driscoll's desk and then opened his arms." There's no hope."

Chief Driscoll motioned him to sit down." I know. I know. They should put the cheerleaders on the offensive line. They could protect McCown better than those bozos. Not that he could complete a pass anyway," Chief Driscoll said, shaking his head.

Barry always wondered why he remained a Jets fan. Nobody opts to be a diabetic or to suffer from hemorrhoids, so why did he choose to be a Jets fan? It was a lifetime sentence of ignominy and frustration. And Chief Driscoll, another transplanted New Yorker, had the same disease.

"McCown is not a bad passer; he just has needs to have a few seconds."

Chief Driscoll laughed. "He's too old. He's afraid to take a hit."

Barry shook his head. "I wish I could disagree."

Chief Driscoll and Barry went way back, to when the chief was a beat cop and Barry still did DUI cases. They first met in a courtroom when Barry cross-examined him about an arrest Chief Driscoll made of a driver who was so drunk that when he got out of his car, he vomited on Chief Driscoll's shoes. The chief was arguing that he had established his collar's inebriation by the shaking of his eyes when he looked to the side, a phenomenon ophthalmologists called end-gaze nystagmus. Barry, who believed one could never be overly prepared for a case, had researched end-stage nystagmus so thoroughly that he determined that it could be elicited in 90 percent of the sober population. With the help of his ophthalmologist, he learned how to do so. He then proceeded to elicit end-gaze nystagmus in the bailiff, the court clerk, and the chief himself with Her Honor watching closely. His client, who was so hungover that he fell asleep during the proceedings, was acquitted.

Several other supposedly open-and-shut cases against Barry had similar results, and for a while, Chief Driscoll resented Barry's ability to use his brilliant mind to get the guilty acquitted. But at the same time, Barry had taught him that the criminal justice system was more of a game rather than a search for the truth. That was good information to have. Thus, both men were aware of the gray areas of their respective professions, and with this history and having completed the requisite foreplay, they came down to the real reason for their meeting.

"Ray, several days ago I had an extremely irate client in my office, a Mr. Cord Campbell." Barry dived right in.

Chief Driscoll nodded, and Barry instinctively knew that he was already intimately familiar with the situation. That was his job.

"I'm hoping that we can come to an accommodation here, a

way to resolve this without courtroom drama, without publicity, and without two dedicated public servants who risk their lives being smeared and perhaps losing their jobs."

If Barry were a younger man, Chief Driscoll would have perceived this as an implied threat. But in this case, he and Barry were on the same page.

"Barry, I just want this to go away. In six months, I'm out of here." He stared off as if he could just see himself enjoying his retirement now. "Fishing at Hilton Head. Sleeping 'til noon if I so desire." He looked at Barry. "I do not want to leave on a sour note."

"Can we begin by seeing what the facts are?"

"I'll do my best," Chief Driscoll responded, "but I can't make promises. I have one of the officer's report here, but I can't give it to you."

"That's fine. I understand your position. Who wrote it? Fletcher?" Cord had informed him of the names of the officers involved.

Chief Driscoll nodded.

"Can you at least tell me why Campbell was pulled over?" Barry now opened his briefcase, producing six pages, a hard copy of the notes of his meeting with Cord.

"Speeding." He said it as if he was stating the weather in December; cold.

"Speeding? Come on, Ray. Unless Campbell is lying to me, that can't be true."

"That's what the report says."

"How was it determined that Campbell was speeding? Radar gun? Speed trap?"

Chief Driscoll stared at Barry, but did not respond.

"What objective evidence establishes that my client was speeding?"

"I can't answer that, Barry."

"Then we have a problem . . . a big problem." That went without saying. But it was his job to say it anyway. "Okay, let's move on. Did one of the officers delete a video that was taken of the incident by

Mr. Campbell's mother?"

Chief Driscoll looked down at the report, but for Barry, this was theater. He'd seen this act a million times. "According to the report, an iPhone was confiscated at the scene but was then returned."

"But why was the iPhone taken? Maybe they wanted to see if a video was taken? Maybe it looked like a weapon? Help me out here."

Chief Driscoll did not respond. He momentarily made eye contact with Barry, then returned to looking at the report. "You know that recording a video can be construed by officers as interfering with an investigation, which is exactly what that woman did."

"An investigation about speeding?"

"Listen, Barry, your client is a rude and arrogant man. My officers tried to control the situation."

"By calling him a nigger? By pointing a gun at him?"

Chief Driscoll's eye shot up. It was obvious to Barry that these particulars were news to the chief. Details of this nature were also left out of police reports.

"You know full well that one of the most dangerous things a cop can do is pull over a car. The only thing worse is investigating domestic violence. Sometimes in the heat of the moment, insults are uttered. Furthermore, a lapse of a split second can result in death. My officers did their job, which is to keep our neighborhoods safe."

"My client claims your officers called him a nigger." Barry went back to the bump in the road Chief Driscoll was apparently having a hard time riding over.

"There is no mention of that in the report." He flipped through the report. More theatre.

"My client claims that one of your officers deleted the video that would have proved this to be the case."

"There is no mention anywhere of a video being deleted."

"But they did grab my client's mother's iPhone."

"Yes, they did. Use of an iPhone constitutes interfering with an investigation."

"That is debatable," Barry responded with a shrug.

"But I will tell you what is mentioned. Your client called my officers white trash. He called them racist thugs. He told them that their houses looked like shacks compared to his. It is possible my officers overreacted, but quite frankly, my men work like dogs to keep this town safe. And people like your client treat us like serfs. My officers acted professionally given this guy's arrogance. He's lucky he wasn't cuffed."

Chief Driscoll was on a roll and getting a little fired up. "And you're forgetting the elephant in the room. Your client signed a form giving my officers the right to search his car."

Barry answered in a calm and quiet voice. "Yes, after one of the officers put his eighty-year-old mother in a four-point position and aggressively padded her down, running his hands up her buttocks and under her brassiere. Any reasonable person would sign the form under those circumstances, especially given that a gun was pointed at him."

Chief Driscoll just stared at him while Barry continued. "Do you know who Cord Campbell is?"

"No, although from the report, it appears he must be quite rich. Was he a jock?"

"He was never an athlete, and the impression that he is quite rich is an understatement. He is one of the most successful hedge fund managers in the country. *Forbes Magazine* estimates his net worth to be over one billion."

"Does he live in northern Westport? What was he doing in that neighborhood?"

"He was stuck in traffic on the Merritt. He tried to take a short-cut. He got lost when his GPS stopped working. He actually lives in Greenfield Hills, a posh neighborhood in Fairfield. But you ask an interesting question."

"What question?"

"You asked me, 'What was he doing in that neighborhood?'"

Chief Driscoll silently cursed his stupidity. That's what looking forward to retirement does to a person. He was losing his political savvy. He brought his hand to his chin. "I misspoke."

Barry paused, folded his hands over his notes, and then leaned forward. "Ray, I'm trying to not inflame a very ugly situation. Don't bullshit me."

Chief Driscoll did not respond.

Barry continued. "Why was he pulled over? Is this a case of DWB; you know, 'Driving While Black'?" He rested back in his chair. "I know you are under political pressure to keep minorities out of these neighborhoods. You have a tough job. Work with me here. I live in Westport, too. I know how these wealthy people think. They are all for diversity . . . as long as it is not in their backyard."

"You have no evidence of that. You can sue the town and the department. The fact remains he signed the form allowing the search." Chief Driscoll was now in cover-your-ass mode.

"Ray." He was intentionally and repeatedly calling the chief by his first name in an attempt to keep it friendly. "I don't know what's going to happen here. But I do know this. Somebody is going to pay for this incident. I will encourage Campbell not to sue. In fact, I'm not sure I'll even take the case if he does. But I'll tell you this; someone will. This single case could put someone's kids through college."

"What do you suggest?" He tried to hide his worried tone. He was partially successful.

"Talk to the officers and get back to me. Why did they pat his mother down? Did they have to call him a nigger? Why did they have to draw a gun on him? And for God's sake, tell me why they stopped him. Campbell is actually a mild guy. All he wants is for the officers to apologize to him, give some flowers to his mother, and he'll forgive them."

Chief Driscoll looked at Barry as if he was from Pluto. "Apologize? Are you serious? For doing their job? For tolerating this rich, arrogant prick's crap?"

"If they stopped him for no reason, they're getting off easy. Campbell is angry, but he is also humiliated. He does not want everyone to read in the papers that his mother was searched while he impotently stood by. This is more about respect than money. If your officers acknowledge what they did—nothing in writing—and simply apologize, we may be able to make this go away. If not, things could get very ugly." He closed up his notes and stood.

"He really expects an apology and flowers?"

"That's it, Ray. It would take five minutes."

"Barry, we demand respect too. Do you know how humiliating this would be for these officers? For our department? For me? For *me*?"

He could imagine. "Ray, I'll talk to Campbell. Nobody has to know. I have been doing this racket a long time, and I know when wealthy people are humiliated, they *can* afford vengeance."

"Barry," he stood, "we simply don't apologize."

Barry sat back in his chair and hung his head. Finally, he spoke. "Ray, he was stopped for a reason. If it gets out that racial profiling was involved here, no one is going to win. No one." This time when he stood, he exited. Nothing else needed to be said.

CHAPTER 4

C hief Driscoll extended his hand, gesturing that his officers, McMahon and Fletcher, have a seat. Even if his office was Spartan, he insisted on good coffee. Thus, the two officers were treated to Shearwater Homacho Waeno, an Ethiopian roast, served in white and green New York Jet mugs. After all, this was Westport.

After some requisite pleasantries, Chief Driscoll began. "Do you know who Barry Hoffman is?"

The question was rhetorical. All police officers knew that Barry was a well-respected criminal defense attorney who had a legendary ability to minimize the jail time for even the most obviously guilty defendants. While many lawyers relied on courtroom theatrics and media-hype, Barry was the lawyer's lawyer; always overly prepared and willing to plea bargain any case to avoid wasting his time, the court's time, and the taxpayer's money . . . as long as all parties were reasonable.

McMahon gave his boss a curt nod, but Fletcher kept his best poker face, trying to look neither defiant nor obsequious. Both men knew they were here to discuss the incident with Cord.

"He and I go way back. He was sitting right in that chair yesterday." He pointed to the chair that Fletcher now occupied, and then continued.

"We discussed the discrepancies between your account and that of his client, Mr. Cord Campbell."

Unwittingly, he was showing Cord respect by using his full, given name, versus the name he really wanted to reference: the troublemaker. But he consciously wanted to be an example to his subordinates. The clock was ticking. He could see the light at the end of the tunnel of all the years he'd put in on the force. There was no need to go splashing through muddy puddles on his way out.

Chief Driscoll paused while waving Fletcher's report in his hand.

"And they are considerable. First of all, why did this get out of control? We have endless hours of sensitivity sessions, and you guys still screw up." He looked from one officer to the other.

There was no response from either.

Finally, Fletcher said, "It never got out of control." He was just as confident and smug as ever.

"It never got out of control? Kevin pulled a gun on the guy." He nodded to McMahon while spatting off at Fletcher. "Hoffman says you called this guy a nigger. Sounds like out of control to me."

Fletcher and McMahon shot each other a look. It was obvious the two had previously discussed how they would handle this situation if they were, in fact, called out on it. They'd both agreed and concluded that if the moment before them ever came, there was only one thing to do.

Lie.

"I never called him a nigger," Fletcher said, his voiced raised as if offended himself by the word.

Chief Driscoll eyed Fletcher suspiciously, searching his face for a telltale sign. Fletcher locked his jaw and stared back.

"You never called him a nigger?" Chief Driscoll said.

"No, sir." Fletcher shook his head emphatically.

"But the report said you took his mother's iPhone."

"We did, but we returned it." He was picking his battles as to what he would and would not deny, that was for sure.

"Then how did this get out of control?"

"Like I said, Chief," Fletcher began to reiterate, "it never got out of control. Not on our end anyway. But that Campbell guy, now he had an attitude . . . a big one."

"An attitude? Everybody in Westport has an attitude. The realtors won't let you buy a house here if you don't have an attitude. Your job is to control the situation. Be polite. Don't raise your voice.

Smile. Be nice. And then pick up your check every two weeks. It's not that hard." Chief Driscoll, realizing he was losing his cool, took a breather.

"Permission to speak freely, Chief?" Fletcher said after giving his superior a moment to gather himself. This expression was used liberally during his boot camp days, which, in truth, Fletcher had never really outgrown. He relished a clear-cut sense of hierarchy.

"Speak! Please! Speak!"

"You read my report. This guy called us trash. He said our houses were shacks; that he paid more money in taxes in a month than we made in a year. In my father's day, we would have yanked this piece of scum out of the car and busted his face."

"That day is long gone, and quite frankly, Officer Fletcher, I do not like *your* attitude."

"You gave me permission to speak freely, sir, so I will do so." Fletcher's tone was respectful as he continued. "First of all, we pulled this guy over for one reason, because he was black . . . and he knew it. This happens all the time. The dashboard computer magically gives us the location of a suspicious vehicle. Every time we pull the vehicle over, it is an African American or a Latino. The majority are trying to avoid traffic on the Merritt. The others are gardeners, cooks, maids, or construction guys. And they always end up pissed, because, trust me, it does not take long for them to figure out that we pulled them over for who they are, not because they are doing anything wrong."

"Yes, and they have a right to be pissed," Chief Driscoll said. Fletcher hadn't shared with him anything he didn't already know. "But if you show the proper demeanor . . . the proper . . . what's the word? Respect. You can control the situation."

Chief Driscoll continued, "You guys know the deal. The town pays us a good salary with fantastic benefits. Hell, we even have this job defined as hazardous duty so that after twenty years, everyone has a fat pension. All we have to do is smile while keeping anyone who might be perceived as scum out of town. We do our job, kiss everybody's ass, and we're fishing in Florida at age forty-five. What the hell is the problem?" He shrugged his shoulder.

Fletcher responded. "Good salary? Sir, with all due respect, you can't wipe your ass with eighty grand around here. You bought in town thirty years ago when it was cheap. Now a goddamn cottage costs $850,000 with twenty grand in taxes. You can get one for 600 grand with an optional roof. We're stuck living in Norwalk."

"Maybe," Chief Driscoll countered. "But talk to the cops from other towns. They're getting punched, kicked, and spat upon by HIV-positive junkies for less money than you guys make. At least once a week, they are involved in a situation where their lives are in danger. You two sit in a car in a safe neighborhood. It's not dangerous work. You could be investigating domestic abuse or breaking up bar fights."

McMahon decided to add his two cents. "I've had to deal with domestic abuse and bar fights in Westport." He could have kept that in his pocket as far as Chief Driscoll was concerned.

Chief Driscoll let out a huge guffaw. "Let's talk about the last domestic abuse case you were called to. If I recall, it was some hot blond trophy wife who called 911 because her seventy-five-year-old zillionaire husband cut up her Niemen-Marcus card after he caught her humping the pool attendant."

"It was actually the guy repairing the patio," McMahon said. "But I was threatened with a pair of scissors when I arrived."

"By the husband?" Chief Driscoll asked.

"No. By the wife."

He tightened his eyes and glared at McMahon, who he had a great suspicion was adding yeast to the bread of the story. "Refresh my memory."

"We arrive and this crazy blonde is screaming at this old guy who is just laughing at her. The repair guy is long gone. She says he can't satisfy her and she has the right to hump young guys. He says she infected the last guy she humped with herpes and that the guy sent him the medical bills. Says her snatch is a 'breeding ground for drug-resistant organisms.' I started laughing, and that's when she comes after me with the scissors."

44

"But with all due respect," Fletcher jumped in, "we do have some dangerous bar fights. Some guy actually pulled a gun on me last year at one of the beach bars."

"Yes, that was quite dangerous," Chief Driscoll genuinely agreed. "But it was not typical. Most of our bar fights are between drunken wimps arguing over bar bills. Or how about that fight the two of you handled at Cedar Brook several years back?"

Fletcher tried to remain serious, but Chief Driscoll and McMahon's laughter overwhelmed him, and he was forced to crack a smile. Soon, all three men were laughing as they recalled the incident at the oldest gay bar in the United States; opened in 1939 and finally closed in 2010.

Chief Driscoll took a sip of his coffee and continued. "If I recall correctly, these two faggots were whacking each other with dildos, and when Kevin approached them, one of them whacked him with the dildo."

"Hit me in the shoulder," McMahon said. "I should have filed for disability on a rotator cuff injury."

"You can't make this stuff up," said Chief Driscoll, shaking his head, hoping the jovial banter would diffuse the situation. "But we have a serious problem here," he continued, ceasing all laughter. "Why the hell did you have to pull Campbell's mother out of the car and search her? What were you thinking?"

"Chief, what happened to me when I did not search that elderly black woman we stopped four months ago?" Fletcher replied.

"Jack, I know you have a difficult job," Chief Driscoll said to Fletcher. "And sometimes, no matter what you do, you're going to be screwed. That's the nature of police work."

A defiant look crossed Fletcher's face. "No. It's not that easy, Chief. I let that woman go, and then she delivered cocaine to some pampered kid who then got in a car wreck while high. Was it the kid's fault? No! Was it the black woman's fault? No! Was it the fault of the parents who spoiled the kid rotten? No! It was *my* fault. Hell, I was formally reprimanded and had to undergo further training—for which I was not paid—on proper procedure. I was passed over for a promotion. And don't tell me I wasn't. And I appreciate your having Kevin come and help me out, but this is not an easy assignment."

The common perception was that the wealthy neighborhoods feared minorities as potential robbers. In reality, this was rarely the case. Most of the robbers were white. The real problem was drugs. Like the lower-class Italians who provided alcohol during prohibition, the poor urban blacks delivered the drugs, not only to the overpampered teenagers, but also to former hippies and potheads that now had the aura of respectability. These blacks were referred to as *mules*, the term for a person who delivered drugs.

But a few years ago, when a sixteen-year-old scion of a Goldman Sachs partner died of a heroin overdose, nobody blamed the distant workaholic father or hot trophy wife that wrecked the family. They blamed the streetwise black teenager who delivered the drugs. Thus, young blacks were stopped indiscriminately. But the drug lords adapted, hiring elderly black women posing as lost drivers or Jehovah's Witnesses.

Four months ago, Fletcher had stopped such a woman but failed to detain her. While preaching the Lord's Word, she managed to deliver some heroin to the fifteen-year-old anorexic daughter of the senior vice president of United Health Care, who then overdosed. While she eventually recovered after a long hospital stay, the political fallout in town was such that all blacks in the wealthier neighborhoods were classified as suspicious characters. Thus, the powers that be wanted all pigmented people stopped and questioned, regardless of physical appearance.

"Jack, you're right; it's not an easy job," Chief Driscoll said.

"So why are you giving me a hard time because we searched her, then?" Fletcher said. "She could have been a mule."

"With her husband and son? How about some common sense here? Why didn't you just say, 'We're sorry, we made a mistake?' Just kiss the guy's butt and let him go."

"And then when they delivered the drugs somewhere, you would be blocking my promotion because I exercised 'poor judgment.' We can't win." Fletcher folded his arms and sat back in his chair.

"Okay, searching the car was reasonable, but did you have to put the guy's mother in a four-point stance?"

"He would have never signed the form if we didn't do that."

A stern look crossed Chief Driscoll's face. "You should have just let him go. There was no need to do that. I hate to do this, but the two of you will be on paid administrative leave until this is cleared up."

There was a long pause. Finally, Fletcher said, "We spoke to our union lawyer. You have no cause to put us on leave."

McMahon nodded in agreement. The two officers were one step ahead of Chief Driscoll.

"That is not entirely correct," Chief Driscoll begged to differ. "You have to request a hearing."

The union lawyer, who was a pretty sharp girl, had given the two officers a trump card that Fletcher now played. "You may be able to place us on leave until our hearing, but we are still unsure how all the suspicious cars in our district magically appear on the dashboard computer."

He paused and looked at his chief, waiting for a response. When there was none, he continued. "We don't know what system is in place there; neighborhood watch, video cameras. Nobody will tell us."

It was now Chief Driscoll's turn to squirm. "What do you mean?"

"I mean, why is it that every black, Hispanic, or otherwise non-white individual automatically appears on our dashboard computer? If we are going to be disciplined for handling this incident poorly—and I am not admitting that we did so—then why are we being blamed for what appears to be a policy that we did not initiate? These are not 911 calls. There is some back-door phone line, or else a bunch of bureaucrats somewhere are looking at footage of minivideo cameras."

Chief Driscoll recognized the implied threat. McMahon and Fletcher were young, but they were learning how to play the game. Any investigation of any so-called racial profiling and the poor treatment of Cord would result in the questioning of the system used to keep undesirables out of the wealthy neighborhoods—a system that Chief Driscoll was complicit in designing and implementing. The resulting imbroglio could implicate his and some powerful politicians whose orders he had followed. Chief Driscoll just wanted to retire, get his pension, sell his house at an obscene profit, and live happily ever after in Hilton Head. His instinct was to bureaucratically destroy both McMahon and Fletcher. But if he followed his instincts, he would have never survived the internecine politics that being a police chief entails. He would follow his reason. And his reason said to come to an accommodation with all parties.

"Let's backtrack here," Chief Driscoll said. "What if we were able to make this situation just go away?"

"How we going to do that, Chief?" McMahon said.

"Campbell is a wealthy man. According to Hoffman, all he wants is an apology from you guys. I told him that we don't apologize, but now, I'm having second thoughts. I just want this to go away."

"Apologize for what?" said Fletcher. "For doing our job? I'm not apologizing to anyone." He looked at his partner. "Let's talk to the union lawyer again." He stood, suggesting he'd had the final word in all of this. He was aware that Chief Driscoll's retirement was just right around the corner. He was willing to wait the situation out. Hopefully, once his chief was gone, so would be the matter with Cord.

Chief Driscoll looked at the two men. "I'll tell you what. I will reassign Jack to regular patrol with Sharon Kline. Kevin, you patrol that neighborhood by yourself. The administrative leave, on second thought, is not a good idea. Let's give it some time. Why don't we just sleep on it? Perhaps cooler heads will prevail."

Just like Fletcher had figured. The wait was on . . .

CHAPTER 5

"What do you mean I can't get an appointment now?" Kwame Baker screamed into his cellphone. "I've been on hold for twenty minutes. You gotta help me. I'm dying! I'm dying!"

Dr. Mason's secretary, Roberta, lifted her eyes to the ceiling. This was the fifth withdrawing Oxy-head she had spoken to today, and her patience was gone. She replied in a bored tone. "Mr. Baker, it's five o'clock. Dr. Mason is about to leave."

"Just have him call in the script then. Please! I'm in so much pain!"

"You know the doctor can't prescribe Oxycodone without seeing you. Besides, it's against the law to call in a narcotic prescription. You should have called earlier."

"I called four times . . ."He was about to add, "you goddamn bitch," but then realized Roberta would simply hang up, as she had done on several occasions before. "I couldn't get through. I got cut off every time."

"Mr. Baker, if you think you are dying, go to the Emergency Room or dial 911."

"They won't do shit. I'll sit there for six hours, and they won't give me a script. I'm in pain! Real pain!"

Roberta looked at the phone in frustration, as if the image of her annoyed face could magically be transported to Kwame's phone and make this problem go away.

"Mr. Baker, go the Emergency Room." She quickly placed the phone in its cradle before she heard a reply.

"Worthless bitch," Kwame screamed.

He had not slept in twenty-four hours. His heart was racing, and his sweaty palms made it almost impossible to hold his cellphone. His emaciated 120-pound frame walked back and forth in his run-down apartment. He tried to focus on the cellphone, but his watery eyes rendered the numbers into random blurs. He ran into his bathroom. There had to be some left. Even though in his mid-twenties, he looked older. His sallow, unshaven, hollowed face stared back at him before he opened the mirrored door to his medicine cabinet. There just had to be some left. He shifted things around. Nothing. For the sixth time today, he gazed at the empty vials. He looked at them again, eyes focusing and refocusing as their water content fluctuated. They all read the same thing, *"No refills."*

Then he had an idea. Grabbing a safety pin, he scratched out the word "No" on one of the vials. Now it read "refills." Maybe the pharmacist would buy it. This was his only chance—especially if he had a chance to use his natural eloquence.

Even though Kwame was the offspring of a crack-addicted mother, he had managed to graduate from high school. While the casual observer may consider this no great accomplishment, it actually indicated a high degree of intelligence. After all, it was well-known that the purpose of the indifferent Bridgeport public school system was to provide employment for the local denizens, not educate students. Perhaps some pharmacist bent on leaving for the day would fall for his gift of gab and not bother to check the pharmacy's computer.

Throwing the vial in his pocket, he threw on his Salvation Army coat, exited his apartment, and shuffled down the stairs, his nostrils inured to the perpetual stench of urine in the stairwells. There was a pharmacy only a few blocks away, but they were used to his pleading. He walked down to the train station and four stops later, he was in downtown Westport instead.

There it wasn't long before he found a cheery pharmaceutical establishment that was open twenty-four hours a day. His mood soured, however, when he entered and found several people ahead of him. Annoyed, he got behind them. His nose started to run. He wiped the mucous on his sleeve. His hands started shaking, and the sweaty palms returned. Then came the "ants," running up his legs, into his groin, and around his buttocks. And they were all biting him, sharp pinpricks that were tolerable but heralded the worst of Oxy withdrawal.

"Come on!" he yelled after several long minutes. He'd only done what most patrons want to do when standing in the long pharmacy line. God forbid one of the customers actually wants the pharmacist to counsel them on the prescription!

Finally, there was only one person ahead of him now, an obese woman whose abdominal fat hung like water balloons over the sides of her tight stretch pants. While yanking on the arms of two squirming toddlers, one black and the other white, she told the pharmacist, "It's your fault if I get knocked up again. I need my birth control pills. They're supposed to be free now."

"It doesn't matter if they're free. You have no refills, ma'am. You have to call your doctor," the pharmacist dead-panned.

"I can pay for them. I just got more money on my card."

"You have to have a doctor's prescription."

"Yo, mamacita! Come on!" Kwame yelled, pushing his empty vial past the woman and toward the pharmacist's face.

"What's wrong with you? Wait your turn," the lady said, her massive body pivoting toward the surging Kwame.

Ignoring her, Kwame said to the pharmacist. "I'm dying. I'm in pain. I need my Oxy now!"

The pharmacist, a listless, graying fifty-year-old woman who confronted similar patients several times a day, knew that keeping a calm demeanor minimized the chance this situation would become uncontrollable. Smiling at Kwame, she took the vial in her hand, immediately noticing that he had scratched out the word *"No."*

She saw no sense in confrontation. She simply said, "These cannot be refilled by law, sir."

"But it says 'refills,'" Kwame responded.

"The pharmacist who typed this made a mistake. This can't be refilled. You need another doctor's prescription."

Kwame had actually started to calm down, but now the woman he had preempted objected.

"Why are you taking care of him? I was here first. I need my birth control pills." She yanked on the arm of one of her toddlers who was trying to escape. The kids started to howl.

Kwame's mellow mood change was short-lived. "Who cares? I'm dying. I have constant pain. I need my Oxy."

"Wait your turn!"

"You don't need no birth control. Ain't nobody tryna fuck yo' ugly ass anyway. That fat ass is all the birth control you need."

This comment was not well-received by the obese woman, who now let go of the hands of her children and lunged at Kwame, swinging her bag at his head and yelling, "Fuck you, junkie."

Kwame batted the purse away and screamed at the pharmacist, "Gimme my Oxy!"

The pharmacist calmly replied, "Sir, you must have a prescription. Perhaps I can call your doctor now."

She had never seen a doctor return a phone call to refill an Oxycodone prescription, but now the situation was indeed spiraling just a little bit out of control. She had to buy time and hope the obese woman calmed down.

It didn't happen. The woman plowed into Kwame, and being twice his size, bowled him to the ground.

The dopamine-starved neurons in Kwame's brain were now firing furiously. He picked himself up and ran toward the pharmacist. He pounded his fists on the counter that separated them, without any apparent concern as to whether his metacarpals could sustain the impact without splintering.

Such displays by addicts and the chemically dependent were routine in the pharmacist's line of work. The only question was whether to call the police. If it were late in her shift, she would not, because then, she would have to be interviewed, and she did not get paid for overtime. But she had six hours remaining in her shift, and having the police cart this lunatic away would allow her to do less work and still get paid. She picked up the phone and dialed 911.

Kwame continued his rampage, first opening several boxes of condoms, displaying them to the obese lady and suggesting she purchase the Magnum XL since her lover would have to be well-endowed to penetrate her. Oxy withdrawal apparently did not dull his sense of humor. The woman, with the desire of self-preservation outweighing the retention of her dignity, exited the store with her children in tow.

Periodically, Kwame would return to the pharmacy counter and bang his fists on the counter, demanding Oxycodone. The pharmacist had now retreated to a cushioned chair and was actually engrossed in one of a series of Danielle Steel novels sold by the pharmacy.

By the time the officers arrived, Kwame was kicking the clear-glass refrigerator, leaving several artistic radiating spirals on the front.

"Stop that right now!" Fletcher boomed.

Kwame was oblivious to the officer's command as he screamed at the pharmacist, "Where's my Oxy? Where's it at?"

Fletcher tackled Kwame, quickly wrestling him to the floor. Kwame's arms were pinioned behind his back and a second officer, Sharon Kline, applied the cuffs. The two police officers grabbed Kwame under each armpit and gently brought him to his feet.

The pharmacist, who was on a first-name basis with all the officers, came forward.

"Sorry, guys. I managed to get two of them out of here today without calling you, but this one was just out of control."

"No problem," Fletcher said. "I doubt if this is his debut. We should be able to keep him off the streets for at least a few months."

It was then that Kwame noticed Officer Kline with her short, black hair, wide hips, and broad shoulders. Unaware of the modern standards of political correctness, he came to a conclusion that he immediately proclaimed for all to hear:

"Fucking bitch dyke cop. Fuck you."

Fletcher, still frustrated by what was now labeled as "the Campbell incident," was in a foul mood. Furthermore, his natural chivalry required that such a comment be avenged. He had first-hand experience with Officer Kline and had considerable evidence that Kwame's analysis was incorrect, although pointing this out publicly would not have endeared him to his wife and mother of his two children. He was withdrawing his fist for a quick blow to Kwame's solar plexus when Officer Kline grabbed his wrist while nodding to the video cameras that overlooked the room.

Kwame, unaware of the fragility of his position, continued to comment on Officer Kline's perceived sexuality. The two officers escorted Kwame out of the pharmacy toward the double-parked patrol car. Kwame was about to utter "ugly dyke" for the umpteenth time when he became acutely short of breath, the consequence of a diaphragmatic spasm induced by a hard jab from Fletcher's fist into his solar plexus. Officer Kline, who was a pacifist at heart in spite of her profession, quietly expressed her disapproval to her lover, but it was too late.

As Kwame doubled over, his right eye was met with an upper cut. The ring on Fletcher's fist tore into his cornea, the clear part of his eye, resulting in a large piece of tissue being displaced. His eyeball then retracted into the socket. Fortunately for Kwame, evolution had provided him with a cushioning fat pad behind his eye, along with a long optic nerve. This allowed for the inner portion of his eye to remain uninjured; however, the surrounding fat pushed into the adjacent bones, resulting in a fracture in the thin bone at the bottom of his eye socket. The problem was that the cornea of the human eye has the most pain fibers per surface area of any tissue in the body. While Kwame was unaware of this anatomical tidbit, he was now brutally aware of the consequence: tremendous pain.

"You sonofabitch!" he screamed while attempting to bring his manacled hands from behind him to cover his eye. As this was impossible, he began screaming furiously and blinking continuously. He did have the wherewithal to close his good eye and conclude that his right eye had lost vision. "You blinded me you, cocksucker."

"You see that? You see that?" Kwame yelled to no one in particular.

Fletcher quickly pushed him into the car, not caring that he fell between the back and front seat. His ranting continued, but when they closed the door, it was harder for bystanders to hear.

"Why did you do that? Are you out of your mind?" Officer Kline said. "We have to take him to Saint V's."

"He got what he deserved," Fletcher said. Fletcher was known to beat a few suspects in his day. "These people have to learn respect."

"Respect? How about unemployment? How about no pension? I was the one who was insulted. It's part of the job."

"Well, these punks have to learn that part of our job is putting them in their place when they mouth off. Just take him to the station, book him, and throw him in the pen. Who cares?"

Officer Kline could still hear Kwame screaming, "I'm blind! I'm blind!"

"Jack, think. If he keeps screaming like that, the prison guards are going to insist that he be taken to Saint V's. We won't be able to control the situation as easily. We have to take him."

Fletcher put his hand on his forehead for what seemed to be minutes. Finally, he said, "Let's go. Maybe we'll get one of those foreign doctors who's easy to intimidate."

Officer Kline wasn't completely secure with Fletcher's anticipations. "But what if we don't?"

Fletcher, not the least bit worried, replied, "So what? No one will believe anything this worthless piece of shit has to say anyway."

CHAPTER 6

D r. Teresa Trybus had had a long day. She had seen twenty patients in the morning and then done ten cataract operations at the hospital. She needed a glass of wine, but she was on call, and walking into the hospital with alcohol on her breath was considered bad form, especially when emergency surgery had to be performed. Thus, she was comforting herself with some Oreos and milk while watching *Downton Abbey* reruns on her 42-inch flat screen television.

The phone rang. "Can't they just leave me alone?" she moaned, throwing her head back against the Chesterfield sofa that highlighted her tastefully decorated living room.

She was trying to avoid the latest guy she had met on Match. com. He suffered from a peculiar abnormality that affected every male who ever filled out a dating questionnaire: acute altitude dementia, which was the inability to remember his height. But at least he wasn't as bad as the last loser, some divorced hedge fund guy who tried to get into her pants before even picking up the salad fork. So much for ChristianMingle.com.

She picked up the phone.

"Doctor, it's the service."

Maybe it was just a patient needing a prescription refill? "I have Saint Vincent's ER on the line."

No such luck.

"Patch me through," Teresa said into the phone receiver, then waited to be connected.

"This is Dr. Patel. Are you the ophthalmologist on call?"

"Yes. What's up?"

"We have a twenty-four-year-old African-American gentleman with a history of drug abuse presenting with orbital trauma."

"What's his vision?"

"What do you mean?"

"His vision. The eyes are used to see, so generally, the first thing you want to know is what the patient can see."

"We didn't check."

"You didn't check? Don't you think that is a particularly germane piece of information before you call me?" Teresa was making no attempt to hide her aggravation, of both having her evening interrupted and the incompetence of the caller.

"I am sorry, Doctor," Dr. Patel said. "I'm trying to do the needful, but there are many patients who are waiting."

"Let me talk to the attending," Teresa said.

"She's doing a code."

"Is he withdrawing?"

"No, we gave him some Oxy."

"Get an orbital CAT scan with coronals. I'll be over in an hour."

Teresa popped an entire Oreo into her mouth and then prepared to head off to the ER.

Having trained in the Bronx and now with her practice in Bridgeport, nothing surprised her. Most doctors would have been unnerved to see a manacled distraught man surrounded by two police officers, but she simply walked into the room and said, "Mr. Baker, I'm Dr. Trybus. What happened?"

Kwame checked her out . . . with his good eye. Teresa was an attractive woman in her late thirties, with long, brown, shoulder-length hair parted in the middle. Her Polish ancestry had conferred her with green eyes and high cheekbones. This combined with her full lips gave her an angelic appearance.

"Fucking pig blinded me," Kwame said, nodding at Fletcher.

Fletcher interrupted. "He fell while resisting arrest. We're always concerned about the safety and well-being of everyone we encounter. Thus, we felt it prudent that he be properly checked." Fletcher could have said that line in his sleep. As a matter of fact, he probably did.

Teresa may have believed him, except that her Bronx training gave her an intimate knowledge of eye trauma and considerable experience with police mendacity. Furthermore, she had examined the CAT scan of Kwame's injury. He had what is called a "blowout fracture." This meant that the thin bone beneath his eye had literally been "blown out" by blunt force trauma to his eye. Ninety-five percent of the blowout fractures she had seen were caused by one of two things: balls or fists.

"Were you handcuffed when you fell, Mr. Baker?" Teresa asked.

"Fuck a fall," Kwame spat. "Like I said, this pig punched me. Had me cuffed when he did it. Pussy bitch."

Fletcher and Officer Kline had rehearsed their story ad nauseum. The problem was that the video camera at the pharmacy clearly showed that Kwame was handcuffed before leaving the pharmacy. It also showed that his resistance was minimal, meaning that the injury had to occur after exiting the pharmacy. Unfortunately, neither were experts on eye trauma.

Teresa looked at Fletcher. "So, he fell after he was handcuffed?"

"Yes," Fletcher replied.

"Lying piece of shit. Pussy punched me after he cuffed me." Kwame was relentless on making sure he was heard.

"This is going to sting for five seconds, then the pain in the eye is going to be gone." Teresa grabbed a bottle of Tetracaine, an eyedrop that numbs the eye, and placed it in Kwame's right eye.

"Ahh!" he screamed. "You got that right, Doc!"

Then the pain was gone, like magic.

"Do you wear glasses or contacts to see in the distance?" Teresa asked.

"Naw. Perfect 20/20 all my life," Kwame was proud to say.

Teresa then asked him to read a sign on the door across the hall. As his right eye was swollen shut, she was checking the vision in the uninjured left eye.

"Consult Room 4," he said.

She then grabbed a tissue box. "Hold this over your left eye."

Kwame complied while Teresa pried open his right eye. "Can you read that sign now?"

"Consult Room 4."

But Teresa noted that he had moved the tissue box, exposing his left eye.

"Keep the left eye covered."

Kwame covered his left eye with the tissue box. "I can't see shit. Told you. Cop blinded me."

"Can you see the number on the top of the clock?"

"Yeah, I see the 12."

With this crude examination, Teresa estimated his vision to be 20/100 in the right eye and 20/20 in the left.

She helped him off the gurney and had him sit on a chair in front of the slit lamp, a special microscope for magnifying the eye. Pulling his head forward, she gently pried open his eyelids and magnified the image of Kwame's eye. The normally white sclera was bright red, the consequence of ruptured blood vessels on his eye's surface. The clear part of the eye, the cornea, had a large abrasion with a deep penetration mark. She rotated her head and espied the diamond-studded ring on the male officer's right hand. She glared at him, but Fletcher held her gaze until she flinched and returned to complete the examination.

Over the next thirty minutes, Teresa dilated Kwame's pupils, carefully checking the front of the eye for the common dangers from eye trauma; cataract, retinal tears, retinal detachments, glaucoma, bleeding in the front of the eye, or ruptures of the eye tissue itself. She took out her miniature flashlight and asked Kwame to follow the light with his eyes. He did fine until she moved the light upward. As his lids were becoming more swollen, she had to gently lift his right eyelid to ascertain this. From this, she concluded that the lower muscle of the eye, what was called the inferior rectus muscle, was either swollen or trapped in the hole in the bone created by the blowout fracture.

"You should be fine, Mr. Baker," she said as she patched the eye shut. "In a few days, the front of your eye will heal and the vision will be normal. The only problem is that you can't look up with your right eye. This usually goes away with time, but sometimes, we have to operate and free up the muscle in your eye."

"Operate? On who's money? I ain't got no insurance."

"Don't worry. I'll take care of you for free. But with a little luck, it will just heal."

She sat down at one of the workstations and typed her name and password, *loyola3,* into the computer. As a product of Catholic education, she used the names of her various alma maters. Unfortunately, the computer was not in a religious mood and rejected her password, informing her that she needed to create a new password. This took several minutes, but finally, she was able to access Kwame's medical records and began typing her consultation report.

In the meantime, Fletcher and Officer Kline walked over to where Teresa sat, Officer Kline smiling and Fletcher glaring. She ignored them for several seconds until Fletcher cleared his throat.

"Can I help you?" Teresa said without looking up.

"What are you going to write in your report?" Officer Kline said cheerfully.

"That is none of your concern." Teresa never looked up.

Fletcher glared at her. "We're making it our concern." His tone was on the verge of being threatening.

"What is this, good cop, bad cop?" Teresa let out a snort. "I can tell you one thing that will be in this report. What the two of you just said to me. And if you want to make any further comments, I will be happy to add them as well." Teresa finally looked up at the officers, flashing a counterfeit smile.

"That would not be wise," Fletcher said.

Teresa turned her attention back to her keyboard and began typing. She then said to Fletcher, "I was never a good speller. Do you spell wise W-I-Z-E or W-I-S-E?"

CHAPTER 7

Connie Vivanti loved to win. Maybe it was because she was the only girl in a family of four boys. Maybe it was that her father never let her win; to the point where he used to hide his money under the Monopoly board and talk her into a trade. Then he would pull the money from under the board, build hotels, and win. Maybe it was the competitive juices acquired from playing high school and college soccer. Or maybe it was simply genetic.

Whatever the reason, being a public defender was the perfect job for her. Although she came from a working-class background, she felt no kinship with her clients whom she considered to be worthless losers: alcoholics, druggies, perverts, women-beaters, thugs, thieves, and pathological liars. She just loved to go into the courtroom and wipe the floor with some hapless underprepared drone from the district attorney's office. What made it great fun was that virtually all her clients were guilty.

But she did have some of her favorites, and Kwame Baker was one of them. This time, she met him in the Visitation Room of the Bridgeport Correctional Facility, the dumping ground for the detritus of the surrounding suburbs. Attired in ill-fitting brilliant orange prison garb, his leg and arms were manacled as he was plopped before Connie by a blank-faced prison guard. His right eyelids were so swollen that it was impossible to see the eye itself.

"It's the lovely Consuela!" Kwame greeted by her baptismal name. Not even a defective eye had dampened his spirits.

And Connie was lovely; a buxom, raven-haired beauty with dark eyes, olive skin, and a figure that caused the eyes of men to linger on her, even when she dressed in modest professional attire.

"Have you dumped that loser yet?" Kwame asked Connie.

Not only were they on a first-name basis, but Connie recalled that during their last encounter, her otherwise stellar representation was encumbered by a temporary depression over a failing relationship. She still managed to plea down his drug possession to time served, but as Kwame pointed out to her, she was off her "A-game" because, "You professional types give it up too easy. Makes you feel liberated. You needs to be more coy."

"He's long gone," she responded. She didn't want to admit she'd actually taken him up on his advice.

"Good news. You need to con-cen-trate on my situation. No piece-a-shit boyfriends messin' up your mind. You didn't hook up with some other loser, did you? You concentrate on me; I'm your new honey. I'm your main squeeze." He pointed at his chest with the two thumbs of his manacled hands.

She had lost count of the number of times she had represented Kwame. At least three DUIs, half a dozen possessions, even a public indecency for simply urinating outside of a bar. They all ended the same: time served.

"Assault, resisting arrest, creating a public disturbance." She had read the police report and was familiar with his case, including the circumstances of the eye injury. "This is not your usual modus operandi, Kwame."

"Modus operan-da-fuck? Over here tossing 'round big words for no-ass reason."

"Not your method of operation. Not your normal way of behaving."

"It's a bunch of bullshit. I just was tryna pick up my Oxy."

"And the eye's okay?" Connie tilted her head from left to right looking at Kwame's swollen closed eye. There was dark bruising underneath it.

"Eye's fine. Doc was right. Better in two days." He brought his manacled hands up to his right eye and pried it open. Connie flinched. The normally white part of the eye was bulging, with sacks of bright red blood protruding over the lower eyelid.

"Doesn't look good."

"But it sees good,"he said.

"Doc called it a blown-out fracture . . . Something like that. She was bad too. Tried to holla at her, but she wasn't feelin' it."

Connie opened the folder that was in front of her. "Says here you fell."

"Come on, you don't believe that shit. Pig sucker punched me like a bitch."

"That's not what it says here." She pointed to the words written on a sheet of paper.

"Ask the doc. She believed me."

"She told you that?" Connie looked up from the folder with a raised eyebrow, waiting on Kwame's response.

"Naw. But I could tell. Pig told her I fell down. But then she looked right at his hand after she looked at my eye. She knew."

"So why did the cop hit you?"

"Called his ho a dyke. Shouldn't a done that. I's asken for it."

"His wife?"

"Naw. The bitch cop who helped arrest me. He's doin' her."

"How do you know?"

"Man, I just knows. Why else would he hit me? Cops take shit like that from niggas like me all the time. No reason to hit me. Unless he's doin' her."

Connie found his analysis quite droll and tried to contain her smile. For the next twenty minutes, she got Kwame's side of the story. But as she listened, her mood soured and her blood began to boil. Yes, her client was a low-life dirtbag, but he wasn't an evil person. And he certainly didn't deserve to get pummeled in the face, even if he called the cop a dyke. This was the third time this month that one of her clients had been used by Bridgeport's finest as an involuntary punching bag.

At the end of her conversation with Kwame, Connie gave him a form to sign. "This gives me the right to interview the doctor and obtain all your medical records."

He signed the form. "No new losers. I'm your man now. You need to concentrate." And he was right.

Connie had never met Dr. Teresa Trybus before, but she knew from their first phone conversation that there was a potential for friendship. Both were single professional women in their late thirties who were economically secure but personally unfulfilled. Teresa had even invited Connie to her Southport condo to discuss Kwame's case upon ascertaining that she was equally outraged at the unproven brutality rained down upon him. She was willing to share any medical insight that might help.

Connie took her up on her offer, and a couple of days after their initial phone conversation, she was at Teresa's place. The condo was not large but tastefully decorated with various seascapes and marine artifacts. More important, it had a view of Long Island Sound. Teresa, like many Connecticut professionals, was an avid sailor. Connie sized her up immediately as a super achiever, with her muscular toned body, the product of heavy exercise and advanced yoga.

"Looks like you escaped Sandy," Connie said while extending her hand to Teresa. She was referring to the hurricane that devastated coastal Connecticut several years ago.

"Not really. My boat was destroyed. Still trying to collect on the insurance. Those guys are nothing more than legalized Mafia. Never missed a premium and now they say the boat did not have flood insurance. I mean, it's in the fucking water. How can it not have flood insurance?"

Although Teresa was a professional, she had a mouth that could make a truck driver blush.

"That's why I like defending criminals. They're much more honorable."

Teresa laughed. "Pinot Grigio?" she offered her guest.

"Sure," said Connie. She welcomed the opportunity to include a kind of sort of girlfriend gesture among their unofficial business meeting.

Teresa led Connie into her kitchen. She extended her hand to a chair for Connie to sit while she walked over to the fridge, grabbed the bottle of wine, and proceed to uncork it. She retrieved two wineglasses, then handed Connie an ample glass. "So how can I help you?" she asked as she remained standing pouring herself a drink. "I've seen the cops whack these guys around many times—more in New York than here—but never saw anyone willing to do anything about it."

"New York that bad?" Connie took a sip of her wine and allowed the controlled portions to slither down her throat.

"Not as bad as Providence, where I interned. Those guys really enjoyed beating up the perps. It was an art form to them. Kept the crime rate a lot lower though." Teresa placed the bottle back in the fridge so that it would keep its chill.

"That's not how the system is supposed to work."

"I know. Just making the observation."

Connie produced the permission form and handed it to Teresa. "That allows you to discuss Kwame Baker's medical condition with me."

She continued while Teresa looked at the form. "I've been doing this a long time, and I guess I should be jaded by now."

Teresa sipped the wine and held the glass in the air, signaling her approval.

"But this is getting to the point where I can no longer remain silent. This is the third client this month that claims to have been beaten by the cops. They can't all be lying."

"Agreed," Teresa said, placing her glass on the countertop. "I mean, who knows, but I'm almost certain this guy was punched. Between what Baker said, the nature of the injury, and the feeble attempt by one of the officers to intimidate me, it seems likely."

"What do you mean, 'intimidate you'?" Connie's ears perked up.

"When I was typing my report, the woman cop was being sweet, but the macho guy kept asking me what I was writing. He kept glaring at me and told me to be careful what I wrote. I told him I would write everything he said to me in my report, so he stopped bothering me, but he wasn't pleased. You would think the bozo would know better than to try to intimidate a woman doctor."

"Can you get the report for me?"

"Sure, let me print it out."

"What do you mean?"

"I have to go to the computer to print it out."

Connie had no idea it was that easy.

"Right this way." Teresa led Connie into her office. Each still cradled their glasses of wine.

Both women sat in front of Teresa's computer while she logged onto the St. Vincent's Website, entering the portal.

Connie watched in amazement as she saw lists of patients' names on the screen. "I thought those privacy laws protected all the patients' information."

"Huge scam. Big Brother, or in my case, Big Sister, is watching. I can access any patient's record I want. I can even see what's going on in the emergency room." She clicked an icon and the list of all the patients currently in the ER appeared. She scrolled down the list and clicked a name. A patient's record appeared. "This stud is being treated for genital herpes. And look, he's married." She pointed to the letter "M" on the status bar. "I should download the record and sell it to someone who wants to blackmail him." She let a mischievous chuckle escape her mouth. "I guess I have a devious mind."

"Unbelievable," Connie said. She wasn't fazed by Teresa's suggested mind-set, but by the fact that millions of patients' private medical records were so easily at one's disposal. "Are all medical records like this?"

"Not yet, but pretty soon. We doctors get penalized if we don't convert to electronic medical records."

"What do you mean?"

"Medicare pays us less money. Soon, private insurance will follow. No electronic records, no reimbursement. No reimbursement, no practice. Very simple."

"Why are they doing this?"

"Because they can." It was just as plain and as simple as Teresa had said it.

Connie thought of all the intimate details of her personal life she had discussed with her gynecologist, who pecked away at her keyboard while she spoke. "I'm not going to doctors anymore." She shook her head like a three-year-old girl refusing to wear a pretty dress.

"Good luck. We're hard to avoid." Teresa moved her mouse around until the record of Kwame Baker appeared. She arrived at her consult report and clicked "Print." As usual, the printer made some mechanical sounds for about thirty seconds until it deigned to print the report.

Connie skimmed the report as it slid from the printer's channel. "You said that the cop hit him."

"No, I said that's what the patient said. I'm still old-fashioned and write my notes in what is called the SOAP format: Subjective, Objective, Assessment, Plan. Subjective is what the patient says. Objective is what I see on my examination. Assessment is my diagnosis or list of possible diagnoses, and Plan is self-explanatory."

"So you're saying that the cop did not hit him."

"Absolutely not. I wasn't there. I don't know what happened. I think the overwhelming likelihood is that the cop did hit him."

"Why?" Connie sipped her wine without breaking eye contact with Teresa.

"I've seen hundreds of blowouts. This was almost certainly due to a punch. But like I said, I wasn't there."

"What's a blowout?"

"A blowout fracture. Let me show you."

Teresa moved the mouse and clicked several icons. A gray and white picture appeared on the computer screen. The picture looked extraterrestrial, with two suns hovering over a horizon with overhanging clouds. "This is what is called a coronal orbital CAT scan. Basically, it cuts the head into planes from the nose to the back of the head." She pointed to one of the suns. "This is Baker's right eye." She then rotated the wheel on her mouse. The two suns diminished in size until they became single points. And they disappeared. Then the suns reappeared as she reversed the direction on the wheel rotation. "When I scroll this scan, we can see the eye in various planes." She stopped until both eyes reached their maximum size. "Look here." She ran her finger below the image of the right eye. "Notice that there is no bone beneath here but there is bone beneath the left eye."

Connie saw what she meant. The horizon was broken under the right eye but not the left.

"That's where the bone was broken?" she asked.

"In a sense, but what actually happened is it was blown out; thus, the name blowout fracture. Each eye is encased in a bony socket called the orbit. It actually consists of parts of seven different bones. When the eye is punched, it is pushed into the orbit rapidly. The increased pressure puts a hole in the paper-thin bone at the bottom of the orbit."

Connie thought about this for a second. "How come this injury isn't more common? It would seem that every boxer would have one."

"No. The blow has to be directly into the eye with an object small enough to push the eye back into the socket with high velocity. In fact, blowout fractures were very common in the bare-knuckle fights on the early 1900s. That's one of the main reasons boxing gloves were invented; to prevent this injury."

"So why are you convinced Baker's blowout is due to a punch and not a fall?"

"I've seen blowouts with falls, but there is almost always another facial injury to go with it. Injuries such as a laceration of the eyelid, forehead, or cheek. Many have broken or displaced teeth. But this guy had none of that. When I see that, it's almost always a punch or a ball—especially tennis balls or baseballs—because they are the correct size."

"Baker showed me his eye. It was all puffed up and beet red. But he said it was fine."

"It is. The puffiness and redness will all go away. Blowout fractures rarely injure the eye itself. The problem with his injury is that the muscle may be entrapped. He can't look up with his right eye."

"Entrapped?" Connie was enthralled by her mini-medical course.

"Yes," and Teresa was delighted to continue instructing her. This is what she did. This was what she knew, loved, and breathed, and what no one could take away from her. "It means one of the muscles of his eye may be stuck in the hole in the bone caused by the blowout fracture. Sometimes the muscle is just swollen from the injury. With a little time, the swelling goes away, and the patient gets better without doing anything."

"You mean the patient can now look up?"

"Exactly. But if Kwame can't do so in the near future, I will have to operate and put a plastic plate over the hole in the bone. Here, take a look."

Teresa clicked a few icons and another view of the eye appeared. "This is a sagittal view, meaning we're slicing the eye from the side." She made a karate-chop-like motion with her hand by her left temple. The eye now looked like a ball but with a small oblong ball in the front. She pointed to the oblong ball. "Here is the lens. Completely undamaged from what I can tell." She moved her finger along the back of the ball. "The retina is flat too. There's no tear or detachment."

She then clicked the mouse and returned to the coronal view. "But look here." She put her finger on the screen. "You see that blur near the hole in the bone? That's the muscle."

"I'll take your word for it," Connie said. It looked more like a blob to her. But what did she know. Teresa was the expert, and even if she wasn't, she sure sounded like one. And she'd sound like one on the witness stand if need be. "But how do you know if you have to operate?"

"I'll see him in follow-up. If he still can't look up with his right eye, I'll go in."

"So you really think he was punched?"

Teresa took a sip of her wine before she'd answered. That

mini-lesson had made her parched. "Not unless he fell on a door-knob." The pleasure of the wine soothing her throat was expressed on her face.

"Would you be willing to testify to that?"

"Sure would, but keep in mind that this is not a certainty. Another ophthalmologist could say it was due to a fall. Like I said, I wasn't there."

"Would you be willing to sign an affidavit also?"

"Of course," Teresa said while standing up.

Connie took her seat, opened her laptop, and placed it beside the keyboard of Teresa's computer. "Give me five minutes."

She pecked away while Teresa left the room and caught up on some household chores.

After a few minutes, she returned to the computer desk just as Connie was finishing.

"Read this over and see if I am accurately representing your opinion," Connie said as she rose from the chair and motioned for Teresa to sit down. "Some of it is written in legalese, but I did my best to use the technical terms you taught me."

Teresa sat down and began reading the document, scrolling through the initial legal procedural comments until arriving at her statement. "I'm amazed you picked up all my medical jargon so quickly. This affidavit is very accurate. You managed to depict my opinion while hedging appropriately."

"Thanks," Connie said. "We lawyers have to be quick studies."

"What do I do now?" Teresa said, turning her head to her new friend.

Connie walked over to the laptop and scrolled to the bottom of the document. "Excuse me," she said as she reached across Teresa and pushed several keys. On the screen appeared a black line.

"Just use your finger to sign your name electronically," she said while pointing to the line. Teresa did as instructed.

Mission accomplished, Connie downed the rest of her wine. "Thank you so much for your help." She nodded toward Teresa's computer. "Are you really serious? You can look at any records in the hospital?"

"Yep."

"Any patient? The X-rays, the lab results, the consult reports? Anything?"

"Big Sister is watching." She winked.

"Could you check on some of my other clients?"

"Not really. I mean, I could, but it would not be legal. They're not my patients."

"I understand that. What I'm asking is whether it's technically possible?"

"Of course, it is. But keep in mind that the system is set up so they know when I'm looking at a patient's record. In other words, the IT people at the hospital will be able to tell the exact time I looked at Kwame Baker's records and for how long. They will know I printed a report. That I looked at the orbital coronal and sagittal scans. Every keystroke I make is recorded in a database along with the exact time."

"In other words, someone is watching Big Sister."

"You got it . . . sister."

CHAPTER 8

"**P**earls?"

Perhaps she was mistaken. Connie locked eyes with her friend and nemesis, Sarah Cornell. Sarah smiled broadly and gave Connie a "Jackie Kennedy" wave. And they were pearls she was wearing.

"Don't let her intimidate you," Kwame said to Connie as he sat at the defense table in the courtroom. "She bad though."

Kwame sat to Connie's left, his legs manacled, but his arms free at Connie's insistence. He actually looked comfortable in the bright orange prison garb like a Wall Street investment banker in a Brooks Brothers suit. This was Connie's first arraignment of the day, and she expected the usual drones from the district attorney's office. But there was the alpha dog: Sarah Cornell.

Sarah was a trust fund débutante from Greenwich who had turned down several offers from Manhattan white shoe law firms to become a prosecutor. Her genetic financial security gave her the freedom to pursue her passion, which was putting bad guys behind bars. She was impeccably tailored: Escada blazer and a navy-blue pleated skirt that descended exactly two inches below her knees. Her ebony Stuart Weitzman pumps had heels that looked like stilts. Her blond hair was pulled back in a bun, highlighting her blue eyes, petite nose, and triangular jaw.

But *pearls*? This entire sartorial splendor just to prosecute perverts, drug addicts, and women-beaters? But that was Sarah's style.

"You can take this fancy bitch," Kwame mumbled without turning his head towards Connie.

"All rise," the bailiff pronounced, ". . . and ye shall be heard."

Kwame mouthed the old English. He had heard it so many times he had it memorized.

"Judge Rita Durazio presiding."

Judge Durazio took her seat, and when espying Connie and Sarah, she gave a huge smile. They were two of her favorites. This was going to be a good catfight.

"Docket number BRG-CV-11-5045668-S, Kwame Baker versus the State of Connecticut. Vandalism, resisting arrest, assault, and creating a public disturbance."

The judge motioned with her right hand, palm up.

Connie rose to her feet. "Not guilty to all charges, Your Honor."

Judge's Durazio's left hand motioned toward Sarah.

"We request $100,000 in bail." Sarah's friendly smile was long gone.

A flabbergasted Connie responded, "We ask that Your Honor release Mr. Baker on his own recognizance. The prosecutor's request is patently ridiculous."

Sarah's eyes locked onto the judge's. "My esteemed colleague's client is twenty-four years old and has been arrested nine times: three DWIs, five for possession, and once for public indecency."

"For taking a piss," Kwame yelled.

Judge Durazio looked at Connie as if she were a child playing Nintendo past her bedtime. "Please control your client, Ms. Vivanti."

"Yes, Your Honor. We apologize," Connie said in a submissive tone.

She leaned over and loudly whispered into her client's ear. "If you say one more thing, I will personally cut your balls off with a butter knife."

He pulled away from her with an astonished look on his face. The judge smiled in amusement.

Sarah continued. "It is unlikely that my esteemed colleague will be able to keep Mr. Baker from the State's hospitality. Thus, he poses a significant flight risk."

"Your Honor, as Ms. Cornell has established, my client has been arrested nine times. He has never left the area and arrived promptly for all legal procedures in the past when he was released on his own recognizance. Furthermore, as my esteemed colleague has pointed out to the Court, he has three DWIs, meaning that his driver's license has been revoked. Also, as my client is not a worldly traveler, he has no passport."

"I went to Jersey once." Kwame just couldn't help himself.

Connie paused and glared at her client, and then she continued. "Sorry, Your Honor."

Sarah rose to her feet. "Your Honor, perhaps my esteemed colleague is unfamiliar with the concept of public transportation, a system of trains and buses that allow passengers to leave the area for a marginal charge. Also, if going to New Jersey does not require a passport, it should."

Like most denizens of Greenwich, Sarah considered New Jersey a third-world country and the slight smile on Judge Durazio's face indicated she concurred.

She continued. "Mr. Baker is a career criminal and a significant flight risk. Our request for $100,000 remains."

Connie responded. "During his arrest, my client suffered an eye injury and needs continuous medical care. As you can see, Your Honor, my client's right eye is completely swollen shut." She pointed to Kwame, and he pointed to his eye, giving off a *yeah-what-she-said* look.

"What is the nature of the care required?" Judge Durazio asked.

"He has what is called a blowout fracture, meaning that the bone beneath his eye..."

"I know what a blowout fracture is, Counselor. I was not put on this bench by spontaneous generation."

"Sorry, Your Honor. May I continue?"

The judge nodded.

"The doctor is of the opinion that surgery may be required depending upon how the eye heals."

"But this can be arranged with the prison, can't it? We send prisoners to doctors all the time." The tone in the judge's voice was such that she really did seem concerned for Kwame's well-being.

"That's true, Your Honor, but there is a gentleman's agreement between prison administration and the police to create what might be referred to as 'logistical difficulties' for any prisoner alleging police brutality."

Sarah was on her feet in a nanosecond. "There is no proof of police brutality, and there is certainly no evidence of any 'gentleman's agreement,' as my esteemed colleague alleges. We will see to it that the prisoner receives proper medical care."

"Ms. Cornell cannot assure that unless she personally promises to drive my client to the doctor."

"Ms. Vivanti is being ridiculous, Your Honor."

"Ladies, please." As much as Judge Duraziow as entertained by the two attorneys' back-and-forth banter, she had to get to the meat of the issue and make a ruling.

"Your Honor," Connie said, "the medical record we have submitted to the Court indicates that Mr. Baker told the attending ophthalmologist at St. Vincent's that he was punched in the eye after being handcuffed."

"Your Honor, the police report indicates this injury occurred when Mr. Baker fell while resisting arrest." Sarah looked at Connie, waiting for her rebuttal.

Connie looked down at her desk, shuffled some papers, and then held up a document. "Your Honor, my apologies for not submitting this earlier, but I just obtained it last night. It is the sworn affidavit from Dr. Teresa Trybus, the on-call attending ophthalmologist at the ER the night my client was seen. She states that the overwhelming likelihood is that a punch, not a fall, caused Mr. Baker's injury."

"Approach the bench, please," the judge ordered.

Both lawyers walked up to the judge's bench.

Sarah turned toward Connie and pointed her right index finger between her eyes. "Did the doctor witness the arrest? Perhaps she was power walking in downtown Westport as part of her exercise routine."

Connie did not respond.

"Did the doctor witness the arrest?"

"Of course, she didn't. Her opinion is based on the nature of the injury."

Sarah turned back to Judge Durazio. "Your Honor, first of all, this affidavit was not presented to all parties prior to this arraignment and should not be considered."

"I will decide what is to be considered, Ms. Cornell," the judge said.

"Sorry, Your Honor. I did not mean to be presumptuous."

"I will consider this document now." Judge Durazio motioned the lawyers back to their respective seats while she read the affidavit.

Connie could feel the argument tipping her way. After years in the legal profession, she saw courtroom drama more as an emotional tide rather than a compilation of legal data. And the tide was now in her favor. She sensed it, and so did Sarah.

When the judge finally looked up, Sarah spoke. "Permission to speak, Your Honor?"

Judge Durazio nodded.

"Your Honor, with all due respect, the doctor's opinion is subject to interpretation, and another doctor may disagree."

"Your Honor," Connie began, riding on the coattail of permission to speak that was granted by the judge to her counterpart, "in the past month, three of my clients have alleged police brutality. They can't all be lying."

"Oh yes, they can," Sarah said. "And Ms. Vivanti has provided no documentation of these cases to the Court. Are we to believe the statement of two dedicated public servants or the rantings of a withdrawing junkie?"

Connie was about to respond when Kwame jumped to his feet. His silence had been far too good to be true.

"That pussy cop handcuffed me and punched me because I called his ho a dyke," Kwame declared as if he'd placed his right hand on the Bible and sworn to it.

Connie threw up her hands in disgust. If she had a butter knife, Kwame would now be singing soprano.

"I'm sorry, Your Honor." Once again, she found herself apologizing on behalf of her client.

Unbeknownst to Kwame, Judge Durazio was one of the few openly gay judges in Superior Court. She glared at Kwame, and Connie felt a seismic shift in the emotional tide.

"Ladies, we have had enough discussion on this case. Bail is set at $100,000."

And down came the gavel.

CHAPTER 9

Cord arrived early for his 6:00 p.m. appointment in Barry Hoffman's office. While hedge fund managers like him were notorious for working ridiculous hours, the markets themselves closed at predictable times that never changed. Tradition still reigned. At 4:00 p.m. Eastern Standard Time, the bell rang and the Dow Jones closed. While some after-hours trading continued, Cord was confident his minions could handle it.

As soon as Cord saw Barry's face, he knew. "So you're not going to help me." He sat in the chair across from Hoffman's desk, stoic.

Barry took his time before responding. "It depends on what your definition of help is." He tapped a pen against the notebook that lay on his desk in front of him. It was almost taunting.

"I see. So we're channeling Bill Clinton now."

Barry ignored the sarcasm. "Cord, you're not looking at the big picture."

"You're not looking at the big picture. I'm not making an unreasonable demand. All I want is an apology."

"No, you're not. You want total humiliation. You want the police officers to literally beg for your forgiveness. That's just not happening."

"Did you have any discussions with the police chief?"

Barry recounted to Cord his conversation with Chief Driscoll. He concluded, "The upshot is this. I can probably bully Driscoll into obtaining an oral apology from the offending officers. I suspect it would be a very tepid apology at that."

"Tepid?"

"Something like, 'we're sorry for the incident, but we're just doing our job.'"

"Which is to keep folks like me out of Westport."

"Cord, can't you just let it go?"

"No, I can't," he yelled. He'd been sitting on pins and needles for this? It didn't seem as if they'd gotten any further in a meeting of the minds than in their last conversation. "Don't give me any of your shine about how I am rich and healthy and powerful. If I can't drive down a street without my mother being felt up by a bunch of legalized thugs, I am not a man. I am a worthless piece of shit." The throbbing temporal veins returned.

Thirty seconds of silence reigned. *Hell hath no fury like a successful nerd scorned*, Barry thought to himself.

"Can I get you a drink?" Barry said.

"No."

"Well, I hope you don't mind if I have one." Barry poured himself a glass of Cognac.

"If I can't get a decent apology, then I will inflict pain. File a discrimination suit against them."

"I won't," Barry said briskly. He had anticipated the request.

"Then I'll find someone who will."

Barry had already anticipated this response too. "Cord, listen to me. You will have no trouble finding a lawyer to take your case. You may even get some money to make it go away; but you must remember one thing. You signed the form giving the police permission to perform the search."

"That was after..." He went silent as Barry raised his hand.

"I know, I know."

"I'll give you a half-million retainer."

"Cord, you could offer me the entire California coast. I just won't take it."

"Barry, this cannot go unanswered. What do you think I should do?"

"You know the answer to that. I have seen cases like this eat clients alive. The only people who win are the lawyers. I'm at the point in my life where I have acquired considerable wisdom."

"Plato's philosopher king. I believe you have to be sixty."

"I'm sixty-two." He took a sip of his Cognac. "It's not worth a heart attack, Cord."

"I'll have a heart attack if I do nothing." He reached into his jacket pocket and pulled out his checkbook.

"I am writing you a check for $5,000 for your time."

"As you wish, but I won't cash it."

"How about to your favorite charity?"

"No. I will accept no payment of any type."

"You really won't help me?"

"I am helping you."

There was another long silence. "I guess I'll have that drink."

Barry poured him a generous glass of scotch. "So what are you going to do?"

"I don't know." He both sounded and looked exhausted as he held his glass in his hand. "But I know this . . . I will not be following your advice."

He took several sips of the scotch, rose, and extended his hand. "I still consider you a friend. I know you believe you are acting in my best interest."

"I still consider you a friend too."

Both men shook hands. Barry walked Cord to the elevator and then returned to his office. He espied the remaining scotch. Even though he'd just refused a case that would make him a high six figures, he hated to see good scotch go to waste. He thought about just pouring it back in the bottle, but then he thought of a better alternative. He grabbed the glass and downed it in two gulps.

CHAPTER 10

Due to his mother's influence, Cord was a churchgoer, and he and his wife attended the Trinity Episcopalian Church in Southport. Initially, the lily-white parishioners had practically assaulted them, seeing them as a testament to their commitment to diversity. They were asked to serve on various committees, join the choir, have tea with the minister, and even participate in the prestigious blessing of the Southport Yacht Club's fleet.

That was until they learned that Cord was a self-described "Clarence Thomas Republican." He did not believe in diversity or affirmative action. He believed in the American Dream. The path to success was hard work on a level playing field. The genteel members of Trinity could tolerate such opinions, but when Cord voiced his opposition to abortion and sodomy, as he insisted on calling it, he found that the toleration of diversity had its limits. The tight lips and grim visages of the Botoxed frosted-blond ladies told him that his opinions were not welcome. So at the insistence of his wife, he kept his mouth shut and smiled vacuously at church socials. Clara loved the church, and as long as his wife was happy, he was happy. Cord had long ago concluded that the key to a successful marriage was total capitulation.

Thus, when the minister asked him and Clara to attend a charity dinner to raise money for intercity youths, he agreed, even though it was his experience that the hosts of such events managed to reap more money that the supposed beneficiaries. It was at this event he became acquainted with Reverend Jeremiah Daniels of the Zion Baptist Church in Bridgeport.

Reverend Daniels was also a state senator and was held in

such high esteem by his colleagues that he was portrayed as "The Conscience of the Senate," due to his advocacy for the poor and those who just got dealt a bad hand in life. Even though Reverend Daniels was a Democrat, he and Cord became good friends.

Reverend Daniels joked to Cord that because of his generous contributions in the past, he was now on the "Grade-A sucker list"— individuals with monopoly money who could be called to give the maximum contribution by law to various politicians, political action committees, and charities. Thus, Cord decided to explain his situation to Reverend Daniels.

Although it had been weeks since his incident with the police, time had not healed any wounds. Cord was still livid over his treatment by the Westport police. While he hadn't ruled out legal options, he decided to pursue political alternatives also. And despite his claim to be "a humble man of the cloth," politicians did not come any savvier than Reverend Daniels.

Reverend Daniels met him at the rectory door.

"Jeremiah, how goes the battle?" Cord asked as he greeted him with a handshake.

"Which one, the Republicans or the atheists?"

Cord laughed while Reverend Daniels continued. "We have you Republicans on the run like wandering sheep in need of a Good Shepherd, instead of that Trump clown. The atheists are more of a problem."

Reverend Daniels ushered him into his office. "Some coffee?"

"Anything a little stronger?"

Reverend Daniels laughed. "You need to hang out with the Catholics. The bishop has the best stash in town. Besides, it wouldn't look good if the senator who just lowered the legal alcohol limit for driving was serving spirits near the house of God."

"Coffee will be fine. Black, please." Cord didn't argue. He hadn't really been serious in his inquiry anyway.

"So what can I help you with? Ethel said you sounded upset when you made this appointment." He looked over his shoulder periodically at Cord as he retrieved their coffee.

A serious look crossed Cord's face. "My family and I have been abused by the police."

Reverend Daniels handed Cord his cup of coffee and then settled into his chair while taking a sip of his own blended brew. The utilitarian office, with its functional oak desk, metal file cabinets, faded carpet, and plastic-covered chairs, revealed that Reverend Daniels was not a fan of temporal pleasures. But his ego wall was covered with pictures of him alongside of political luminaries like Bill, Hillary, Barack, Michelle, as well as myriads of state and local politicians. But Reverend Daniels had all these centered around his favorite: his picture with Steelers coach, Mike Tomlin, who in Reverend Daniels's opinion, had a place in heaven already reserved beside the right hand of God. Reverend Daniels had actually been a fair defensive back in the days, and his insistence on wearing his clerical habit did not hide his athleticism.

As the two men sat comfortably across from each other, Cord recounted his incident with the officers, even describing in painful detail the humiliating search of his mother. He finally stated that he not only wanted an apology, but for the police officers to give his mother a bouquet of flowers.

To his dismay, he noticed no outrage in Reverend Daniels's face as he described his travails. Perhaps it was just a politician's poker face. But when he was done, Reverend Daniels steepled his fingers and turned his head toward his ego wall.

"Are you serious? You want these police officers to apologize? And give your mother flowers?" It didn't go unnoticed by Cord that the man couldn't even look him in the eyes while saying it.

"That's what they made my grandpappy do years ago in South Carolina when he forgot to duff his cap to a white woman."

"Sounds to me your grandpappy got off easy."

"As are these cops. I could sue them, the town, go to the media, and maybe even get them fired. But even if I couldn't get them fired, I could publicly humiliate them. That's not what I want. I just want them to bring Mom a bouquet of flowers and apologize."

"Maybe even have them shine your shoes while you're at it?"

Reverend Daniels said. He saved his sarcastic tone for an occasion when needed to clear up any confusion as to whether it was his intention or not.

"That's definitely a thought." Cord would make him regret holding back.

"I can't help you with this problem," Reverend Daniels finally said, still not bothering to make eye contact.

"What do you mean?"

"Just what I said. I can't help you."

"Can't you get ahold of the attorney general?"

Reverend Daniels held up his cellphone. "Cord, I can get the AG of Connecticut, the U.S., or both."

"Are you saying you can't help me, you won't help me, or both?"

"Both."

"Both? Why?" Cord said incredulously.

"I am involved in delicate negotiations with the police unions, the governor, and our suburban communities to prevent the outright slaughter of our black youth. What you are asking me to do will destroy these negotiations.

"You have to understand something, Cord. Black men are dying like flies, and nobody cares. Thirty-three in Hartford, twenty-seven in New Haven, and twenty-three here in Bridgeport in this year alone. When twenty white kids got shot in Newtown, everyone went ballistic. But when black youth are slaughtered, nobody cares."

He paused for effect. "Do you know how many funerals I have gone to in the past two years? Fifty-seven. Fifty-seven wailing mothers clinging to me, hugging me—begging me to do something. And I *am* doing something. We've banned assault weapons, put up more streetlights, video cameras, even created several midnight basketball leagues. But we have found that only one thing works, and that's cops on the street." He'd rambled all that off as if making a campaign speech.

He turned to look at Cord. "But there is a problem. The cops don't want to stand on the street. They want to sit in their patrol

cars and drink coffee and gobble donuts. And even that's dangerous. Look how those two cops got killed in New York a few years
back. And you know something? I don't blame them. Nobody in
their right mind would want to walk the midnight beat in any of our
inner cities."

"But this is because we don't demand it," Cord insisted. "We
pay these people. They have Cadillac health insurance and fat pensions. If they don't want to protect us, they shouldn't take the job."
If Reverend Daniels had been trying to support his reasoning why
he wasn't going to help Cord, he'd failed miserably.

"I wish it were that simple. I'm on the verge of getting something done, but it's going to cost money. I've been in negotiations
with the police unions and finally got them to agree. But they don't
just want time-and-a-half. They want double time. Plus, they want
two cops together at all times. It's going to cost a fortune, and the
cities don't have it. So what did I do? I groveled. And I got some of
the suburban reps—even Republicans—to agree to less money for
their towns so that Bridgeport gets more to hire these cops. Now
I have the governor on board. We're on the verge of stopping this
senseless violence by our angry young men."

His deep brown eyes locked onto Cord's. "But I can tell you this.
If I make an issue of your predicament . . . demand that some cops
genuflect before you . . . Do you know what the chance is of my
getting this done?"

"Jeremiah, one of those cops put their grubby paws on my
mother! The cops won't even say why they pulled me over. But
we all know it was DWB." Cord hated to raise his voice considering
Reverend Daniel had been very even toned and diplomatic. But he
was fed up.

"Cord, I have to look at the big picture. I'm trying to save black
lives. Can't you see that? Don't you have another connection? Can't
you just find another lawyer? Why do you need me?"

"Because you're my friend." He'd thought Barry was his friend
as well.

Reverend Daniels could not hide annoyance. "Cord, you live in the white man's world, a suburban nirvana. A land flowing with milk and honey. You are the fourth wealthy member of our tribe to ask me this month to use my political influence to punish some white man for the indignities the rest of us tolerate routinely."

He began to mock the requests that had been made to him. "Jeremiah, I had to wait forty-five minutes for my dinner at Guido's while the white people got served first. Pull their liquor license. Jeremiah, this rent-a-cop kept following me when I was at the Darien Boutique. Audit them. Jeremiah, how come my kid didn't get the lead in the school play? It's racism pure and simple. Get that teacher fired."

He sat back in his chair. "I even had a lawyer from our tribe who wanted me to impeach a judge."

Cord raised his eyebrows. "Impeach a judge?"

"Funny story actually, if it wasn't so telling. She's sitting in the court room with her white client who is accused of shop lifting. The judge starts talking and then this lawyer realizes that the judge thinks she is the criminal and that her white client is the lawyer."

Cord let out a guffaw. "If I got upset every time something happened to me like that, I would be in a state of perpetual outrage."

Here, Reverend Daniels paused for effect. That was one thing he had learned in politics. Raising his voice was a sign of weakness—that you were playing a losing hand.

"Meanwhile, I spend my evenings looking at the corpses of dead, young black men; at least the ones who did not have their faces shot off and have a closed casket."

He turned to Cord and looked him straight in the eyes. "Cord, I *am* your friend," he said quietly. "But you can't just come in here and demand I pull some strings that I'm not even sure I can pull. I appreciate your generosity to my charities, but I just can't help you."

"I did not give you money in return for favors." Cord didn't hide the fact that he was indeed offended. "I have never asked you for anything before. I gave you money to help our people. And forcing these thugs with badges to apologize sends a message."

Reverend Daniels understood where Cord was coming from, but

he wasn't moved nonetheless. "We live in the white man's world. If our people are to survive and thrive, I need their help, *especially* the help of the police."

"That's where you're wrong," Cord said, his voice raised ever so slightly. "All we need is for the white people to leave us alone. My family lived in the segregated South for generations, and you know something? We were better off before than we are now."

"You grew up in the South. My granddaddy moved from Alabama to work in the Pittsburgh steel mills. We all have horror stories about the segregation in the South. The cops, the Klan, the constant indignity of being called 'boy' and 'nigger' to your face. How can you say that?"

Cord, who considered himself an amateur historian, responded, "Because segregation gave us what we don't have now, which is economic independence from white people."

Reverend Daniels thought about this. "You mean our own businesses?"

"Exactly. In my great-grandfather's South Carolina, we had our own schools, funeral homes, garages, insurance companies, farms, doctors, lawyers, grocery stores, bars, restaurants, and even our own speakeasies. And most importantly, we had stable families. After Reconstruction, whitey left us alone, but only for a while."

"Because the racism was always there."

"No, that's what everyone wants to believe, but it's not true . . ." Cord was now on a roll. "What we're hearing is politically sanitized nonsense that made paternalistic white liberals out to be heroes. You are right. The racism was always there. But the real reason was that the whites couldn't compete."

"Couldn't compete? Are you *serious*?" He contorted his face to show his disagreement.

"Dead serious. Remember, I'm a businessman. Do you know what the Flexner Report is?"

"No idea." Reverend Daniels was now mesmerized with Cord's analysis.

"The Flexner Report was a document issued by Dr. Abraham

Flexner in 1915. Its reported purpose was to improve the standards of American medical schools." He rolled his eyes as he said "standards."

"The real reason was to close down our medical schools. My great-grandpappy couldn't continue in medical school when they closed it down, even though he was a brilliant man."

"We have our own medical schools today," responded a skeptical Reverend Daniels.

"Sure, but only two, Howard and Meharry. I give to both of them. But we had over a dozen in 1910. The problem is that we were producing too many doctors. Good doctors who knew what they were doing. In fact, we had a higher percentage of doctors in 1900 than we do today in spite of so-called affirmative action that you liberals are so proud of."

"So what was the problem, Cord? I confess; this is news to me." He didn't mind admitting he wasn't the smartest man in the room.

"The problem was whites couldn't compete. You have to understand that the average white person likes green more than he hates black. Believe me, I know. I deal with these guys all day. They couldn't care less if I had purple skin that glowed in the dark, as long as I make money for them. And I do. So when some dirt-poor, racist, white tenant farmer needed a splinter pulled out of his leg or a broken arm set, he went to a black doctor rather than a white doctor because the black doctor charged half as much. White doctors couldn't compete, so they closed us down."

"It was like that with everything," Cord continued. "Did you ever hear of the expression 'nigger-rigged'?"

"Of course," Reverend Daniels said, suppressing his chuckle.

"Do you know what it means?"

"Fixing something cheaply?" he answered. "I've done that a time or two with the an aluminum foil ball on the television antenna to get better reception." This time he did chuckle.

"Cheaply but effectively," Cord said. "Our garage mechanics, like my daddy, were masters at fixing cars for next to nothing. These racist whites would go to their white garages and be told they needed a new carbonator or muffler, and that it was going to cost a fortune. They got tired of getting ripped off. So they came to us. We would find a spare part or patch something. Problem solved for a tenth of the price. 'Nigger-rigging.'"

Cord shook his head. "It was like that for everything: labor, food, even female companionship—if you know what I mean. Whitey couldn't compete. So what did they do? They got the Klan to terrorize us, and then they got their racist cops and judges to deny us Rule of Law. When we bought guns, they made it illegal for us to own them. In Tulsa, Oklahoma, they bombed us in 1921. Got a plane, flew over our neighborhoods, and dropped bombs. Killed dozens. For some reason, that 'little event' never got into the history textbooks."

Silence ensued during which it appeared that Reverend Daniels was reflecting deeply. Finally, he said, "You have a point, but I have no choice."

"No choice? You're *not* serious." Cord couldn't believe after he'd schooled Reverend Daniels that he was still unwilling to help him.

"You are right, Cord, in everything you say. I am aware that we traded violent racism for paternalistic racism. I deal with it every day. In fact, I like to call it 'Consensual Apartheid' and nowhere is it worse than here. Connecticut is more segregated than Mississippi was during the height of Jim Crow. You can count the number of whites on one hand in our public schools here in Bridgeport, and you can count the blacks on one hand in the public schools in Westport."

Reverend Daniels sat back in his chair. "And I think your point that at least with violent racism, you know where you stand, is also well taken. You can fight it then. We used to grovel to white people to prevent them from beating, shooting, and lynching us. Now, we grovel for them to give us money to support us."

"So why don't we fight? The first step would be to help me!"

Reverend Daniels shook his head. "You are asking me to fight a system that is on our side most of the time. A system that is fighting for our right to vote, our right to get a job, get affordable health insurance, and who created voting districts that give us representation. That's the real killer."

"Voting districts? Why is that the real killer?" Cord said with the tone of disbelief in his voice. Perhaps now it was time for him to learn something new.

"Cord, you may know black history, but you are clueless when it comes to black politics," Reverend Daniels replied.

"So enlighten me." Cord's previous irritation was now replaced with curiosity.

"Our people were originally Republicans. The party of Lincoln. In fact, the first president to invite one of us to the White House was Teddy Roosevelt."

"I know, I know," Cord said quickly. "He was ahead of his time."

"Like I said, you know your history but not your politics. Teddy couldn't care less about our rights. He needed our help."

"What help? We had no political power back then."

"Believe it or not, we did," Reverend Daniels responded. "The Republicans to this day like to cite this as proof of their open-mindedness. Complete nonsense, of course. Roosevelt had upset the powerful Wall Street Republicans by breaking up their trusts and monopolies. 'Malefactors of great wealth,' he called them. But back then, there were no primaries. Women couldn't even vote, but black men could. In fact, all those so-called heroic suffragettes you read about were the biggest racists around. Their main argument was that if the stupid nigger men can vote, why can't we? That never made it into the history books either."

"Each state had delegates appointed by the party. And in the South, the Republican Party was black: the legacy of Lincoln. With all the Northern Republicans up in arms, Roosevelt charmed the Southern Black Republican delegates. That's how he got re-nominated. But his distant cousin, Franklin, used the Great Depression to get us hooked on the government, and we've been with the Democrats ever since."

"So what does that have to do with voting districts?" Cord asked.

"Since we were giving the Democrats all our votes, we wanted to see some blacks in government—assemblymen, councilmen, congressmen, and senators. But as the Chinese say, 'Be careful what you wish for; you may get it.' Getting our districts came with a price. We had to support the whites' agenda."

Reverend Daniels paused, as what he had to say next was an admission of his own perceived cowardice. "In return for affirmative action, welfare, and affordable housing, we had to allow white liberals to destroy our family structure."

"Now you're preaching to the converted," Cord said. "Free birth control, abortion, prime-time porn, and no-fault divorce are what have destroyed our families."

"You got that right," Reverend Daniels said.

"But why do you support this nonsense?" He thought for a moment and then answered his own question. "I guess it's because our people do."

"Not true," said Reverend Daniels. "My congregation was livid with me when I voted to allow the gays to get married. Years ago, I preached sermons telling my congregation they would burn in hell. Then I was forced to vote for it. I lost count of the times members of my flock called me a hypocrite. I told them that I had learned compassion for these people, but they didn't buy it, and they could tell that I didn't buy it either."

"Why?"

"Because of my poor wife," Reverend Daniels said, nodding.

"Your wife? She supported this nonsense?"

"Do you know what sarcoidosis is?"

"Sarcoid what?" Cord asked. Twice in one sitting, Reverend Daniels had stumped him with something he'd not heard of.

"Don't feel bad. Nobody knows what it is. None of the doctors understand it, but poor Norma has it. The body attacks itself—the lungs, the heart, the skin, and the eyes. The disease was invented by the devil himself. We spend all our time in doctors' offices—all sorts of specialists. And they help us. Norma would be dead or blind if it wasn't for them."

"I am truly sorry to hear that, Reverend. But what does this have to do with voting for gay marriage?" Cord felt compassion in his spirit and referred to the man as reverend.

"I have a poor congregation. They can't afford to pay for our health insurance. If I lost my seat, Betsy would lose all her good doctors. There is no way I could afford to pay them."

"How can you lose your seat? You got 85 percent of the vote last time, if I recall correctly."

"Eighty-seven percent," Reverend Daniels corrected.

"Because those goddamn white liberals in Westport and Greenwich would not support me if I didn't vote the way they said."

Reverend Daniels glared at Cord. "Now you got me taking the Lord's name in vain. I apologize, Jesus." He looked skyward.

"These people are not even in your district. Why do they matter?"

"Because they write the check. This liberal socialite from Westport walks into my office." He nodded to the entryway, "Right through that door. Doesn't even knock. Sits right in that chair where you're sitting and dictates to me that I have to vote for gay marriage or I will lose my senate seat."

"To a Republican? In Bridgeport?"

"No, Cord, to another Democrat. She and all her liberal friends were going to find someone to run against me in the Democratic primary. Give her all the money she needed while cutting off all of mine. No way I could win. I lose the seat, I lose our health insurance, and my poor Norma has no doctors to care for her. So I have to be Stepin Fetchit for these people."

Cord hung his head. "I'm sorry I asked you for this favor. I was rude and arrogant. Is there anything I can do to help you at this time?"

Reverend Daniels looked directly into his eyes. "I would encourage you to fight this indignity against yourself and against our people. Just don't do anything crazy."

Cord hopped into his Lexus. He had played by the rules and gotten nowhere.

He turned on his talking book, *David Copperfield*. His MIT education had only required several token humanities courses, and he was always trying to compensate. Steerforth was shaking down David at boarding school when he pulled into the driveway.

To his annoyance, a newspaper in a yellow plastic bag littered his driveway. It was the *Connecticut Post*. He never ordered it. They just randomly threw copies on his driveway, along with an order form.

Even though he thought they should pay him to read it, he removed the yellow cover and heaved the thicket of coupons and fliers into the trash. Once inside his house, he realized no one was home, so he was able to grab a glass of Pinot Noir without his wife's disapproving looks. He retired to his favorite place on the planet, his wraparound front porch.

He started leafing through the newspaper on his way to the Sports Section when a headline with the term "Police Brutality" caught his eye. He focused on the article and read the following:

Police Brutality Alleged
By Patti Becker

What appeared to be a routine arraignment in Superior Court on May 20 became a legal brawl as public defender Connie Vivanti alleged that her client, Kwame Baker, was savagely beaten during his arrest. Baker, twenty-four years old, of Fairfield Avenue, was arraigned on multiple charges, including vandalism and resisting arrest. Baker, who interrupted the proceedings on several occasions, had a right eye that was completely swollen shut. Sarah Cornell of the district attorney's office, argued that the police report indicated that Baker sustained the injury during a fall while resisting arrest. Vivanti presented the Court with the sworn affidavit of Dr. Teresa Trybus, stating that the nature of the *eye injury was more likely caused by a punch than a fall. Officers Fletcher and Kline were involved in the incident. Bail was set at $100,000 by Judge Rita Durazio.*

Cord read the article three times, each time more slowly. He then entered his kitchen to refresh his wine and grab a pair of scissors. Returning to his porch, he carefully cut out the article, folded it, and placed it in his wallet. He sipped on the Pinot. The lengthy finish lingered in his mouth. A small smile crept across his face. Yes, he had played by the rules and had lost. But now, they were going to play by his rules. He picked up his iPhone and called his old college roommate.

CHAPTER 11

C hief Driscoll walked into his least favorite room on the planet, the office of the Westport first selectman.

"We have a problem," he said.

Gwen Trudeau walked directly up to him, placing her face three inches from his with her trademark infinite self-confidence. The first selectman of Westport replied, "I would say that is an understatement. Sit down."

Chief Driscoll complied while Trudeau circled around the oak desk that had been in her family for generations. Her scent of the women's cologne, Alien, followed her.

Everything about her was perfect. Her coiffed auburn hair lay comfortably across her tanned forehead framed with perfectly symmetrical bangs that ended in semicircular curls. Her makeup enhanced her turquoise-blue eyes. The off-red lipstick was meticulously applied. Fifty years of age, she was without wrinkles even though neither a plastic surgeon nor a Botox needle had ever touched her. She was attired in a kelly-green cashmere sweater that fit tautly over her perfect figure in a way that made her look simultaneously professional and sensuous. Stud emerald earrings provided the pièce de résistance.

This was her town. Her ancestors, French Huguenots, migrated to the colony of Connecticut from New Rochelle almost three hundred years ago. She considered the WASPs in town—even the patrician Episcopalians—to be newcomers. But she welcomed the recently invading Manhattan Jews. They kept the town's real estate values in the stratosphere, even after the so-called Great Recession. More importantly, they shared her passion for education.

Westport's public schools were not only the best in the state, they were the best in the country. If you lived in Westport, there was no need to blow $55,000 a year on Choate or Hopkins, unless you wanted your obnoxious teenage kids out of the house. Even though she was a product of Miss Porter's, each of her five children attended Westport public schools. The two oldest were off to the Ivies.

The schools were not the only reason everyone loved Westport. It was also safe. As she bragged to the invading Manhattanites, "You don't have to bother to lock your doors." In fact, after her first term as first selectman, she commissioned a $5,000 poll to determine the main concerns of her constituency. Not that such a poll was necessary; she was so popular that the Democrats had not even bothered to field a candidate. But she was curious. The results were interesting. Her constituency had no concerns. Like her, everything in Westport was perfect.

But there had been some incidents. Minorities bringing in drugs, shoplifting, making scenes at restaurants and insisting upon hanging out on Sherwood Island, one of the town's so-called public beaches, while blasting rap music. Thus, it was Chief Driscoll's job to keep these people out. It was that simple. As she'd told her husband after she had one too many glasses of Sauvignon Blanc, "The value of real estate and the quality of education is inversely proportional to the concentration of melanin in the skin of the population." She had a natural aptitude for mathematical analysis.

Trudeau did not consider herself a racist when she was younger, having enjoyed the company of black men during her sexually explorative phase. Her friends had warned her, "Once you go black, you never go back." That was . . . until her "Nubian Stallion," as she insisted on calling him, impregnated her. She never understood why women said having an abortion was such a gut-wrenching decision. Strolling into her parents' country club with a mixed-race child was not an option. And she quickly concluded that while dealing with blacks and patronizing them with vacuous platitudes was a political necessity, living or socializing with them was not.

"Tell me about this Campbell situation."

Chief Driscoll suspected she already knew the details. She never asked a question unless she already knew the answer. Her spies were everywhere. He responded, "Two of our officers, Fletcher and McMahon, stopped an African-American male named Cord Campbell for speeding. He became indignant, and they suspected he may have been carrying drugs into the neighborhood. When they requested to search the car, he became verbally abusive. I believe my officers did their best to handle a difficult individual. No one was injured, and Campbell signed the form giving our officers permission to search the car."

Trudeau stared into Chief Driscoll's eyes to see who would blink first. This was one of her favorite tricks. Her eye doctor had informed her that if she placed numbing drops in her eyes, this was a contest she would never lose. Chief Driscoll considered himself pretty good at meeting people eye-to-eye. But after about thirty seconds . . . he blinked.

She smiled coldly. "You discussed this situation with Attorney Hoffman?"

"Yes. We are old friends."

"Friends?" She tilted her head and looked at him like the family lab did when her son returned from college; like she hardly recognized him. "Do you think you perhaps should have contacted me first?"

"You are quite busy with your job and your family. I hated to bother you."

Trudeau nodded. "I appreciate your kind consideration, but your judgment is somewhat flawed. Do you know who Cord Campbell is?"

"Hoffman told me he was one of these hedge fund guys worth millions."

"He's worth *hundreds* of millions. Maybe a *billion*. He's the richest African American in the country after Oprah. Worth more than Jordan or Tiger."

"Then why was he driving himself?" Chief Driscoll said. "Those guys usually travel by limos or helicopters."

"I should be asking you that question. I was wondering the same thing myself."

"I don't know." Now he returned his version of the family lab. Unlike her, he didn't ask questions if he already had the answer. It was a waste of breath. He was saving his breath for retirement.

"You don't know . . ." Her voice trailed off, and she paused. "Did one of the officers erase Mr. Campbell's mother's iPhone? Did one of the officers put Mr. Campbell's mother is a four-point position?"

Chief Driscoll stared blankly at Trudeau.

"Did one of your officers call him a nigger? Do you know *any-thing*? Anything at all?" Chief Driscoll remained silent. *She may win the blinking contest,* he thought, *but I will win the silence contest.*

After about thirty seconds, Trudeau continued. "So *why* do you think we have a problem then?"

"Is this conversation being recorded?"

Trudeau laughed as she reached into her desk and pulled out a black oblong box almost a foot long with protruding black fingers. "Monstro 10. Blocks everything: cellphones, Wi-Fi, video, recording devices. Every politician with a brain has one."

Chief Driscoll did not look particularly relieved but continued. "Fletcher and McMahon suspect that there is a mechanism to target undesirables. They refused to answer any incriminating questions about the incident. They implied that should any disciplinary action be launched against them, they will publicly state this, or at least have their union lawyer do so."

"Do they understand the implications of this threat?"

"We can't let this become public," Chief Driscoll said.

"No, *you* can't let this become public. These are *your* men. *You* need to handle the situation."

She took a sip from a rectangular bottle containing a green liquid. When she saw Chief Driscoll's absorption in the product, she explained. "Asparagus juice. Plenty of antioxidants. Plus, it goes with my outfit. Looks like you could use some, Ray."

Chief Driscoll just nodded while Trudeau continued. "What

does this Campbell person want anyway?"

"He wants an apology. He wants my officers to go over to his house, give his mother a bouquet of flowers, and apologize."

"You're not serious?" She let out a harrumph, her shoulders slightly bouncing up and down a couple of times.

"My men were as opposed to the idea as was I, but now, I'm having second thoughts. This could get ugly."

She glared at him. "Do *not* apologize under *any* circumstances," she shouted. "Under *no* circumstances. These people need to understand the pecking order around here."

"I told Hoffman the same thing, although not in those words."

"And speaking of pecking order . . . Your man Fletcher seems to be out of control. Beating up a withdrawing junkie? Can't you keep your staff under control?"

"There is no evidence he touched that guy."

Trudeau gave Chief Driscoll a look of mock confusion, squinting her eyelids and creating crows' feet. "Do I have STUPID written on my forehead, Chief Driscoll?"

She reached into her purse, grabbing a small mirror. She gazed at her face in the mirror for several seconds, tilting it up slightly. "Hmmm. No, I didn't think so. Can't see it written there. I like to check periodically, though. My teenage children seem to think it's written there."

"The prosecutor effectively argued that there was no evidence of any abuse by Officer Fletcher or any of my staff."

"Oh, she did, did she? Did *you* speak to her?"

Chief Driscoll's silence telegraphed the negative answer.

"I had a drink with the prosecutor, Sarah Cornell, last night. Sarah and I are old friends. Dated her older brother at Harvard. An arrogant prick who became even more arrogant when he got into the Porcellian Club. On his third wife now. Poor thing. I pity her."

Chief Driscoll just nodded. He thought about acknowledging that he actually knew what the Porcellian Club was, but he didn't want to give her the satisfaction of responding with her continuous jabs to establish her social superiority. Twice in his career, he had pulled guys over for DWIs—both totally shit-faced—who had kept yelling, "Do you *know* who *I* am? I'm a member of the *Porcellian Club*. You can't do this to me."

And they were right. In both cases, the judge practically saluted when they walked into the courtroom; then, without even bothering to hear the arguments, the judge threw out Chief Driscoll's arrests on the grounds of "gross violations of due process." God, how he hated these people.

Trudeau placed the mirror back in her purse.

"Sarah was in a good mood. She apparently got a huge bail on this junkie, even though it was obvious to her that Fletcher smashed his face and broke his eye socket. She and one of the public defenders, Connie Vivanti, are always having contests to see which one of them can execute the grossest miscarriage of justice. She said she won by a mile. Makes up for all the times that Vivanti beat her on obvious domestic violence cases."

"Officer Fletcher denies touching that suspect, and I believe him." And that was a prime of example of thinking one thing while saying another.

"You are missing my point, Chief. Whether or not Campbell was abused by your officers is irrelevant. Whether or not Fletcher beat this lowlife is irrelevant. What *is* relevant is that you have violated the Caleca Rule."

"The Caleca Rule?"

"Yes. It is named after Tom Caleca, my brother's chief resident, while he was an intern at Columbia. Apparently, my brother had refused to see a patient in the emergency room because he was too busy caring for other patients. The attending physician heard about this and berated Dr. Caleca for my brother's perceived negligence. Dr. Caleca informed my brother that he was a 'worthless, pampered, entitled socialite faggot who should be pounding down martinis on his yacht rather than trying to play doctor'; an assessment that, incidentally, was quite accurate. When my brother responded that he can't be in two places at one time, Dr. Caleca responded, 'You can screw up all you want, just as long as I don't hear about it.'

My brother named it 'The Caleca Rule.'"

She took another sip of the green elixir. "So you see, if your officers want to harass black tycoons or beat pigmented lowlifes, that's fine with me—as long as I don't hear about it. Because if I hear about it, that means other people will hear about it. It means that it will end up on Facebook, or get tweeted and retweeted and quadruple tweeted. And it means that someday, the press will ask how we know when Mr. Campbell and his kind are being pulled over when they are in the wrong neighborhood."

Chief Driscoll's eyes flashed with anger. He could only take so much humiliation. "This was not my idea. *You* are the one who told me that cameras were to be placed in that neighborhood so that our staff knew when undesirables invaded. I had no input into the decision."

"Chief Driscoll, I take exception to your tone. But you are correct, of course. It was my decision. But once the decision was made, you embraced it. You even helped the coders construct the algorithms. You sat down with Cozy Bed Security and told them what color skin to look for. You even *supervised* the instillation of the cameras."

She grabbed another piece of paper from her desk and waved it in his face. "These are the notes from your meetings with the coders."

"That's not entirely true," Chief Driscoll responded. "I recommended young, white males be included, but they couldn't figure it out."

"You are not entirely correct. You wanted them to target white males with tattoos. The technology did not exist to do that. At least not yet."

"There is no way I am taking the sole blame for this. This was *your* idea." Chief Driscoll spoke sternly while still trying to be respectful.

"You are correct, Chief Driscoll," she didn't hesitate to admit. "It was my idea. If you go down, you can drag me with you."

"Those cameras have to go," he said.

"Now you're making sense, Chief." This time she said the word chief as if before he didn't deserve to wear the title, but somehow, from the beginning of the conversation to now, he'd earned the right.

She paused for effect. "So tonight—around 2:00 a.m.—I want you to personally remove those cameras."

"*Me*? What if I'm seen?"

"Who else? Fletcher? McMahon? Me?"

"Why can't you order the company to do it?"

"Are you out of your mind? I'm going to have enough difficulty covering up their involvement. We are both getting our hands dirty here, not just you."

"I'm not doing it. You created this mess. *You* fix it."

She glared at Chief Driscoll. "If this becomes public knowledge, we will have reporters from the *New York Times* prancing around here. Do you *know* what that means?"

She stood up, placed her hands on her desk, leaned forward, and glared at Chief Driscoll. "It means we are the lead story on the local news, maybe the national news. It means Twitter hashtags such as #westportracists and #trudeaumustgo. It means Al Sharpton, Jesse Jackson, Colin Kaepernick and Black Lives Matter minions prancing around our town green. It means a scapegoat must be found. Do you know *who* that scapegoat will be? Do you know what that could mean to that scapegoat's pension?"

Chief Driscoll, a veteran of many internecine bureaucratic battles, knew he was beaten. He hung his head and said, "I'll see what I can do."

"That's not the right answer, Chief Driscoll. Are you going to personally take down those cameras tonight?"

He nodded.

"Say it," Trudeau barked.

"I will take down those cameras tonight."

"Please shut the door when you leave."

CHAPTER 12

Cord remembered college like it was yesterday. It was said that nobody normal ever graduated from MIT. He suspected it was true in his case. He was sure it applied to his old roommate, Joe Montalbano. Joe had grown up in the Bronx, one of the few students of Italian descent admitted to the Bronx School of Science, a major feeder for MIT.

Cord and Joe were paired together freshman year as roommates. MIT, like many colleges, had figured out that a major determinant of student satisfaction was the relationship incoming freshmen had with their initial roommate. Thus, the school pioneered a computer algorithm—now used across the country—that attempted to maximize the probability of roommate compatibility. This algorithm concluded that the son of a black garage mechanic would get along fine with the son of a first-generation Sicilian barber. The computer was right. Upon meeting Joe, Cord asked him directly if he would have trouble rooming with a black.

Joe replied, "A Sicilian is an African who knows how to swim. Just as long as you're not a Red Sox fan, because if you are, then we *are* going to have a problem."

Within one month, their fellow students were calling them "The Brothers," as they did everything together.

MIT students were an arrogant bunch. While the students down the street at Harvard bragged they would someday rule the world, the MIT students responded that they were the only ones who understood it. The average person was clueless as to why a car started when the ignition button was pushed, why you could play poker on an iPhone with someone from the Faroe Islands, or even how an airplane could fly. But many MIT students not only knew the answer to all these questions, but could actually design the devices that made such things possible.

But even by MIT standards, Joe was arrogant. When some Asian kid from California bragged about how he got an 800 on the math part of his SAT, Joe responded, "How long did it take you to finish?"

"One hour and ten minutes," the poor guy responded.

Joe grinned. "Dumb shit. It only took me forty-five minutes."

Joe aced all the calculus, computer, and physics courses, and soon was excelling in campus politics, having been elected as class president. His data—Catholic, genius IQ, natural leader, analytical mind and working-class background— were then inputted into another computer algorithm, and the answer that spat out was CIA Operative. By the middle of his sophomore year, Joe had full security clearance at the Pentagon, where he had a part-time job analyzing sensitive military data and playing the war games that determined what levels of nuclear submarines, missile defense systems, and missile silos were necessary to decrease the probability of a nuclear confrontation.

Cord, on the other hand, was targeted by a different kind of shadowy organization, but this one had its address on Wall Street: Goldman Sachs. Black and brilliant, this combination was a gold mine for the politically savvy financial insiders whose opulent lifestyles depended upon mathematical wizardry and political connections. And there was nothing like a black face to maximize political connections, especially a black face that did not need affirmative action to be there.

Cord and Joe continuously updated and compared their respective careers as they plowed through college. Joe found it fascinating that his pal learned how to make a bundle on oil futures while serving an internship at Goldman Sachs. Cord couldn't believe that Joe could actually predict when a coup in some third world armpit would occur. Their friendship grew. When Cord would occasionally remind Joe that his white skin gave him an upper hand, Joe's response was that blacks whined too much and let white people push them around. And this is why Cord loved him. Their friendship was strong enough that Joe had the freedom to say what he thought, not what he thought Cord wanted to hear.

But it was in the fall of their senior year when they were watching television in the lounge of their dormitory when Cord finally realized that his friend had a point. A story appeared on the national news. A psychotic black woman from the Bronx, Eleanor Bumpurs, had just been killed by a police officer in an attempt to evict her. According to the newscaster, this obese sixty-six-year-old black woman had brandished a knife after cops had forcibly entered her apartment. The cops' response was to blow her away with a shotgun. The broadcast then segued to a gathering of black protesters led by a local minister screeching outrage over what they viewed as unrepentant police brutality.

"Unbelievable," Cord said.

But Joe just laughed.

Cord was accustomed to Joe's bizarre sense of humor, but even this annoyed him. "What's so funny?"

"Those idiotic protesters," he said while looking up from his electrical engineering textbook.

"Don't you think it's justified?"

"Justified? Are you out of your goddamn mind? That's why you blacks are always getting screwed. You're a bunch of pussies. You believe in this 'peaceful resistance' bullshit. Do you know what would have happened if they shot a Sicilian grandmother with a shotgun?"

"Well, if you know everything, what should we do?"

Joe smirked. "Shoot the damn cop that killed her."

Cord just looked at him dumbfounded while Joe continued. "If the cops did that to an old Sicilian woman, there would be no pussy protests or priests asking for some rigged grand jury to investigate. The goddamn cop who blew the woman away would have an 'accident,' and then the rest of the thugs on the police force would get the message."

"No way," Cord said, struggling to believe this. "You think the

Mafia would handle it?"

"Damn right. The Mafia is not a bunch of thugs running around like in *The Godfather*. It's a system of government designed to deal with official tyranny. Sicily was always ruled by outsiders: Greeks, Arabs, French, Normans, Spanish, and now Italians. The Mafia is just a shadow government that countered these invaders."

"And they kill cops?"

"If they don't get the proper respect, yes. And not just cops; politicians and judges too."

Joe continued. "Sixty years ago, my Uncle Louie had a few too many and was staggering home singing to himself. He wasn't bothering anybody, but these two Irish cops approached him in front of his porch and started pushing him around. He started mouthing off, so they whacked him with a billy club. When my Aunt Rita ran out of the house to confront them, they called her 'a dago cunt' and smashed her jaw, knocking out a few of her teeth.

"The cops enjoyed whacking the Italians, and this was the last straw. Uncle Louie spoke to Mr. Gaudio, the local councilman, who then walked into the police station and politely suggested that the offending officers offer my aunt an apology. Believe it or not, it was the 'dago cunt' comment that got her and my uncle more upset than the lost teeth. The cops just laughed, telling Mr. Gaudio that if he came back, they would give 'the dago cunt another few whacks just to keep you wops in your place.' Mr. Gaudio graciously thanked them for their time."

Joe was enjoying himself now. He closed his textbook and continued. "About three weeks later, one of the cops was cleaning his gun . . . and guess what?" He paused for effect. "He accidentally shot himself in the head."

Joe threw his hands in the air. "These things happen. Our community was distraught. We sent a huge bouquet of flowers to his funeral home. Mr. Gaudio penned a letter expressing appreciation for his years of fine service and how he was beloved by all. The bereaved widow was besieged with cannoli, home-grown tomatoes, wine, and sauce with the best meatballs on the planet."

Joe sat forward in his chair and stared at his friend. "And what do you think the other cop did?"

Cord responded. "He apologized?"

"You're fuckin' right he apologized. He came to Aunt Rita and Uncle Louie's house with a bouquet of flowers, got on his knees and begged their forgiveness. Which, incidentally, was granted. And to this day, the cops in Aunt Rita's neighborhood tip their hat when she makes her way up Arthur Avenue with her walker."

This may have been where the idea of an apology first lodged itself in Cord's mind. But he knew that Joe would help him because of another incident altogether. During their senior year, they were in a bar together when some guys started giving Cord a hard time.

"Hey, MIT bro. How about those College Board scores?"

This annoyed Joe more than Cord. There were not many Italians at the Bronx School of Science, and there were even fewer blacks. Even the elite public schools in the liberal bastion of New York City—The Bronx School of Science, Stuyvesant, and Brooklyn Technical—had no interest in diversity. You took a test, and you got a score. If that score was high enough, you were admitted. There was no affirmative action.

But few people knew this, and working-class Italians and blacks had to endure snide comments until they proved themselves. Especially galling to Joe was that, unlike the other groups, the Italians and the blacks never had their parents spending thousands of dollars on prep courses to learn how to game the test. In fact, when his scores arrived in the mail, his father looked at them and said, "Gooda boy. Now sweepa the floor."

Thus, Joe looked into alcohol-glazed eyes of the preppy punk who had articulated this insult and responded, "He got 800 in math, pal. Higher than your total score."

He paused and then continued. "I bet you douchebags even struggled to score the 400 you get for just signing your name."

"This eight-ball got 800? You're lying." The guy looked at Cord and said, "What's four plus four?"

His friends that accompanied him laughed contemptuously,

hoping to goad Cord into a confrontation. Normally, it would not have worked, but tonight, Cord was on his fifth scotch and soda, and he was going to put these clowns in their place.

Cord held up his hands in mock surrender. "All right. All right. I'll make a bet with you guys since you're so smart."

One of the guys, who was even drunker than Cord, shot back, "What is it?"

Cord smiled. "I'll bet you $20 that if you give me $50, I'll give you $100 back."

They made him repeat the bet several times. Then the guys spoke among themselves for about a minute and then reached into their wallets, with one guy accumulating a total of $50.

"Here you go, genius," he said as he shoved the money in Cord's hand. He then sneered at him. "Where's our $100?"

Cord smiled at the guys, but Joe knew trouble was coming. "You guys won the bet," Cord said to them.

"We know we won the bet. Give us our $100." Their stances were becoming threatening.

"No," Cord said. "The bet was for $20." He reached into his wallet and attempted to hand a twenty-dollar bill to one of the guys who just slapped his hand.

"Where's our hundred?" the hand slapper yelled out.

Cord just laughed. "I thought you guys were smarter than me. You bet me $20 that I would give you $100 if you gave me $50. You won the bet. I'm not going to give you $100. I'm giving you $20. Like I said . . . You won the bet."

A look of comprehension crossed the faces of the group. One of the guys yelled, "You tricked us, you black piece of shit."

Joe stepped forward. "We were minding our own business, and you assholes started bothering us. Now, you have suffered the consequences. Leave us the hell alone."

"Give us our money back!" one of the guys screamed while puffing up his chest.

Joe grabbed the twenty-dollar bill from Cord's hand and shoved it into the guy's face, his nostrils flaring. "Here it is. Take it or leave it. And if one of you guys lays a hand on my friend, I swear, I will slit your throats in your sleep."

Their faces turned ashen hearing that. One of the guys took the twenty-dollar bill, and they promptly left the bar.

It was with this story in mind that Cord had contacted his old friend. While they had stayed in touch, mostly through Christmas cards and phone calls, they had seen each other only a half dozen times over the last thirty years. Cord had been busy building his empire and raising his family while Joe, although married with several children, had been posted as a CIA operative in various hot spots throughout the world. Every time Joe spoke to Cord, he joked that his poor wife was a single mother.

Cord sat on his front porch as he saw his old friend's car pull up into his driveway. He walked out and extended his hand. "How's life in the fast lane?"

Joe grabbed his hand and hugged him. "It's so great to see you. Sorry Carol couldn't make it. Where's Clara?" He looked over Cord's shoulder to see if she was nearby to greet him.

"She's inside cooking some lasagna. It's better than yours was."

"That's because the tomatoes in Cambridge were lousy. Even the best cook can't make a good lasagna with poor ingredients."

Slightly shy of six feet, Joe hadn't changed much in the past thirty years. There was no incipient paunch, and his hair remained jet-black, but his face had aged appropriately, and he now wore glasses.

Joe surveyed Cord's 8000 square-foot Tudor house. The lawn was freshly cut. A panoply of bushes and flowers surrounded the driveway, and he could smell the newly-laid cedar mulch. "These digs seem a bit squalid for a man of your stature."

Cord put his arm around him. "Market's a bit volatile, so we're slumming it."

"Obviously," Joe laughed as they entered the house.

The inside of the home made as much of an impression on Joe as the outside had. The large open foyer made him feel as though he'd just walked into city hall. He imagined if he shouted out, an echo would bounce off the oval-vaulted ceiling. The hardwood floors were freshly waxed, and the crystal chandelier sparkled as it dangled from above. *Slumming my ass,* he thought as he swept the space with eyes.

Clara smiled when she saw Joe. He had been the best man at their wedding. "You still like Bourbon?" And even though she hadn't really seen him since the wedding, she still remembered his favorite drink.

"Sure," Joe responded, a hint of surprise in his eyes that she remembered.

Clara winked and then went to retrieve the drink.

Cord's parents soon joined them. Herman embraced Joe, and to Cord's embarrassment, immediately launched into the story of how Joe had prevented his son from being arrested when he had tried to purchase all the clothes in a store after he was accused of shoplifting. Cord's mother did not say anything, but her facial expression made it obvious she did not enjoy the story as much as her husband either.

The five of them sat down to a simple dinner. In spite of Cord's wealth—he could afford to hire a bevy of servants—Clara preferred the simple life; a life minus a regular staff like some of their neighbors had. Like her husband, her skin was jet-black, and she was close to Cord's six feet in stature. Her hair was starting to gray, but her skin was free of wrinkles, making her appear ten years younger than her age of fifty-three. Her attire was simple but elegant; pressed navy-blue slacks with a beige blouse. Her father had been a dentist, and although her mother had occasionally hired cleaning people, she could not tolerate servants, maids, or even handymen in her space. When major work needed to be done, Clara and Cord stayed at the Marriott in Trumbull until the work was done and the house completely cleaned. Cord found this annoying, but as he always said, "Happy wife, happy life."

After the first bite, Joe agreed with his friend's earlier declaration. "You're right, Cord. Clara's lasagna is better than mine."

They made small talk, Clara trying her best not to brag too much about their children, one who was in medical school and the other two who were thriving in college. She attributed their successes to their religious upbringing and strong family, while Cord's parents nodded in agreement.

Joe gobbled down three portions of lasagna while washing it down with a 1985 Lafite Rothschild. Cord rarely drank social status wines, especially at $3,000 a bottle, but he indulged his old friend. Joe was poorly paid for the service he provided to the country that Cord loved—warts and all—and this was the least he could do.

Besides, Joe knew wine.

CHAPTER 13

The dinner ended, and Clara suggested that Cord and Joe go to "Versailles," as she called her husband's hideaway that was the entire attic. Cord's parents retreated for their usual early bedtime.

The two men walked down a corridor to an elevator as Cord started a conversation. "Dad's hips make it hard for him to take stairs, although he is too proud to admit it. Put this in for him, and now I find I like it too."

The elevator quietly ascended three floors to the attic and opened to an expansive room that was the product of a brilliant mind that was too cheap to hire an interior decorator. To the right was a leather semicircular sofa surrounded by a seamless Philips Design Line flat-screen television. Glass-enclosed Renaissance paintings along with pictures of various planets and nebulas were scattered randomly along the mahogany walls. A generously stocked bar was on the left.

Joe walked across the maroon carpet. An Olhausen slate pool table under a Tiffany lamp dominated the center of the room. Farther back was a felt poker table. Along the back wall were several pinball machines and video games: Asteroids, Pac-Man, and Joe's and Cord's personal favorite from college—Xaxxon.

"Check this out." Between two of the gabled windows, Cord opened an oak door that led to an expansive hardwood deck, and a state-of-the-art telescope usually reserved for small university observatories.

"This is a beauty," Joe said as he walked onto the deck. "What's the mirror size? Ten inch?"

"Twelve," Cord replied. "Problem is there is too much light pollution. Have to go to Litchfield County to do some serious gazing."

Cord grabbed the keypad attached to the three-mirrored Cassegrain Celestron telescope. He pushed several buttons, and the telescope moved until it was pointing directly upward. "Take a look."

Joe peered into the eyepiece. "Ring Nebula?"

"You got it, pal. You never forget anything, do you?"

"Just a lucky guess. I assume you took those pictures." He nodded toward the pictures.

"That's what I do to relax. One of them was printed in *Astronomy*."

"Congrats. But you did not call me to show me your pictures." Joe had enjoyed the evening with his friend and his friend's family, knowing that the evening of enjoyment had dues of some sort hanging over it.

Cord hung his head, slightly embarrassed that his friend had been on to him from the jump. "You're right, Joe. The thing is . . . I have been humiliated beyond belief. What I want to do is illegal and immoral. But I'm going to do it anyway. Now, I don't want you to feel obliged to help me."

The two men walked off the deck, and Cord closed the door. He walked over to the bar and poured two ample glasses of Louis XIII Cognac, neat. He reached under the bar and grabbed one of his humidors.

"Take your pick," he said as he opened the ornate inlaid wood lid.

Joe chose a Cohíba Espléndido. "You don't mind?" It was a $60 cigar.

"Good choice. I'm having the same." Cord picked out his own cigar then returned the humidor to its place.

"Doesn't Clara get upset with the smell?"

Cord flicked a switch underneath the bar. A barely perceptible humming sound emanated from the roof. "Air filtration system. Don't ask what it put me back. Actually designed it myself."

"The value of an MIT education," Joe smiled and shook his head.

"The system works so well that Clara never smells a thing. It fact, it works too well. The bitch down the road claimed the smell was making her kid's asthma worse. Turns out the kid didn't even have asthma. She's just one of these snooty liberals who thinks everyone should eat rabbit food and do yoga and isn't happy unless she is whining about something. Cost me over two-hundred grand in legal bills to get the right to smoke a cigar on my own property."

Cord lit his friend's cigar and then his own. The two men sat on two leather chairs by the bar. Cord sipped nervously on his Cognac. He was about to have to relive The Moment again. He wasn't looking forward to his blood pressure elevating.

Joe began. "What happened?"

Anger flashed in Cord's eyes, but then his face softened. "It's too humiliating to recall."

"Cord, I'll do anything for you. But you have to toughen up here. I can't help you if you don't speak to me."

For the next ten minutes, Cord recounted the incident where the cops had stopped him, and his legal and political attempts to obtain justice. When he finished, Joe remained silent for almost a minute.

Finally, he said, "Do you know why they stopped you?"

"Because I'm black."

"Yes, but how did they know? You said these cops came from nowhere. They never saw you. How can you say that they stopped you because you were black?"

Before his old friend became even more agitated, Joe answered his own question. "They're using face recognition software. They have micro cameras embedded somewhere. In the telephone poles probably. The leaves get in the way when you put them in the trees. Don't worry, I'll find them if they haven't removed them already. We'll get these pricks."

"I knew it was something like that," Cord said.

"This is beyond outrageous and cannot go unanswered. We no longer have cops in this country. We have Storm Troopers. But you have to understand something, Cord. These cops are just following orders. My friend, if you want your revenge, I can arrange it. I can arrange to have these cops terrified or even killed, but that won't attack the underlying problem."

"I know. It's the whole system: the politicians, the prosecutors, the judges . . ."

Cord took a puff on the cigar and continued. "Remember that story you told me about your aunt and uncle? How the local Mafia killed one cop and the other came and apologized? That's what I want. I want those cops to come to my house, give my mother a bouquet of flowers, and apologize. I don't want their money. I don't want to hurt them. I don't want them to be fired or lose their pensions and health insurance and their livelihood. You'll have to scare them, but no violence, unless it's absolutely necessary. I just want an apology."

Cord had what felt like all the money in the world. He could have hired the best assassin money could buy if it was death he wished upon the cops. But it wasn't death. It was just an apology. It was acknowledgment. It was respect.

Joe paused and stared into space, pondering the situation. He then made eye contact with Cord. "What you're asking is possible, but some degree of terror is necessary. You're going to have to have cojones the size of cantaloupes if you want to pull it off. You're asking that the cops humiliate themselves. You're asking that the power structure and the local law enforcement hierarchy acknowledge that you are the ultimate arbiter of justice and not them. And I assure you, this will not happen unless some terror is rained upon them," he said adamantly. He then rested back in his chair, took a puff from his cigar, and said, "But I will help you."

Cord exhaled. That was the answer he hadn't necessarily expected from his friend, not so easily, but it is the answer he'd hoped for. But still, he had to consider the risk involved. "Joe, think about your answer here. We're like brothers, but brothers do not ask each other to destroy their lives. I cannot ask you to do anything that would imperil your career or the financial security of your family.

Think about what you're saying."

"Cord, did you ever see those movies like *Mission Impossible* where the CIA is portrayed as an unaccountable shadow government that can do whatever it wants?"

"Sure. *MI II* was the best one. But it's just fiction."

"Believe it or not, it's true. We are a shadow government, and we can do whatever we want. With the Homeland Security Act, our domestic powers, which were once quite limited, have been greatly enhanced. I could arrange to have a few cops knocked off and never be caught in a million years, if that's what you want."

Joe paused then continued. "The problem here is not my getting caught. It's you."

"Joe, I don't give a shit if I get caught. Just as long as nothing happens to you."

"But what about your kids? Your wife?"

"They'll be fine. There's enough money for the next ten generations of Campbells. But there may be a way to pull this off with no chance that I'll be caught." Cord, although one might assume was erratic in his thinking and resolution, had at least thought some things out.

He reached into his wallet and pulled out a copy of the article from the *Connecticut Post* detailing how Kwame Baker alleged that he was beaten by the police. He gave it to Joe. Joe's eyes shifted from left to right as he read the article. "I'm not following you, Cord."

"If we go after the cops for beating this guy, they can't trace it to me. I had nothing to do with it. I have not called this man. I have not Googled anything on this case. I have not investigated it in anyway. I have not discussed it with anyone. There is no way they can figure out that I'm behind it. The cops will be totally bewildered."

Joe shook his head. "Are you familiar with the concept of criminal profiling?"

"Vaguely. It's when the cops try to determine the characteristics of the person who would commit a particular crime."

"Exactly right. And that is what will happen here."

He sipped on the Cognac and looked at the glass. "You didn't have to waste the good stuff on me."

"For you, anything." Who was Cord kidding? He had to bring out the big guns when making such a request.

"Thanks."

Joe continued. "What you have to understand is that criminal profiling has greatly improved over the past decade due to the huge amount of data that is available on the Internet, especially from social media, medical data, and credit card companies. Privacy is dead. Complex computer algorithms now enable the police to determine, with increased accuracy, who would commit a given crime. Just like the algorithm at school that made us roommates. This, combined with DNA technology, enables many culprits to get caught. It has even solved some previously very cold cases."

"But how could they catch me if I helped this poor junkie get justice?"

"Think about it, Cord. You have some poor junkie in jail unleashing a vendetta against the cops who beat him. The police will check out his family and quickly conclude that they have neither the skill nor the resources to obtain revenge. They will then sit down and try to come up with a profile of someone who would arrange this. They will conclude it is someone who is black, wealthy, and has been recently arrested or harassed by the police. Probably someone local. Furthermore, they will conclude that this is an individual of very high intelligence, not someone who came into his money as an athlete or through the entertainment field. This individual probably went to an elite school or has a graduate degree: a doctor, a lawyer, or has an MBA. And they will plug this information into a database. And guess what? One name will pop up and ring like a slot machine that hit the jackpot: *Cord Campbell*. And they will come after you and arrest you."

Cord pondered his friend's words. He'd made all viable points. "Can't we make it look like some behind-the-scenes force is doing this? Sort of like vigilante justice?"

"That is what you will claim, but they won't buy it."

———

"I don't care. I want to put these people in their place. If I get caught, I get caught." Joe could—purposely or unknowingly—try to talk Cord into coming to his senses, but his mind was made up.

Joe leaned forward and looked directly into his friend's eyes. "Do you understand what you are saying? Do you understand what this could mean to Clara and your kids? Are you really serious about this?" He'd be doing Cord an injustice and wouldn't be as good as a friend as Cord thought he was if he didn't reiterate this point.

"Dead serious."

"Let me repeat myself. Are you *really* serious about this?"

"Joe, I can't live with myself. My blood pressure has skyrocketed. My doctor wanted to put me on Zoloft, but I refused. I never understood how pills can change one's circumstances. I doubt it would help me."

"How much are you willing to spend?"

"As much as it takes."

"Are you willing to go to prison?"

"Yes. But I will have the finest legal team trying to keep my out."

"Are you willing to spend enough money so that they won't dare keep you in prison?"

Cord's jaw dropped. "What do you mean?"

"What if I told you there was a way to extract revenge in such a way that the power structure would crumble at your feet."

"I'd do it in a heartbeat." That answer he didn't even have to think about.

"Cord, is it true that you are worth over a billion dollars?"

"It is."

"Are you willing to spend $30 to $50 million? And I don't want a nickel of it."

"Oh no. You help me out here, I will make you a multimillionaire. On that I insist."

"But are you willing to spend that much?"

"Joe, maybe I have not explained myself. I don't care. If you told me it was a billion, I would pay it. If you told me I would go to prison, I would go. This isn't just about me. I know you work for the CIA, and that sometimes, rules have to be bent. But our government is out of control. The cops blew away a kid in Ferguson for jaywalking. For fucking *jaywalking*! And they strangled that poor guy for selling cigarettes. And it's not just because they were black that I'm pissed. I've been doing a lot of reading on this. The cops have been pulling this crap forever. Now with video cameras they're getting caught. So their response is simply to lie, threaten, and intimidate, like they did to me when my mom recorded them."

Cord continued. "In New Haven, the cops went to the wrong house, threw a flash bomb in the door, killed someone, and guess what happened? Absolutely nothing. In Enfield, they caught a cop on videotape beating the crap out of a handcuffed guy—a white guy— and guess what happened? Absolutely nothing. The state's attorney said there wasn't enough evidence. What the hell do they want? The videotape was all over YouTube, but there is no outrage. And then when they are supposed to protect us, they cower in fear, like that pussy cop in Florida did when all those kids will being killed by that lunatic. The fucking press is useless. The cops probably threaten the journalists if they make an issue out of these outrages."

"Cord, you're preaching to the converted," Joe responded. "In a way, the CIA is a shadow government that counters the cops and FBI. That's why there is so much rivalry among us. You don't know the half of it. Police forces around the countries have become paramilitary organizations—complete with tanks, Humvees, riot gear, and automatic weapons. You are not the first person to approach us. But some of my colleagues and I have been waiting for someone like you to put these cocksuckers in their place."

"Why me?"

"Because you have the cash, and you have the balls, which is a rare combination. There is another point too. After they arrest you, you can claim you know nothing. The fact that we are avenging Kwame Baker will make it appear that we are independent. All you have to do is keep saying that you know nothing. They'll know you're behind it, but they won't be able to prove it."

"So how is this going to work?"

"Before I explain this, I want to make sure that you understand what could happen to you. You could be imprisoned. You could be raped. You could be killed."

"What about my family?"

"Family is off-limits. The political power structure knows that if they attack the family of guys like you, their families are fair game too."

"That's all I need to know. What do I have to do?" Cord's family had always been his main concern. It was because of them he was hell-bent on revenge.

"Actually, not much. I assume you have money stashed in numerous foreign banks. Guys like you always do."

"Of course."

"Where?"

"Several places that promise absolute secrecy. The Caymans, the Seychelles, Singapore."

"Great. All you need to do is give me the account numbers and passwords. I will launder the money through a dozen shell companies and render it untraceable. Then the fun and games will begin."

Cord got up and flipped a hinged picture of the Andromeda Galaxy on the wall, revealing a safe. He dialed the combination, opened it, and grabbed a piece of paper. "Here it is, buddy," he said while handing it to Joe.

"Thanks for your trust. How much is in these accounts?"

"About one-hundred million."

"Cord, I can't give you all the details because you will need what in this business is called 'plausible deniability.' A fancy way of saying what you don't know can't hurt you."

"That's the way my wife runs our personal finances when I ask what something costs."

"I'm going to meet with a close friend of mine called a fixer. All I need from you is for you to write down the names of the cops who harassed you and this junkie. I will arrange to have a few disposable encrypted cellphones brought to your house. They are just like the tapes in the old *Mission Impossible* episodes. One call and they self-destruct. I will also place GPS trackers on all your cars. We will be placing bugs in numerous spots so we can follow what is happening to you. I'll contact you sporadically but don't ever call me unless absolutely necessary."

Cord found a piece of paper and wrote down the names of Fletcher, McMahon, and Kline.

"I've heard the term *fixer* before. But who are these guys?" he asked as he handed the paper to Joe.

"Usually, they are retired CIA operatives, Navy SEALs, or Delta Force. They're just like the guys in the movies . . . Tom Cruise in *Mission Impossible* or Matt Damon in *The Bourne Identity*. People like that actually exist."

"Are you like that?"

"No. I'm not athletic enough. I'm more like Matt Damon in *The Good Shepherd*, the brains behind the scene."

"As I suspected." He was an MIT graduate after all. The brains behind the power; physical power, that is. "So what do these fixers actually do?"

"They're like guys who run the drug cartels in Mexico. They give people with authority an offer they can't refuse, 'Plata o Plumba.' 'Silver or Lead.' Everyone complains about corruption; but often, these police officers in Mexico don't have a choice. They either accept a bribe to look the other way in drug trafficking situations, or they will be killed."

"And there are similar situations here?"

"All the time. The fixer I'm going to use just had a case where a federal prosecutor was going to imprison the owner of a piano company for importing ivory for his keys. The law even says that there is an exception for musical instruments, but this prosecutor didn't care. He told the guy to come up with three million in fines to avoid prison or they would go to court, which would cost him five million in legal fees, and he may still end up in prison."

"You know, now that you mention it, I've heard about these guys. Goldman Sachs uses them occasionally."

"Goldman Sachs is the fixers' biggest customer."

"So what happened in this case?" Cord's curiosity was piqued.

"Just routine. My buddy kidnapped the prosecutor while he was jogging. Hooked up his testicles to a few electrodes and just kept flipping the switch until he agreed to drop the case."

"The prick got what he deserved."

"He did indeed."

"What else do they do?"

"The biggest market is to force women into having abortions."

"That's disgusting."

"I know. The guy I use won't do it."

"Thank God. So why do the other fixers go around doing abortions?"

"They hardly ever do them. Just threaten to do them."

"I don't understand."

"It's very simple. In the good old days, when a woman told a guy she was pregnant, the guy just sneered in her face and said, 'How do I know it's mine?' But, now, the woman simply says, 'I'll get a court order to check the DNA.' This has led to an entire class of attractive women who have figured out that spending fifteen minutes on your back with the right guy means you don't have to work for the rest of your life. Once the baby is born, you get millions in child support. That's the law."

"You mean they get pregnant on purpose?"

"Exactly. Most major cities now have websites where women can find out where the local athletes, rock stars, and other traveling big shots are hanging out. Hell, there are even apps that connect to Google maps to trace these guys. Women figure out if they are ovulating, then all they have to do is pick up one of these guys, get pregnant, and here comes the big payola. Same thing happens to rich, married guys all the time."

"So the fixers force these women to have abortions."

"It's usually not necessary. They just offer them fifty grand and they comply."

"Why would they? It's not that much money comparatively."

"Because if they don't, they are kidnapped, drugged, and brought to an abortionist who then does the dirty work. The abortionist then washes out the woman's womb with a little acid, meaning she can never get pregnant again. The word gets out, and the other women are more agreeable when offered cash."

"The world is not a nice place."

"Yes, the veneer of civilization is quite thin. Are you still sure you want to do this?"

"Joe, our ancestors had balls. Your ancestors got on a ship and went to a country where nobody spoke their language. And they thrived. Mine were packed like sardines in slave ships. And they survived. Now, we are just a bunch of wimps playing it safe. I'm tired of playing it safe. I am tired of protecting what I have. I want justice. I want respect."

Joe Montalbano smiled at his old friend and held up his glass in a salute. "Then you will have it, my friend."

CHAPTER 14

Joe hated the Midwest. He never understood how anybody could ever live here. It took hours to drive through the endless miles of amber waves of grain. Yes, the Bronx was noisy, congested, and violent, but at least it wasn't boring. And here he was, sitting in Nowheresville, Oklahoma, at a bar where the walls were covered with pictures of covered wagons bearing the letters OU. Holding on to a past that was probably pretty dismal didn't say much for the local perspective.

"What kind of port do you have?" Joe said.

The bartender raised his eyebrows and laughed. "Son, you are a long way from home."

Yes, he hated the Midwest. "Just give me any non-lite beer you have on draft."

"There's only one."

"I'll take it."

Joe saw two pictures of intense-looking men. "Who are those guys?" He pointed.

The bartender just shook his head. "You *are* a long way from home."

He plopped the beer in front of Joe and continued. "Those are the fourth and fifth persons of the Blessed Trinity—Barry Switzer and Bob Stoops. Switzer gave us Sooners three National Championships, and Stoops gave us one."

Joe actually knew about Switzer. He just didn't remember the face. The reason is that the man he was about to meet, Trip Pilgrim, had played for Switzer in the 1980s. Middle linebacker, if memory served.

Joe looked at the bartender. "You know, I've always wondered this. What exactly is a Sooner?"

The bartender scratched his head. "Not really sure. It has something to do with the pioneers."

Just then, Joe felt a hand on his shoulder, and there was his colleague, Trip Pilgrim. "A Sooner is an individual who settles on government land before they are permitted to do so," Trip explained. "The term has been generalized to someone who attempts to gain an unfair advantage. It originated when our state was still a territory, and President Grover Cleveland, to encourage more settlers, gave land away for free. A specific date was set for the giveaway, but some arrived too early to stake their claim. They were called Sooners."

The bartender replied, "I was close."

Trip sat beside Joe and looked at the bartender. "Dewar's and water. Easy on the water."

The bartender complied.

Trip was a retired member of the First Special Forces Operational Detachment-Delta, more commonly known as Delta Force. This elite branch of the U.S. Army consisted of only 800 men, all capable of extreme physical and psychological feats. Trip could do two hundred finger-tip pushups, run ten miles in an hour, stay underwater for two minutes, and still do the iron cross on the gym rings. And he was forty-nine! Of the two hundred seventy-four in his class who tried to become Deltas, Trip was among only eight who were chosen.

The CIA had a branch called the Special Operations Group, and there was considerable overlap with Delta Force. This is how Joe knew Trip. They had worked together in Iraq and Afghanistan but had met in Peru, where they worked together on a few assassinations of leaders in the Marxist group, the Shining Path.

Joe hadn't seen Trip in several years, and he remembered him having a full head of shortly cropped blond hair. Now, he was completely bald.

"What happened to your hair?" Joe asked.

"Since going private, I find the shaved head makes it easier to intimidate people. Avoids unnecessary violence."

And Trip *was* intimidating. At six foot three, he radiated power. There were no bulging biceps or forearms, just sinewy arms attached to massive hands that looked like they could rip out your throat in a matter of seconds. And they could. His chest was not broad, but tapered rapidly to a thin waist and whip like legs that could flex into a crippling groin kick, rotate to a fatal kick to the temple, or directly kick in the face and displace an opponent's front teeth. He had learned this French martial art, Savate, when he had worked with the French Foreign Legion in Algeria. But the scariest thing about Trip was his stare. His deep-set azure eyes combined with his thin lips and high cheekbones could overawe even the most amoral member of the Hells Angels.

"Family okay?" Joe asked. He was following Cord's suit of being easygoing before jumping into serious business.

"Couldn't be better. At first, I was upset when we only had girls. But I'll tell you something. Girls love their daddy. Megan just turned eleven, and she can deck any boy in her class. Taught her Savate. Won't have to worry about unwanted advances with that one. Judy is eight. Not as athletic as Megan but a good student, just like her old man. Got them in a good Christian school. Teaches them right from wrong. None of this secular humanist crap. Molly is just four and has already established that she has a mind of her own."

Joe had noticed that many Delta members came from conservative Christian backgrounds. He theorized that the concept of good and evil inculcated in them at a young age made them perfect tools for discreet military operations that required killing and torture. No concept of moral relativism. We were good. They were bad. Nothing else to know. Just do what we want or we get out the blowtorch. And for those who are tortured before they die, no big deal. Since they were going to be tortured in hell for eternity, what are a few more minutes?

"How's your crew?" Trip asked.

"We're fine. Carol still gets upset when I'm away too long on a mission. Thank God, we live on the same street as her mother and sister. Even though the kids are bigger, they still need to be watched."

"How's Peter doing with his basketball?"

"Okay, but he's not tall enough. Of course, he's only fourteen and not done growing."

"And Michelle?"

"She loves ballet and soccer, like every other girl in the neighborhood. Great student though. She's going to be my MIT girl."

It was apparent the men were more than just acquaintances. They were friends who kept tabs on each other's lives and family because they actually cared. It wasn't just small talk.

Both men sipped on their drinks reflectively until finally Joe said, "Let's get down to business. We can't talk here." Catching up time was over.

Joe put two ten-dollar bills on the table for a six-dollar tab. The bartender looked at the money. "We're not starving around here, son. No need to be so generous."

Joe grabbed one of the tens. "Is that better?"

"Still a bit much, but I thank you." The bartender nodded and scooped up the bill.

"Thank you for the fine service."

Trip and Joe exited the bar. A Corvette convertible was parked by the side of the bar.

"Silver. My favorite color." Joe's lips spread into a smile.

"Shark-gray metallic," Trip said.

"Looks like the fixer business is doing well," Joe said as he circled admiringly around the Corvette.

"Never better. But it almost upsets me that business is so good. Our government is at war with its people."

The two men sat in the car. Both were used to always finding a venue where listening devices could not be found. The bar was not a safe place to talk. Trip's car was since he swept it daily for listening devices.

"Now I'm getting doctors," Trip continued. "My last client was a plastic surgeon in Colorado. One of my retired buddies has a young daughter. His wife turns her head for a second and their three-year-old daughter pulls a pot of boiling water down on her leg. Lucky, it didn't hit her face. She has these horrible burns that need all sorts of skin grafts and multiple operations as she grows. The goddamn government won't pay for it. So he takes his daughter to this gal and she finds out my buddy is a retired Delta. She says her daddy fought in Vietnam, and when he came home, some college kid from Columbia spat in his face and called him a baby killer. She tells my buddy he is a hero and thanks him for protecting her freedom. Fixes his daughter's leg so you can hardly tell she was burned. Doesn't charge him a dime. Not a goddamn dime."

Trip stopped for a second then continued. "One day my buddy stops in the doc's office for a follow-up, and she's literally in tears. Some fascist from our government comes into her office and say she violated some Hippo law."

"Hippo law?" Joe raised an eyebrow.

"Maybe it's Hipaa. I don't remember. It's some medical privacy law that Clinton pushed to protect all the faggots with AIDS. Anyway, this thug tells the doc she has to come up with a million bucks or they were going to throw her in jail."

"What did she do to break the HIPAA law?" Joe had known what his buddy was referring to all along, but he didn't want to correct his friend and come across as being some smart guy. He saw no need to flaunt his intellect.

"She was throwing out some old records. Put them in a garbage can. Not allowed to do that says the government. You have to shred them. So this fascist looks in the garbage behind her office and says she broke the law. 'A million bucks or we haul your ass in jail,'" Trip mocked. "Poor woman told my buddy she will have to mortgage her house to pay. Her husband is so pissed off he's talking divorce. And they have three kids. My buddy says to the doc, 'Don't worry.'"

Trip spread his hands. "He calls me up and gives me this cocksucker's name and asks me to take care of it. Tells me he'll pay my fee. I tell him don't worry about it. This one's on the house. I trail the guy and wait until he's in a hotel room by himself in Oregon. I sneak in his room while he's sleeping, politely wake him up, and tell him that the case against the doc is going to be dropped."

Trip laughed. "You should have seen this guy. He's some retired cop from your neck of the woods. Not even forty-five years old. Must have a sweet deal there. Big guy. Muscles all over the place. He looks at me and says, 'Take off that ski mask.'"

"Probably not a wise move," Joe deadpanned.

"I told him I would be happy to remove the mask, but I would have to gouge his eyeballs out first. The dumb bastard stands up and yells, 'You don't know what you're dealing with!' and throws the slowest roundhouse I've ever seen. I step back and kick the point of my shoe right in his nuts. Goes down like a sack of potatoes."

"*He* was the one who didn't know who he was dealing with."

Trip laughed again. "I give him a few minutes to recover and placed my hand on his throat. He literally craps in his pants. And I tell him to say, 'I will never bother the nice doctor again.' I make him say it twenty times. And I tell him that if I ever hear of him or anyone bothering that doctor again, I will put him in intensive care for two months. A week later, the doctor gets a letter saying that the investigation has been dropped."

Joe shook his head. "I hate to say it, but this country is going to end up like Sicily. People with money are going to hire guys like us to fight the government."

"You're right," Trip said. "I have more work than I know what to do with. I just smashed the face of some trial lawyer who was suing a doctor for saving a baby's life. He dropped that case fast. I smashed the kneecap of some bureaucrat who was telling some farmer he could not clear part of his land because of some varmint. Some crap with the Endangered Species Act. I let him know that if he bothers that farmer again, he was going to be an endangered species himself."

Joe nodded. "You always had a good sense of humor."

"But why do we have to do this?" He spoke with seriousness while shaking his head. "We are run by bureaucrats and lawyers and thugs posing as cops. Think the Constitution is a piece of toilet paper. Hell, my daddy fought against these types in World War II and grandpappy did the same in World War I. Now we have the same scum running our country. What did they fight for? You and I have spent our life defending our country, our way of life, and now we have government at war with its people. Hell, the country is barely worth defending anymore. We have a bureaucratic and legal class of scum balls and perverts who just want us to pay taxes for all this bullshit—global warming, abortion on demand, can't pray in school. Hell, in one of the public schools, you are no longer allowed to say boys and girls because it pisses off the perverts."

"I don't get it."

"Some crap about transgender. I don't get it either."

"Well, Trip, you're going to love this job. This guy is my best friend from college, and I will do anything for him."

"You mean Cord? You talked about him all the time. Said how rich he was becoming. Said you should have done the same thing."

"Yep."

"He's black too."

"Yeah. I remember. What happened to him?"

"Police humiliated him, and he wants revenge. No expense spared."

For the next five minutes, Joe explained to Pilgrim how Cord had been stopped by the police for no crime other than he was driving while black in the wrong neighborhood. He saw the rage in Trip's face as he recounted how his mother had been searched and violated. He also told him how Cord wanted to get revenge on the cops who beat Kwame Baker.

When he was done, Trip just shook his head. "If those scumballs had done that to my mom, they would all be dead. Slow, painful deaths. Hell, I would videotape me whacking their heads with baseball bats along with my specialty, a little blowtorch action on the testicles. Then I'd put it on the Internet. If they put me in the gas chamber, I couldn't care less."

The left corner of Joe's mouth raised. "I *knew* you were the right man for the job."

"You're right. I used to think those blacks were just a bunch of crybabies, but now I agree with them. With all these video cameras, these cops can't lie any more. Hell, they killed that poor, fat, black guy in New York for selling cigarettes. They blew away that kid in Ferguson because he stole a few cigars. They stuck a billy club up that poor guy's butt in New York. And then that pussy cop in South Carolina shot that guy in the back eight times while he was running away. And that's when they get caught. Imagine the shit that goes on when no one's looking. I actually agree with that Kaepernick guy, but he shouldn't have kneeled during the anthem."

"All he wants is an apology. He wants the cops to bring his mother a bouquet of flowers and beg for their forgiveness."

"We can do that. But probably have to kill one to get the other one to do it. We'll see . . ." Trip was thinking out loud now.

"But there is one thing I don't understand. Why does he give a shit about this junkie—what's his name—Kwanza Baker?"

"Kwame Baker," Joe said. "I think it's a black thing. He feels that justice shouldn't only apply to people with money. Also, the cop who beat Baker was one of the cops who pulled him over."

"So we're going to go after three cops then?"

"We'll see. One cop, Fletcher, was involved in both incidents. He's the real prick. The other, a woman, was involved in the beating of Baker. A third cop, McMahon, was Fletcher's partner when Cord was harassed."

"Let's ride." Trip started the car and pulled out of the parking lot. Joe looked ahead. More amber waves of grain.

"I think best when I'm driving, especially in my 'Vette. So what's your plan?"

"Cord wants to go after the cops who beat up Baker first. I was thinking of a little video action to begin with."

Trip gave Joe a dejected look. "Video action? That's boring. I'd like to bust a few heads."

"You'll get your chance. But the videos will be great fun."

"And I suppose you expect me to place all these cameras."

"It's one of your many talents."

"Then when they come down hard on Baker, maybe you can bust a few heads, but that's really not what Cord wants."

"How do you know they'll come down on Baker?"

"Because they'll have no choice."

"But don't you think they'll figure out he had nothing to do with it?"

"Of course. They'll use criminal profiling, and they'll figure out it's Cord. Unless they are stupider that I think. Which is not really possible."

"Then what?"

"Then the real fun begins. They'll arrest Cord, and we'll swing into action."

"So what prelims do I do?"

"The usual . . . video cameras in all the players' offices and domiciles. Taps on all phones. GPS trackers on cars and clothing. Remote control smoke bombs and a few real bombs. Triangular speakerphones for the negotiating. Voice-changing software and a few tablet-controlled guns. I'll get you all the equipment. I'll take care of the keylogging on their computers and jailbreak their cellphones. I've purchased a couple of buildings through shell corporations. Then you just sit tight until the time comes to rock and roll. I've already hacked some of the computers already."

"Do you think we'll need that much stuff?"

"Probably not," Joe said. "But you can't be overprepared."

"Sounds straightforward. But how do we spring your buddy once he's in jail? You don't expect me to single-handedly invade the prison and bring him out. I'm good, but I'm not *that* good."

Joe smiled. "You won't have to. They'll let him walk out."

"We're in Oklahoma here, buddy, not Colorado. If you're smoking that weed, it's illegal here."

Joe spoke for the next three minutes about how he surmised they'd ultimately let Cord walk out of prison. His old friend did not interrupt.

"Nothing's changed. You're still a goddamn genius, or maybe

it's just that devious Italian mind."

"Sicilian."

"Whatever. This is going to be the most fun I've had since we vaporized those Taliban clowns. But this is going to cost millions, in equipment alone."

"Tens of millions." Joe didn't blink.

"And this guy has that kind of money?"

"He's the second richest black in the United States. Only Oprah has more. You have an account, right?"

"In the Seychelles. I'll get the number for you when we get to the house."

"You should have it memorized."

"You MIT guys are obnoxious. What am I going to get here? I'm charging $200 an hour now."

"You're having decimal point problems, pal. You'll get at least a mil. No expense is being spared. You're the best, and I want the best. I'm not patronizing you, it's just the truth."

"That will put me on easy street. Won't have to worry about the girls' education. I thank you."

"Don't thank me yet. You may be cursing me in a few weeks."

"No way. I never get caught." He spoke with the utmost confidence.

They drove for several minutes until they pulled up to a modest split-level house on a cul-de-sac. As they walked up the driveway, they were greeted by a tall blond woman who, if Joe recalled correctly, was once a cheerleading captain.

"Joe, great to see you again." She gave him a polite peck on the cheek. "Trip," she rested her hand on her husband's shoulder, "the steaks have been marinating for five hours."

"Thanks, gorgeous. I'll fire up the barbecue." He kissed his wife on the lips and then turned to his friend. "Joe, come on in and say hi to our girls."

CHAPTER 15

"**M**ommy, everyone is using this bad word in school that begins with 'f'."

Cheryl Fletcher looked down at her eight-year-old daughter. She had hoped that sending her daughter to All Saints Grade School would have enabled her to avoid this question until at least age eleven, but Catholic education was not what it used to be. There was not a single nun in the school. Only a bunch of teachers biding their time until they got offers to teach at the public schools, where the pay and benefits were better, and there was a pension plan.

She looked at her daughter sternly. Cindy was attired in her plaid school uniform with a little silver cross attached to her lapel above the school emblem. She looked back at her mom. "Is it really a bad word?

Cheryl grabbed her knees, bent forward, and looked her daughter in the eyes. "It's a *very* bad word, and I don't want to ever hear you use it. And your father will be very upset if he finds out you ever said it."

Her daughter's eyebrows knitted in bewilderment. "Then why is Daddy doing it if it's so bad?"

Cheryl tried not to laugh. It seemed obvious to her that whoever was educating her daughter on the birds and the bees explained to her daughter that this was necessary for her to exist. "Sweetheart, don't you worry about that. You'll understand these things when you get older."

But her daughter still appeared to be confused. "Yes, but what does fu . . . that bad word mean?"

"Cindy, you'll understand when you get older, but it's a bad word."

"But if it's so bad, why is there a video of Daddy doing this bad thing on the Internet?"

Cheryl's heart just about stopped beating. Or maybe it did, for a second or two. She stood up straight and glared at her daughter. "What are you talking about, young lady?" She had an emotional concoction of fear and anger in her heart. She did her best to keep it out of her eyes. Sometimes if children saw anger in their parents' eyes, they said what they thought the parent wanted to hear out of fear. Well, all Cheryl wanted was the truth.

"That's what all the big kids were saying. They kept watching it on the iPhones and laughing. They kept saying that Daddy was doing that bad word."

Her daughter then witnessed her mother's face drain of blood until it was completely white. "What's wrong, Mommy?"

Sickness had now been added to the brew. Cheryl was sick to her stomach. It was in her heart; it was in her eyes. It was in every ounce of her being. "Go to your room." She turned away from her daughter.

"But what's wrong, Mommy?"

"Go to your room *now*!" she roared.

Cindy knew that when her mother spoke in this tone, immediate obedience was mandatory, and she scurried up the stairs. Cheryl then entered the den and turned on her computer. Instead of the usual screen saver of her two daughters in their Brownie uniforms, there was an image of her husband with a female officer in what appeared to be a store. Across the image was written the words *"Actions have consequences."* She clicked on the arrow superimposed on the image. The image began to move as a muffled voice narrated the video.

"What have we here?" the voice said. *"It looks like Officer Fletcher is about to punch a handcuffed suspect."* She saw her husband's balled fist about to hit a handcuffed black man in the stomach. She then saw the female officer grab his wrist and point her chin upward.

The narration continued. *"But look. Officer Kline sees the video camera and stops her friend. How magnanimous."*

The video then showed a mug shot of a scrawny-looking black man with his right eyelid so bruised and swollen that the eye itself could not be seen. He had a surprisingly calm look on his face.

The narrator continued. *"But what happened here? Our suspect, Mr. Baker, has a black eye. The good officers said Mr. Baker fell. But that's not what Mr. Baker said. He says that Officer Fletcher punched him in the stomach and then in the eye after they handcuffed him. His lawyer even told this to the judge. But the judge did not believe Mr. Baker, which is why he is still in jail."*

The video cut to a scene of her naked, aroused husband walking into a bedroom. And it wasn't their bedroom. She screamed with outrage.

The narrator continued. *"Now it's time to celebrate with Officer Kline."* She saw an attractive black-haired woman in a bed smiling as Cheryl's husband approached. She recognized her as the same officer in the video. Cheryl screeched again.

"What's wrong, Mommy?" Her daughter had appeared out of nowhere and was now in tears.

Cheryl hugged the screen to prevent her daughter from viewing it. "Go to your room now! Go to your room now and start packing. We're going to visit Grandma and Grandpa."

"But, Mommy—"

"Cindy, please listen to Mommy. Please. Please." She briskly wiped her tears away, causing her skin to redden.

Her daughter left the room, and Cheryl looked again at the screen, making sure her daughter did not return. By now, her husband was gyrating under the sheets with the cooing Officer Kline.

The narration continued. *"Officer Kline seems to be in a frisky mood. Hopefully, Officer Fletcher is not using bootlegged Viagra."*

She had seen enough. The humiliation was unbearable. She clicked off the screen and ran up the stairs. She grabbed two suitcases and threw them on her bed. After unzipping them, she ran into the bathroom and scooped up her toiletries. With no attempt at organization, she heaved them into one of the suitcases.

"Mommy, what are you doing?" Cindy asked, entering the room.

Cheryl forced a smile. "We're going to see Grandma and Grandpa."

"But why do we have to pack? Are we staying overnight?"

"Yes. Grandma and Grandpa want to see us."

"But they live so close. We never stay overnight. I won't be able to talk to my friends on the computer."

"Don't worry, dear. You can use Grandma's computer." With her things all packed, she walked over to Cindy.

"But it doesn't work. They don't have video chat."

Cheryl kept smiling at her daughter as she nudged her out of the room and walked her to her own bedroom. "Don't worry, sweetheart. I'll figure it out for you. You can talk to your friends tonight."

Cheryl rapidly emptied out several of her daughter's dresser drawers and threw the contents into a princess suitcase. She then stormed into her other daughter, Molly's, room and did the same, filling up one of Molly's oversized duffle bags.

"Is Molly coming too?"

"Yes, sweetheart. She's at school practicing with the band. We'll go pick her up."

"Why can't Daddy pick her up?"

"We'll see Daddy later."

"Are you mad at Daddy?"

"No, sweetheart. I love Daddy, and Daddy loves me." This was a prime example of someone saying just opposite of what they felt inside. Love was not what Cheryl would call what she felt for her husband at this moment. It was more like hate, disappointment, and disgust. But she wasn't about to share those sentiments with her child. "Now get in the car. We're going to visit Grandma and Grandpa."

She zipped the duffle bag up and threw it over her shoulder. Cindy was in charge of her princess suitcase while Cheryl towed her larger suitcase. She started to walk down the stairs but everything was a bit much to carry. She decided to leave the larger suitcase on the top of the stairs and come back for it. She and Cindy made their way through the kitchen and entered their garage. Opening the trunk of their Honda, the increasing adrenaline enabled Cheryl to easily toss the duffle bag and the princess suitcase inside. It took up most of the available room, so the next one would have to go in the backseat.

With Cindy following her back into the house, Cheryl ran back upstairs and grabbed the other suitcase.

"Cindy, let's go. Grandma and Grandpa are waiting," she called out as she dragged it down the steps.

"But, Mommy?" Even with their bags packed, Little Miss Cindy was still bound and determined to put up a fuss.

"Let's go, sweetheart." Cheryl loved that fact that her daughter was an excellent student, but now her high intelligence was annoying her. She grabbed Cindy by the hand and escorted her out to the garage.

"Get into the car."

"You forgot Elmo."

"You can go grab Elmo, sweetheart. But hurry." All Cheryl wanted to do right now was to get out of there. Why couldn't that child of hers just cooperate?

After heaving the other suitcase in the car, Cheryl ran back upstairs to hurry Cindy along.

"Where's Elmo? Where's Elmo?"

When Cheryl entered her daughter's bedroom, she found her running around in circles beginning to get hysterical.

Cheryl had just seen that thing. But with a zillion and one things going through her head, she couldn't easily recall. "Think. Think," she told herself as she began to pace. She had to think. She was still in control of the situation. Then it hit her. "He's by the television!"

Cheryl ran down the stairs and found Elmo lying face down on the couch. "I've got Elmo. Let's go."

Her daughter slowly came down the stairs. Within seconds they were back in the garage.

"Get into the car," Cheryl told Cindy. There was not enough

room in the back with that oversized suitcase thrown in the back-seat, so she opened the front door. "Get in, sweetheart."

"But you said I was too little for the front seat."

"Just get in the car!" Her daughter reluctantly complied.

Cheryl slammed the door shut and ran around to the driver's side. She pushed the garage door opener and started the car. Placing it in gear, she rapidly pulled backward but abruptly stopped as the garage door was not fully open.

"Mammy, I don't have my seatbelt on yet. It's dangerous."

"You can put it on as we drive."

She hit the gas. Just as she was about to exit the garage, a police cruiser turned into her driveway, causing her to slam on her brakes. She tried to veer to her left, but the cruiser blocked her from moving.

"Aaarrghhh," she screamed.

"Mommy, it's Daddy." Cindy was happy to see her father and began bouncing up and down in the car.

Cheryl pounded her fists on the steering wheel. In her rearview mirror she saw her husband quickly open the door on the passenger side of the cruiser while one of his colleagues, Kevin McMahon, got out of the driver's seat. She opened the door and started running toward the street. She had no idea where she was going to run to. Her brain was telling her to run and her feet were listening.

Without even saying a word, Fletcher easily blocked his wife's path and positioned himself to where she practically ran into his arms.

"Let me go! Let me go!" she pleaded, tears forming in her eyes.

Fletcher grabbed her around the waist and carted her into the garage like he was carrying a piece of lumber. He did not want to handle the situation with his wife in the middle of the street for the entire neighborhood to witness.

"I said let go of me!" Cheryl continued to scream while she pounded away at his torso and kicked her feet, her sandals flying onto the garage pavement.

His jaw clenched tightly as he carried her into the house.

"Daddy! Let Mommy go!" Cindy yelled after getting out of the car and following them into the house. Tears gushed out of her eyes as she watched her daddy handle her mother like he would a criminal on the street.

"Hold up, Little Lady." McMahon grabbed Cindy, pulling her back gently as to give Fletcher a head start.

Cheryl's feet continued to flail. She kicked over a vase of flowers Fletcher had brought home to her yesterday.

"Let go of me, you worthless piece of shit. I'll kill you. I'll kill you."

Trip and Joe sat on cushioned chairs in the basement of an abandoned building in Bridgeport. The walls were concrete blocks, and the floor was gray cement.

Joe had purchased it with untraceable cash through a shell corporation in Singapore. Trip laughed. "Joe, I must protest these working conditions. And you could have at least gotten us some popcorn."

"Stop complaining. Look how comfortable the chairs are." He tapped the arm of the chair. "Plus, I got you eighteen-year-old Macallan Scotch."

"I prefer Glenlivet."

Both men directed their attention to the Dell laptop with an eighteen-inch screen they'd been watching for the past hour or so.

"Home movies are becoming a lost art. But I must say, the Fletcher family is resurrecting the genre," Joe said.

"Yes, but we should have popcorn," Trip protested.

"Good thing we placed a camera in the garage too. We would have missed some of the action."

"But we should have popcorn."

Both men watched as Fletcher gently set his wife down on the living-room sofa.

"You can't get away with this!" Cheryl yelled. "You can't get away with this. My brothers will kill you."

"Cheryl, calm down. Calm down. It's not what you think." Fletcher smiled benevolently.

His petrified daughter stood over in the corner. McMahon had placed her there and was now holding an oblong, black three-inch by two-inch plastic box, a wireless camera detector. He pulled out the antenna and held it up, scanning the room.

"Wrong model, moron. Where'd you buy that piece of crap? Walmart?" Joe said to the monitor.

While most Americans conceptually grasped that the advent of modern technology combined with social media had destroyed personal privacy, they had no idea how the government or well-financed individuals could follow their every action, intrude on their personal lives, and drain their bank and brokerage accounts. Officers Fletcher, McMahon, and Kline were about to have their lives intruded upon in ways they could not possibly fathom.

Joe was not only a master of modern eavesdropping equipment; he had personally designed some of the latest developments. Poor McMahon was attempting to find miniature video cameras and microphones with a piece of equipment that was as obsolete as the bow and arrow during a nuclear attack.

Trip had personally placed the cameras whose lenses consisted of fiber optic cables the diameter of a pinhead. His favorite spot was in the screws of light switches, but they were everywhere— embedded in library books, sequestered in picture frames, and masked inside overhead lights and chandeliers. These cameras were connected to wafer-thin transmitters that instantly conveyed high-resolution images to underground signal amplifiers that were within one-hundred feet of the house. From there, the signals were boosted into cyberspace, where they would exist in perpetuity. Joe could watch them in real time, save them, place them on YouTube, edit them, and transmit them to anyone at any time. The microphones were even smaller; twice the diameter of a human hair.

But this was just the beginning. Joe had instructed Trip to place sophisticated keylogging software into the computers of the three officers, both at their offices and home, giving him multiple options of ways to terrorize everyone involved in Cord's situation. Every time someone touched a key on those computers, the information was relayed to Joe's mainframes and routed through various databases throughout the world, until he had an untraceable encrypted database with the passwords, e-mails, word documents—anything typed or received—at his disposal. He could drain Fletcher's wife's 401K at will and send her life savings into cyberspace through untraceable networks, never to be seen again. He could access the medical records of McMahon's children and even prescribe medications for them—making it appear that the prescriptions originated from their doctors' offices.

Every time someone viewed a Web page, logged onto Facebook or did a Google search, Joe could trace when and where. He knew that Officer Kline liked to play Internet backgammon, McMahon liked Internet poker, and Fletcher was partial to porn featuring buxom blond farm girls copulating with dwarfs.

Not only that, he had jailbroken their cellphones so that every text, e-mail, and Web site view was documented. That's what happens when you clicked onto messages that say, "You have some unclaimed money at our bank." Trip had also placed GPS trackers in the personal and official cars of the officers.

Joe shook his head in disgust as he watched McMahon say to Fletcher, "It's all clear. No cameras. No microphones. No need to continue behaving."

"They're still in the Stone Age," Joe said.

It had dawned on Fletcher and McMahon that if Officer Kline's bedroom was bugged and equipped with video cameras, their houses could be similarly invaded. But now, with his partner's reassurance that all was safe, he could put his wife in her place.

Fletcher's benevolent smile became a malignant snarl. "Listen, you goddamn bitch. I'm tired of tolerating your crap. I'm lucky if I can get you to put out once a month. What did you expect?"

She stood up from the couch and thrust her fist at her husband. He caught it in his massive hand.

"Did you see that; domestic violence?" Joe said in mock horror.

McMahon looked at Fletcher. "Control the situation, Jack."

"I'll show you control." He slammed his open palm into his

wife's abdomen with such force that she fell back onto the couch and propelled it into the wall. His wife's face turned temporarily blue as she lost her breath, her shoulders heaving as she grasped the side of the couch.

Their daughter came out of her terrified trance and ran toward her mother. "Mommy, Mommy. Are you all right?"

"You shut your mouth!" Fletcher yelled at his daughter.

"The big kids were right." She pointed her finger at her father. "You were doing that bad thing on the Internet."

Fletcher's hand was coming down to slap his daughter in the face when McMahon grabbed it. "You have to calm down. Let's get a better handle on this. We need to talk to that punk Baker now. Let's get out of here."

McMahon smiled at the young girl. "Cindy, sometimes Mommies and Daddies fight. That doesn't mean they don't love each other, and it doesn't mean they don't love you."

"Daddy just hit Mommy. Do you think I'm stupid?"

Joe watched the screen. "A precocious one."

"I think Officer Fletcher needs to work on his parenting skills," Trip added. "Maybe an anger management class would help too."

McMahon scooped up the young girl and took her upstairs. Fletcher glared at his wife. She was now able to breathe normally, but the look of defiance had been replaced with a look of terror. Fletcher placed his massive hand around her throat, being careful not to squeeze so hard that he would leave a bruise. She grasped his wrist with both hands and tried to pull his hand away. It was like trying to move a tree trunk.

"You listen to me very carefully, Cheryl. You are powerless. You can't call the cops. You can't call a lawyer. If you do, I will kill him. You are not going to destroy my family. Guys like me are always going to get some side action. Hell, I nailed one of your college pals in the bridal party the night before our wedding. Get used to it. I can't help it if women find me irresistible."

He continued. "I could kill you right now. And I could get away with it. Now, are you going to calm down?"

She looked into his blazing eyes and concluded that he wasn't bluffing. She would have to bide her time. Maybe she would forgive him. What choice did she have? So she just nodded her head.

"Rather full of himself, don't you think?" Joe said.

"Guys that bully women are always pussies," Trip said.

"He's lucky he didn't marry a Sicilian. She would shoot him in the spine while he slept and then cut his balls off." Joe said.

Trip responded. "I can't wait to put him down."

"You may get your chance," Joe said. "You may get your chance."

CHAPTER 16

Kwame's head bounced off the concrete wall of the interview room for the second time. He looked at the camera lens suspended in the upper corner of the left ceiling.

"No luck this time, asshole. It's disconnected." Fletcher grabbed the front of Kwame's orange prison shirt and with one hand, curled his limp, 115-pound frame until his feet were six inches off the ground and his eyes were so close to his that he could see them dilate with fear.

His eyes began to refocus. "I'm tellin' you, man, I don't know what you're talkin' about." That Kwame sure did know how to take a lick and keep on giving lip.

"Listen, you worthless piece of shit. We're just getting started here. How did you get that video camera into my partner's apartment?"

"I don't have no camera. What partner? What you talkin' about?"

"You think you're smart? You think I'm an idiot?"

McMahon tapped his colleague on the shoulder. "Let me talk to him." He was always up for a game of good cop-bad cop.

Fletcher released Kwame suddenly. His knees buckled as his feet hit the floor. His ankle twisted on impact, causing him to stagger until he reached his outstretched hand to the wall, regaining his balance.

Fletcher retreated while McMahon approached the inmate, gently grabbing his arm. "Mr. Baker. I'm sorry. Let me help you up."

He guided him into the chair and then took a seat across from him, cautiously placing his open his hands on the metallic desk with the palms up. Studies had shown that this submissive gesture by the interrogator increased the chance of confession by 18 percent. Fletcher stood behind him, folding his arms across his expansive chest and burying his knuckles into his biceps so that his arms bulged from his tight uniform shirt. He glared at Kwame, whose face now displayed both the emotions of fear and confusion. Yeah, they had the good cop-bad cop routine down to a science.

"Mr. Baker, let me explain the situation. There is a video on the Internet that shows Officer Fletcher and Officer Kline arresting you in the pharmacy. This is followed by a video of Officer Fletcher and Officer Kline together in Officer Kline's apartment. This video is destroying Officer Fletcher's family, and we would like to know how you arranged to tape this video and place it on the Internet."

Kwame's eyebrows rose. His right eye was no longer closed shut, but there was still some blood in the eye itself. "Look, yo, I been in this jail ever since you cuffed me. I didn't make no video. How could I?"

Fletcher leaned over the table, his arms like tripods supporting his expansive chest. "We know that, you dumb shit. You paid someone to do it. Who did you pay?"

Kwame sat back in his chair. "Paid someone? Paid them with what? I got no money. I know nothing about no video. What's the video show?"

"That's none of your goddamn business," Fletcher snarled.

Kwame smiled for the first time. "I was right. It shows you doin' her. That's why you mad."

Fletcher brought his hand back and was about to slap Kwame. McMahon brought his hand up to stop the blow. Both men were thinking the same thing. If Kwame knew nothing about the video, how could he have so quickly deduced that that the video showed Fletcher and Officer Kline copulating? They had discussed ad nauseam how this video had been produced and concluded that Kwame must have had connections with criminal elements to extract his revenge. The problem was that the poor guy was such an obvious loser that they could not imagine anyone going to bat for him, let alone risking the full force of a police investigation.

McMahon continued. "Mr. Baker, help us out here. This video was made as way of getting revenge against Officer Fletcher and Officer Kline for supposedly beating you, which is something they never did."

"You *did* beat me," Kwame shot at Fletcher. "Why do you think my eye is still red?"

"You were resisting arrest." Fletcher was adamant. He said it like it was the stone-cold truth.

"Here we go; cops doing what they do best. Lyin'. I ain't got nothin' to do with no video, but I'm glad you got what's comin' to you. God's punishin' you for lyin' and hittin' me. You not allowed to do that. You ain't even allow to have me in here without my lawyer."

McMahon raised his hand attempting to maintain peace while Fletcher balled his fist.

"Where do you buy your drugs? Who's your source?" McMahon asked.

"I ain't got no source. I just buy from whoever be on the corner when I can't get a doc to write me a script."

"What about your gang friends?"

"Gang friends? You serious?" Kwame sucked his teeth. "I ain't in no gang. Niggas in gangs get killed all the time. Besides, you think gangs would do videos? Y'all obviously not too bright. Not their modus operandi."

McMahon did not know how Kwame knew what modus operandi meant, but he was not about to ask for clarification. They had bigger fish to fry . . . more like a humongous whale. "Who have you spoken to?"

"What do you mean?"

"Spoken to you, dumb shit. As in moving your mouth."

"You mean here since you locked me up? I ain't spoke to no one." Kwame shook his head to back up his statement.

"How about that doctor?"

"I'm supposed to see her, but there be a problem with transportation. I ain't seen her yet."

The problem that McMahon and Fletcher had was that they knew he was telling the truth. The only visitors that Kwame had seen since being taken into custody were his public defender, along with his aunt and his stepsister. This was documented with video footage and log books. They also knew that his appointment with Dr. Teresa Trybus had been cancelled. In fact, they arranged the cancellation. They just wanted to see his reaction to the question.

McMahon got up and whispered into Fletcher's ear. "We've got to stop. The Bridgeport guys are going to start getting nervous. They can only look the other way for so long. There's going to be too big of a gap in the disc."

Most jails had interview rooms for suspects, and these were equipped with video cameras attached to DVD recorders. When the technology was first developed, Bridgeport's Finest would simply turn off the video when they wanted to beat suspects. This worked fine . . . until a clever lawyer who was defending a suspect that the cops had pummeled used the GPS feature of one of the cop's iPhones to determine the time of an interrogation. She then correlated this to the log book of the interview room and determined that the interview had not been documented because the camera had been turned off. The offending cop had been placed on paid administrative leave for a few weeks and the city settled for $1.3 million without admitting fault. The cop then returned to active duty. This was because there was a specific clause in the union contract that prohibited the firing of a police officer unless it was proven he or she committed a crime—what the force jokingly referred to as "The Nigger-Beating Clause."

The result was that everyone was happy. The beaten suspect got rich. His lawyer took a fat fee. The cop kept his job, and the clueless taxpayers got the bill. But greater care was now taken to make sure there were no long gaps in the log book or on the discs.

Both officers abruptly left the room. McMahon told one of the jail guards to escort Kwame back to his cell. They then walked to a corner of the room where they had some privacy.

"Do you have any idea how humiliating this is?" Fletcher said.

"This punk has the power to destroy my life, and we're letting him get away with it."

McMahon shook his head. "That's not what's happening. He has nothing to do with it. How could he? This was a very sophisticated, well-financed operation. Somebody has it out for us and is using Baker. It has to be somebody with a lot of money."

Fletcher looked up to make sure no one was eavesdropping and then continued in hushed tones. "When the public defender tried to get him out on bail, she produced a statement from that doctor. I remember that bitch from the ER at St. V's. She gave a statement that accused me of beating that turd. She's probably rich and maybe she's one of those liberal do-gooders. She got snarky when I tried to get her to edit her report."

"Well, then let's pay her a visit," McMahon said.

⸻ ⠶ ⸻

"This chair's too tight."

Teresa gazed at the 350-pound mass struggling to wiggle his expansive posterior into her examination chair. She twisted a lever on the side of the chair and swung the armrest out laterally. The patient's pink abdomen spilled over the seat of the chair, revealing a green tattoo of an open-mouthed cobra with black fangs and a red protruding tongue.

"You need to get a better chair."

Teresa ignored the remark and perused the chart. Alex Dugan. Age twenty-seven. She looked at the list of medications Mr. Dugan had been prescribed: Prozac, Adderall, and Neurontin—the trifecta of the dysfunctional. The list went on: Metformin, Crestor, OxyContin, Ambien, Diovan, Prilosec, Advair, Viagra. She stopped reading after Viagra.

She looked up at the corpulent being who was now scrolling through the messages on his iPhone. Who would want to have sex with this thing? She couldn't even comprehend the mechanics. His blond hair was shaved close to his scalp. Horseshoe-shaped earrings—that looked like the Greek letter Omega—hung from each earlobe. A metallic nose ring that was one inch in diameter traversed his nasal septum, encircling his nostrils. Dried mucous was at the base of the ring. An orange metallic circle pierced his lower lip. Blue Chinese figures were tattooed to both sides of his neck. A gold chain descended to his chest where it was attached to a small closed fist with an erect middle finger.

He slouched in his chair, continuing to scroll through his messages with his thumb.

"Mr. Dugan, I'm Dr. Trybus. How can I help you today?" She could think of plenty of things this being needed help with, yet the million-dollar question was, what could she possibly do?

He continued to scroll for another ten seconds. Finally, without lifting his head, he said, "I need more contacts." She could see a tongue stud as he articulated his demand.

"Are you wearing them now?"

"Wouldn't be here if I had them."

"Did you bring the box for your contacts with you?"

"What box?" He was now texting something. She was amazed how he texted so quickly with both thumbs, especially given the thickness of his hands.

"The contacts usually come in a box that gives the prescription strength along with the brand and size and shape of the lens."

"Naw. I don't have that. Just get me some new ones."

She turned to the back of the chart and saw a photocopy of his Medicaid card, the state insurance for the poor. She would receive $53.57 for examining this patient, and Medicaid did not pay a fee to fit contact lenses.

"Your insurance doesn't cover contact lens." He finally looked at her. His lips sneered, causing the gold ring on his lower lip to tilt. "I know that. I buy them online. I just need the prescription."

"But you didn't bring the box. I have to refit you."

"So fit me. And I want the blue ones."

"Your insurance doesn't cover the fitting of contacts."

"How much is it?"

She usually charged $150, but there was not enough money in the universe to make her fit this germ. "It's $750." So she was discriminating. Did that make her a hypocrite, considering she loathed individuals who discriminated against others? Perhaps. But this lowlife had discriminated against her with his poor manners. He would not have taken the same tone with a male doctor.

He finally stopped texting and glared at her. "That's a rip-off."

"What I can do is give you your glasses prescription. Just go to Walmart and they'll give you the contacts."

"I need them now."

The only reason Teresa even took Medicaid was because she felt obligated to help the poor. That was the influence of the nuns. But this patient and others like him were making her reconsider.

Suddenly, her secretary knocked on the door. "Dr. Trybus, there are two gentlemen here to see you."

The door then flung open and two police officers barged in. She immediately recognized one of them as the officer who had brought Kwame to the emergency room the night she cared for him.

Fletcher glared at her. "Examination's over, Doc. We need to talk."

Her secretary protested. "You can't just walk in here while Doctor is caring for a patient—"

McMahon turned toward her. "Please, ma'am. This is police work. Do not slow us down or you will be arrested for interfering with an investigation." Didn't seem so much like good cop now.

Teresa returned Fletcher's glare. "Do you have a warrant?"

Teresa, like most law-abiding citizens who rarely encountered the police, watched too much television. McMahon said to her, "Doctor, we are investigating a crime and do not need a warrant to do so. We are simply asking questions. We are not searching the place."

The patient now put in his two cents. "I need my contacts. I can't see shit." The sense of entitlement emanated in his voice.

Fletcher turned his head toward the patient. "Hey, Piggy, get your lard ass out of here." After all, Fletcher had read the CliffsNotes for *Lord of the Flies* in high school.

"I have my rights."

Fletcher walked over to the patient and smirked at him. "I'll show you your rights, Piggy."

Fletcher grabbed his nose ring and started pulling. The patient literally leapt out of the chair, grabbing Fletcher's arm.

"Ouch!" he screeched to no avail. Fletcher kept pulling on the nose ring while the patient continued screaming.

"Still want to discuss your rights, asshole? You open your ugly mouth again and I'll rip this thing out of your face." He led the patient out of the examining room and released the nose ring. The patient staggered and grabbed his nose.

Teresa did her best to conceal a smile. What a great way to get rid of an unwanted patient.

McMahon then looked at Teresa's secretary. "He's having a bad day. Best not to irritate him." He gently pushed the secretary away from the door and shut it.

Teresa was now alone in her examination room with the two officers. She walked briskly toward the door only to be clotheslined by Fletcher's bulging arm.

"Have a seat, Doctor. We have to talk," McMahon said politely.

She started pushing on Fletcher's arm.

McMahon shook his index finger at her. "No, no, no, Doctor," he said in a calm, soothing voice.

"You have just assaulted a police officer."

"Assaulted a police officer? I just touched his arm," Teresa said.

McMahon just smiled at her. "Not only have you assaulted a police officer, but you have verbally admitted that you assaulted a police officer. We can arrest you right now if we wish to. So please, calm down. We just want to talk."

Teresa took McMahon at his word, not that she had any choice. She let go of Fletcher's arm but defiance was still on her face. "I don't have to say a word to you."

"Let's cuff the bitch now. Take her down to the station," Fletcher barked.

Teresa's defiant glare quickly changed to one of fear. "I haven't done anything."

"You assaulted me, Doc," Fletcher said this with a roguish grin.

"I'm calling my lawyer," she said while pulling an iPhone out her white coat.

McMahon blocked the door while Fletcher circled in front of her. He grabbed the iPhone from her hand and placed it on a counter full of eyedrops and oddly-shaped equipment.

"You're not calling anyone, Doc."

"I have my rights."

"You're new to this, aren't you? You assaulted a police officer. You have no rights. Sit in your chair there. Shut your mouth and speak only when spoken to." Even though this was clearly a threat, McMahon hadn't used a threatening tone, just a sugary-like convincing one.

Teresa sat down in her examination chair, the look of defiance slowly returning to her face. McMahon pulled up one of the other chairs in the room and sat in front of her. "We'll be out of here in a few minutes if you just answer a few simple questions."

She nodded.

"Have you spoken to anybody about your care of Mr. Kwame Baker?"

"I spoke to his lawyer."

"Connie Vivanti?"

"Yes."

"Did you speak to anyone else about the case?"

"No."

"Are you sure?"

"Yes. Connie told me not to. Besides, it violates patient confidentially to discuss cases. We are not allowed to do that without the patient's permission."

"But you did produce a statement to the court that you thought we abused Mr. Baker."

"That's not what I said. I said that the injuries he sustained were not consistent with a fall. I have seen that type of injury many times.

It is almost always associated with a fist or a ball. I did not witness the injury taking place, so I can't say for sure what happened."

McMahon pondered this. The entire charade was now going to come down to the next question. Her response to this question would determine whether she was going to be placed in handcuffs and taken to the station, or if the two officers were going to simply leave her office.

McMahon asked, "Did you arrange to have a video taken of Officer Fletcher?"

"What video?"

McMahon read Teresa's facial expression, looking for even the slightest hint of culpability. He saw none. He looked up at Fletcher. The two locked eyes just long enough to visually agree that Teresa was just as clueless as Kwame had seemed to be.

Teresa waited for the next question, even though they looked as though they were waiting on her to elaborate on the one she'd already asked. She couldn't elaborate on something she knew nothing about. So little did she know, but she'd passed their brief interrogation with flying colors. It was not her answer that mattered. It was the look on her face—a look of total non-comprehension and innocence. Like most police officers, Fletcher and McMahon were accomplished at picking out liars. And that look told them that Teresa was not lying. It also meant that they had no idea how this video had come into existence.

"Doctor, we thank you for your cooperation and apologize for the inconvenience." McMahon stood.

A look of relief crossed her face. Fletcher laughed. "Look at the bright side, Doc. We got that fat piece of shit out of your office. Doubt if you'll see him again."

She continued to stare at the officers but had to fight hard to suppress a smile. Yes, these two guys were thugs, but they dealt with the detritus of society on a daily basis. If every patient she dealt with was like the entitled germ on the public trough that Fletcher had just heaved out of the office, she would be a thug too. Yes, they had abused her and terrified her. But deep down, she was glad they existed. It was Friday. The dirtbag they had ejected was her last patient. She was about to go to her spacious condo in Southport, sit on her porch overlooking the Sound, and drink $30 glasses of Amarone. These two guys would return to cleaning up the shit that rarely encroached on her life. As Jack Nicholson said in her favorite movie, *A Few Good Men*, "You want me on that wall. You need me on that wall."

Trip and Joe watched on their monitor as McMahon and Fletcher walked into the reception room.

McMahon tipped his hat to the terrified secretary. "Have a nice day, ma'am. Sorry for the inconvenience."

"Pleasant fellow," said Joe. "Too bad we couldn't get a camera in the prison, though, but at least the GPS tracker on their cruiser proves they were there. Nice job with the wiring. The doc has four different rooms to see patients. Must have been a lot of work."

"Don't mention it," said Trip as he pushed a handful of popcorn in his mouth. "I think I'm making some progress on the face recognition software . . . Found two crevices in those stone pillars that had some scratches. Like you said, that's probably where the cameras were, but they got rid of them."

"My bet is that when they heard that Cord was making noise, they removed them immediately."

"Who did? And what made them think that was a good idea to put them there in the first place?" Trip said.

"God is always watching, but now, someone else is watching: Google. I went through the local newspapers. The neighborhood where Cord was pulled over had some high-profile drug overdoses and the local politicians said they would do something about it. I got the names of some of them and checked out their Google searches. Several of them, including the first selectman, Googled face recognition software."

"First selectman?" Trip raised an eyebrow.

"That's what they call mayors in many Connecticut towns. Some holdover from the colonial days . . . Anyway, this first selectman—her name is Gwen Trudeau—sent several e-mails to a company in Mumbai inquiring about their services."

"Doesn't prove anything though."

"Yeah, but I love India. Still corrupt to the core. I'll make a few phone calls and with all of Cord's money, it's just a matter of time until we find the right palms to grease. With a little luck, we may be able to get the actual video feed of Cord being profiled."

Trip laughed. "That will make a great YouTube video."

"That it will," laughed Joe, scooping up a handful of Trip's popcorn.

CHAPTER 17

Connie was livid. She stared defiantly at Judge Durazio.

"Your Honor, this is an outrage. Officers Fletcher and McMahon took my client into an interrogation room without the benefit of counsel, made wild accusations, and threw him up against the wall while he was in handcuffs, smashing his head."

Sarah leaped on her feet. "What evidence does Ms. Vivanti have that this happened?"

Connie walked behind Kwame, who was slouched in his chair in orange prison garb, both his feet and hands manacled. He had lost ten pounds since his previous courtroom appearance, with three-day-old stubble protruding from his concave cheeks. He continued to stare blankly at the table as Connie placed her hand on the back on his head, feeling the protruding hematoma.

"Come over and feel his head for yourself, Sarah."

Sarah glared at her and then turned her face to the judge. This case was taxing their friendship. "I repeat myself, what evidence does Ms. Vivanti have?"

Judge Durazio was trying her best to hide her fear. She had been forced by the politicians to revisit the bail hearing as the Kwame Baker situation was spiraling out of control. Everyone had seen the video of Fletcher and Officer Kline *in flagrante delicto* and listened to the chilling narration, linking it as retribution for the alleged abuse of Kwame. Her instructions were to find out how this happened, even if she had to bend the rules.

"The prosecutor has a point. What evidence do you have?" She raised her head and tightened her jaws as she waited on Connie's response.

"You have my client's statement, Your Honor. Plus, you have the statement of Dr. Teresa Trybus, who was also harassed by these two officers."

Sarah shot back, "That is not evidence, Your Honor. That is the statement of a man who has been arrested almost a dozen times, now bent on slandering two dedicated public servants. He could have received this injury by falling or by an assault from another prisoner. And Dr. Trybus's statement is totally irrelevant."

"It shows a pattern of behavior, Your Honor."

"Your Honor, why are we arguing? I'm sure the police department will permit Ms. Vivanti to view the video of the interrogation room."

Connie chuckled. "Perhaps Ms. Cornell is tired of being a prosecutor and would like to have a second career as a stand-up comedian."

"I do not tolerate sarcasm in my court, Ms. Vivanti," Judge Durazio said.

"I beg the Court's pardon, Your Honor," Connie said.

"Let's ask Her Honor for an order allowing us to view the tape. Is that unacceptable?" Sarah said.

"Sounds reasonable," Judge Durazio said to Connie.

Connie looked over at Sarah, and a sarcastic sneer enveloped her face. "It is not reasonable, Your Honor. The officers turned off the video camera while they were beating my client. In fact, Officer Fletcher even pointed this out to my client while he was hurling him against the wall."

"Evidence, Connie, evidence. One L. Remember?"

Kwame continued to stare at the table in front of him, oblivious to the discussion. His previous cockiness was now gone. He had acquiesced to his fate.

Connie responded, "If Your Honor is willing to order the prison to make the disc from the interrogation room available for forensic analysis, the defense will be more than amenable."

Judge Durazio's eyes narrowed at this request, but she said nothing. Sarah responded, but without her usual voice of confidence.

"That may not be prudent, Your Honor. That disc contains crucial evidence in other cases that I am prosecuting. Forensic analysis could take at least three weeks and even damage the disc."

"The prosecution is correct," Judge Durazio said, relieved that Sarah had managed to keep her from tipping over into that batch of quicksand. "This issue has been before this court before, and cases have been delayed and disrupted because of technical problems in forensic analysis of the prison DVD recordings."

Connie smiled and turned both palms upward. "Your Honor, the DVD machine at the prison is capable of copying the disc. Please issue an order for a copy of the disc under the supervision of myself, Ms. Cornell, and the video technician from our department."

"We cannot use a copied disc as evidence. It must be the original," Sarah shot back.

Judge Durazio was now up against the wall. Copied discs were used as evidence all the time, but she had to protect the criminal justice system. Thus, she forcefully said, "The prosecution is correct; we cannot use a copied disc."

"Your Honor, this is an outrage. I have been a public defender for ten years and refusing to allow a copy of a videotape or disc is unprecedented. You are excluding evidence that proves my client was beaten by these two officers."

Judge Durazio banged her gavel with such force that Kwame tried to jump out of his chair, but was impeded by his leg manacles. "Ms. Vivanti, you are perilously close to contempt. Do not imply that any action of this court is less than in full compliance with laws of this state. Both of you, in my chambers. Now!"

———— ((•)) ————

Judge Durazio pointed to the two chairs in front of her desk, and Connie and Sarah sat down. She reached into her top drawer for a packet of Philip Morris Filter Kings. She banged the pack against her fist, pulled out a cigarette, and lit it with a Bic lighter.

Before either woman even thought about commenting on her action, she said, "I don't give a shit what the smoking policy is here. *I'm* the judge, and I need a goddamn cigarette."

She sat down in her high-back chair, inhaling the cigarette with such force that both the ladies noticed the orange end visibly shrinking.

She pointed her finger at Connie. "You, young lady, are a pain in the ass."

"I am representing my client," Connie said, not the least bit offended by the judge's name-calling. She knew she was a pain in the ass. She got paid to be a pain in the ass. "The reason you will not release the disc is because it will prove that the video camera was turned off when my client was being abused."

She was right, of course. It was common knowledge that a tampered disc, even a copied one, could not survive a forensic analysis. This is because when the video camera sends a signal to a DVD recorder, the recorder processes the image and turns it into pixels, tiny dots that create the images. If the video camera or the DVD recorder is turned off, there is an abrupt space in the disc, since there are no pixels being placed on the disc. Forensic software can find this abrupt space. Furthermore, the software could tell the exact time when the video camera was turned off. Other video cameras at the prison would prove the approximate time that Fletcher and McMahon were in the building. Not only would they be implicated, but also the prison employees who enabled them. Connie knew that Sarah and Judge Durazio would never let this happen. They would protect their own.

Judge Durazio gave a furtive glance to Sarah, who then rotated her chair so that she was no longer facing the judge, but looking directly at Connie.

A perplexed Connie looked back and forth at the two women and finally said, "What's going on here?"

To her surprise, it was Sarah who spoke. "Connie, you have to help us out here. Judge Durazio and I have been getting calls from terrified police officers and politicians. It's bad enough that anything we say can be immortalized, but now our bedrooms can be invaded. I even received a call from Senator Bentley who was extremely concerned about this incident."

"As did I," Judge Durazio added.

"I still don't understand what's going on here," Connie said just as oblivious as Kwame had been outside in the courtroom during the hearing.

"Did you watch the video?" Judge Durazio asked.

"Of course," Connie said. "Everyone has watched the video. I think it has over a million hits at this point. I'm amazed that Fletcher's wife has not filed for divorce. Can you imagine the humiliation?"

Both women merely nodded. Judge Durazio continued. "What we are seeing here is an assault on our legal system, an assault on Rule of Law. The only reason I allowed this hearing is to find out how your client was able to extract his retribution."

Now it all made sense to Connie. No wonder the judge had excluded the press. There was never any intention of freeing her client. This hearing was a fishing expedition.

"My client had nothing to do with that video. How could he?" Connie said.

Judge Durazio looked directly in her eyes. "Connie, Sarah and I both know you are right. We know that Fletcher punched your client the night he was arrested. We know that Fletcher and McMahon beat him in jail, and we know that these two cops harassed the ophthalmologist who took care of your client, the same woman who had the guts—or stupidity—to point this out in an affidavit."

Sarah nodded in agreement while Connie's jaw dropped. And here she thought her nemesis had just been out there trying to kick ass in the courtroom when all the while she was trying to cover everybody's ass.

"So why won't you release my client, or at least give him a reasonable bail?" Connie asked.

"I can't give him bail now that this has happened. You're a little young. Still idealistic," Judge Durazio said. "You don't realize that society has disintegrated. The family structure is gone. These people are reproducing like rabbits, creating a class of thugs that Sarah and I have to keep off the street. And our brave police officers—these poor guys and gals—have their fingers in a dyke that is in constant danger of breaking."

"That doesn't give them the right to beat my client."

"These men and women are cursed at, spat upon, punched, and sometimes shot. Sometimes, they snap. And it wasn't the end of the world until these goddamn iPhones with their video cameras put these unfortunate incidents on the Internet for all to see."

"Well, a video showed the world when a cop in South Carolina shot a man eight times in the back after stopping him for a broken taillight," Connie said.

Judge Durazio flicked some ashes on the rug. "That cop did society a favor. Piece of scum had been arrested ten times, had four children, and refused to pay his child support. If he were still alive, he'd produce four more mouths for the taxpayers to feed."

Connie was outraged at this thinking, but had the sense not to respond. She would be in Judge's Durazio's courtroom multiple times in the future.

Sarah looked directly at her. "Connie, we're friends. I would be upset if this happened to my client too. But we cannot allow this to go unpunished. It will destroy the criminal justice system. Whoever did this invaded Kline's apartment. The experts say that the equipment was the best available. We are dealing with pros. We even found the same equipment in my office and in this office." Professionals who had an eye for this type of thing, unlike Fletcher and McMahon, had done their due diligence in locating some of Trip's handiwork.

"Are you serious?" said Connie.

Judge Durazio nodded in agreement and then pointed to the light switches. "The camera lens is so small that it was placed in the middle of the screws over the light switches. There were six of them—all attached to sophisticated receivers that immediately placed all images in cyberspace. There were minuscule microphones all over the place. Senator Bentley arranged to have some

FBI specialists help us out. Our local police do not have the expertise. I just hope they found all of them."

"But why do you think Baker is involved?" Connie asked.

"Who else could it be?" Sarah responded. "The video specifically says it is retribution for beating Baker. They even had Baker's mug shot, you know, the one with the closed eye? How the hell did they get a hold of that?"

"My client told me he doesn't have the slightest idea how this happened," Connie said.

"Well," Judge Durazio interjected, "I am going to interview him personally, and I expect your cooperation."

Connie's jaw dropped. "Your Honor, this is unprecedented. My client still has rights. You cannot just interview him off the record."

Judge Durazio stared at her for several seconds. "Young lady, when our criminal justice system is under attack, I can do as I please."

It took all of Connie's self-control not to accuse the judge of judicial misconduct. But she knew if she reported this to the Judicial Review Committee, Judge Durazio would never be sanctioned. Judges abused their power all the time, and smart lawyers just sucked it up. Otherwise, they would be punished with unfavorable rulings in the future. Thus, she nodded in agreement.

Judge Durazio pressed a button on her phone and said, "Bailiff, bring the prisoner to my chambers."

In several seconds, the potbellied bailiff delivered a shuffling Kwame.

Sarah stood up and gestured to her chair. "Mr. Baker, please take my seat."

"I can stand," he said.

"Sit down, Mr. Baker," Judge Durazio said.

Kwame continued to stand, his eyes downcast. Finally, Connie stood up and gently grabbed his arm. "Please, take my seat, Kwame."

He complied, his eyes remaining downcast.

Judge Durazio stared at him. "I have some questions for you, Mr. Baker."

"You gonna let me out?" he asked, perking up some.

"I'll ask the questions here."

Kwame looked up at her, his submissive expression quickly changing to one of defiance. "You gonna let me out?"

"Mr. Baker, you are not in a position to negotiate."

"You gonna let me out? Yes or no?" Kwame was persistent, that was for sure.

"Kwame, just answer a few questions for Judge Durazio," Connie said.

Kwame suddenly became animated. "Why should I say shit to this dyke? She just gonna put me back in prison, and pigs gonna come back and beat me again."

"What did you say?" Judge Durazio asked, appalled.

"You got a hearing problem, dyke? I ain't answerin' none of your questions."

Judge Durazio tensed and forcefully pushed her cigarette in the ashtray. Her childhood had been torture. Her sexuality was obvious by age five, and she was ostracized by all as soon as she attended kindergarten. Lonely, painful years. In fact, she never even accepted herself until she attended Smith. Eventually attitudes changed. She was now respected for what she was, a brilliant gay woman. But now this germ was reminding her of the pain she had once routinely suffered. And she was not going to tolerate it.

Her voice became a menacing snarl. "You listen to me, Mr. Baker. You have no respect for this court, and now you will learn the price of your insolence. You will remain behind bars for years if you do not cooperate. You cannot talk to me like that."

"I can talk to you anyway I want. You got the problem here, not me." Kwame was never moved by the threats those in authority made against him. Why should he be? Most of the threats had been carried out and he was still standing.

Sarah said, "What problem do you mean?"

"I don't have to talk you, whore. You just lyin' to protect the cops. They probably fucking you too."

"Kwame, there is no need to be so rude," Connie said.

Kwame turned to look at her. "Whose side you on? You supposed to be *my* lawyer. I'm being abused because these muthafuckas be letting it happen, and you says *I's* rude?"

"Kwame, some very powerful people are threatening the police officers who arrested you. Do you have any idea who they are?" Connie hoped the expression on her face and the tone in her voice reflected to Kwame that she really was on his side, which is why she was trying to protect him.

"I told that pig cop I got no idea, but now I do."

"Who?" All three women spoke simultaneously and waited with bated breath.

Kwame looked from one woman to the next. He had to admit that it felt good inside to finally have people actually waiting to hear what he had to say. His voice was finally going to be heard by these people. "God." Kwame continued, "God is punishing the bully cop and his whore partner. And God is gonna punish this dyke and this here whore." He nodded his head from the judge to Sarah. "My grandma used to read the Bible to me. God is always watching, and God's gonna give you what you deserve."

Judge Durazio sat there for a moment with tight lips and disgust on her face. "Get used to your cell, Kwame. You're going to be there a long time. Bailiff, get him out of here."

The bailiff proceeded to remove Kwame from the room.

After Kwame was gone, Judge Durazio began to calm down, helped by a second cigarette. "You can't reason with people who believe in imaginary beings. What do you think is going on here, Connie?"

"I spoke to my client at length about this after Fletcher beat him a second time. This is the first time that I have heard that your office and Sarah's were bugged in a similar fashion to the police officer's."

Sarah interjected, "I know the FBI agents that Senator Bentley arranged stated that this equipment was top of the line, but private detective agencies have very sophisticated equipment now. They are way ahead of what the government is using, at least to my knowledge. You have to understand that huge amounts of money are at stake here. These agencies are very good at discovering infidelity because it greatly enhances settlement talks in ugly divorces. It is not unusual for a wife to walk away with tens of millions of dollars."

"What are you saying?" Judge Durazio said.

"I'm saying that for as little as $50,000, Kwame or one of his relatives or friends could launch this vendetta. Even less."

"I honestly believe Baker does not have the slightest idea how this is happening," Connie said. "Not to mention Kwame and his entire family together probably couldn't scrape up fifty grand."

"I agree," Sarah replied. "But on second thought, that does not mean that someone, without his knowledge, couldn't have arranged this. He could have a family member who is in the Crips or a family member who is an athlete, a rapper . . ."

Connie finished her sentence for her. "Or simply a successful professional."

"Sarah, when we find out who this is," Judge Durazio said, "I am personally going to see to it that he spends the rest of his life in prison. All my life, I have struggled for justice and Rule of Law. But sometimes . . . We have to bend the rules."

Sarah Cornell nodded in agreement, but Connie Vivanti did not respond.

CHAPTER 18

J oe sat in the secure Bridgeport bunker and scrolled down on the screen of his laptop. What voice should he use? He had it down to Marlon Brando, Robin Williams, or James Mason. Obviously, James Mason was the way to go. His baritone could be simultaneously intimidating and harmonious; but, Joe was a Robin Williams fan, to the point where he downed a bottle of Chianti in honor of his memory the day of his unfortunate death.

"What do you think, Trip?"

"It's a no-brainer. James Mason. But if I know you, you're going to go with that pinko Jew." Trip's opinions were always predictable.

"Who are you going with?"

"Arnold, of course," Trip replied.

This software had actually been Joe's creation, although he codeveloped it with some of his CIA colleagues who hailed from the evil Cal Tech, MIT's main rival. The software digitalized the voices of movie stars with unique voices by going through every movie, television appearance, or voice-over the star had ever performed. You spoke into the microphone; the software processed your voice, and out came the voice of the movie star you chose. The royalty fees were humungous, but that was the advantage of working for a government agency dedicated to national security. There was always an infinite amount of money available.

Joe flicked on the switch of his microphone and screamed "Good Morning, Westport!" just like Robin Williams once did in the movie *Good Morning, Vietnam*. His voice was then projected into the office of Sarah Cornell, two towns away.

McMahon jumped up from his chair while Fletcher reached

for his gun. Chief Driscoll froze, and Sarah, the only woman in this sea of testosterone, remained calm. She quickly ascertained that the voice was emanating from the left bottom drawer of her desk. Opening the drawer, she rummaged through some papers until she found a triangular speakerphone at the bottom of the drawer.

"Love that lipstick. Goes well with your earrings," the voice through the phone said.

She picked up the triangular speakerphone and gazed at it, quickly ascertaining that it also contained a video camera. The meeting at her office had taken an unanticipated turn.

"Please place the phone on the desk." She felt the machine vibrate as it spoke. She found herself eerily complying with the machine's request.

"Who are you?" Sarah said.

"I'm Robin Williams. Don't you recognize me?"

"Robin Williams is dead," said Fletcher, whose initial fear had now been replaced by anger.

"Such a clever boy, Officer Fletcher. But I am alive and well, and I am here to teach you some manners."

"This is Chief Driscoll of the Westport Police Department. Will you please identify yourself?"

"Who I am is not the issue here. The question is 'Who are you?' Are you stand-up individuals who accept responsibility for your behavior and atone for your sins, or are you arrogant weasels who believe you have the right to beat people and lie to cover up your malfeasance?"

"What are you talking about?" Chief Driscoll said.

"Chief Driscoll . . .*pleeease*. You know what I am talking about. We are responsible for entertaining your community with the sexual exploits of Officer Fletcher. We think he may actually have a future in the pornography industry, although he may have to work a bit on his stamina. We have much more fun and games planned for you."

Fletcher stood up and slammed his fist on Sarah's desk. "Listen, you cocksucker, if I ever get my hands on you, I will *slowly* tear you apart limb by limb."

"We are aware of your physical prowess, Officer Fletcher, but we have never seen you with a worthy opponent. Let me introduce you to my colleague."

Trip spoke into his microphone and the German accent of Arnold Schwarzenegger filled the room. "You are a bully and like all bullies, you are a pussy. Picking on handcuffed men, helpless women, and fat slobs with nose rings. You will be terminated."

McMahon's face turned ashen while Sarah spoke. "What are you talking about?"

Joe, with the voice of Robin Williams, spoke. "Please check your e-mail, Ms. Cornell. You will see two e-mails, one titled *Domestic Bliss* and another called *A Visit to the Eye Doctor*. Click on whichever one you want."

Sarah looked at the three men and saw terror in Fletcher's eyes. She clicked *Domestic Bliss*. Immediately, she saw Fletcher's hand around his wife's throat. Her hand covered her mouth in horror as she heard the threats Fletcher hurled at the poor woman. Chief Driscoll stood up and walked over to Sarah's chair. He watched the video for several seconds and then glared at Fletcher and McMahon.

"We think this is an excellent example of a home movie—a dying art—that we would like to resurrect. We can't wait to show it to Mrs. Fletcher's parents and to her brothers and sister. Should make for some interesting family discussions, wouldn't you say? But check out the other video now."

Sarah continued to watch the first video in horrid fascination until Chief Driscoll grabbed the mouse, exited the pop-up screen with the first video, and clicked on the e-mail titled *A Visit to the Eye Doctor*.

He and Sarah gazed at the screen, which began with Fletcher grabbing the nose ring of the obese patient and continued with their intimidation of Dr. Teresa Trybus.

Arnold's voice came out of the speakerphone. "You guys are really tough. Can't wait to see how you handle some *real* competition. But I hear you Connecticut cops have good dental plans."

Robin William's voice returned. "You have to excuse Arnold. He hasn't been the same since his divorce. Bad manners. There is no need for such threats, Arnold. There is no doubt these pleasant people are going to do what we ask."

"What do you want?" Sarah said. She just wanted it to be over with before she became the target.

"Not much. We ask that you merely drop all the charges against Kwame Baker, and then when he is released, Officers Fletcher and McMahon must personally visit him and apologize for their behavior. We believe Officer Kline has suffered enough from the humiliating video. Given that there is no evidence she struck Mr. Baker, there is no need for her further involvement. The officers are then to take Mr. Baker to Dr. Trybus's office so that he can be properly cared for. While they are there, they will also apologize to Dr. Trybus. It's really very simple. And then those videos will never see the light of day. In fact, I would strongly suggest you delete them now."

"I will not drop any charges against Baker," Sarah said. "I will not allow you to intimidate me and the justice system."

Fletcher stood up and pointed his finger at Sarah. "You do what he said, bitch. You're not the one who is going to have those videos destroying your life. Kevin and I could lose our jobs if this became public."

Sarah stood up and yelled back. "Listen, Jack. I'm tired of cleaning up your crap. They're right. You are a coward. I am *not* dropping the charges against Baker."

Fletcher puffed up his shoulders and was about to respond but the pleasant voice of Robin Williams preempted him. "Officer Fletcher, calm down. Ms. Cornell is a reasonable person. She just needs some simple persuading."

Sarah stared at the speakerphone. "I don't care if you have videos of me doing it with a Shetland pony, I will never accede to your demands. Never!"

The mellifluous voice of Robin Williams responded. "Ms. Cornell, please log into you E-Trade account."

"What do you mean?" she said, her voice shaking ever so slightly.

"Am I not making myself clear? Or perhaps you don't recall your password. It's yaZ1979. The name of your birth control pill, plus your year of birth. Remember that the password is case sensitive—you have to capitalize the Z. I must admit though, we expected a little more imagination in your password creation."

Arnold's voice came out of the speakerphone. "We also tried all the names of your former lovers. It took a while since there were so many combinations. Don't worry; it's just a matter of time until we get some scenes of you fornicating too."

"Arnold, please. Such bad manners. After this is over, we are going to see Arnold attends finishing school."

Sarah gasped as she opened the account. There was a total of $57.23 in an account that once had over $10,000,000, which amounted to a large portion of her trust fund.

"You bastards," she screamed. "You give that money back to me."

"How do you know it was us? Maybe it was just a bad day in the market."

"You give that money back to me. I'm going to call the SEC and find that money and put you in jail for the rest of your life. My family has connections in the highest places."

"Ms. Cornell, please calm down. We are very impressed with your family connections and do not want to generate ill will. But the fact of the matter is that your money has been rerouted by a dozen transactions that are impossible to trace. For all you know, it could have been used to purchase several rare gold coins that are now in a safety deposit box in Zurich, or maybe it has been converted to stacks of cash stored in duffle bags in the basement of a house in Topeka. Trust me. It's gone. But don't worry, not only do we plan to replace every penny, we will even add in the LIBOR interest rate for the days it's been MIA while you prepare the documents to drop all charges against Kwame Baker. We are very reasonable people."

"How do I know I can trust you?" It didn't take Sarah long to realize she needed to put on her catcher's mitt and play ball too.

Arnold's voice came over the speakerphone. "Because we are not like you. We do not lie and cheat. Our word means something. We are people of honor—not worthless trash like you and the three cowards in that room."

"Would you like me to take out a few bucks to send Arnold to finishing school? He really needs it."

"I can't believe this crap," Sarah said under her breath.

Williams's voice continued. "We really don't want to take your money; but, you are not in a strong negotiating position. Our demands are not unreasonable. Everyone still has a job, and you can keep this among yourselves."

"You won. How much time do we have?" Sarah said.

"Ten business days. But I want to hear you and the good officers say it."

"Say what?" said Chief Driscoll.

"I will have Mr. Baker out of jail in ten business days," the William's voice said.

"Say it, Ms. Cornell." The pleasant tone was now gone.

"I will have Mr. Baker out of jail in ten business days," she said in a dry, defying tone.

"Again." Clearly, it wasn't a tone Arnold appreciated very much.

"I will have Mr. Baker out of jail in ten business days," Sarah repeated. She hadn't lost the attitude, so Joe made her repeat it ten times until she did.

Then he both made Fletcher and McMahon each repeat ten times, "I will graciously apologize to Mr. Kwame Baker and Dr. Teresa Trybus."

"And one more thing," the Arnold voice added. "You will record your apology to Mr. Baker and to Dr. Trybus on your iPhone and send it to the e-mail address we will provide to you. And we expect these to be sincere apologies, hat in hand."

The Robin Williams' voice concluded. "You may have some second thoughts about living up to the agreement we just made here. Trust me . . . It would not be a wise move. We can make your lives infinitely more miserable. And it would be so unnecessary. There is simply no excuse for bad manners. Goodbye, and have a nice day."

Sarah looked at the three men. "How is this happening?'

A possible explanation entered Chief Driscoll's mind, but he held his tongue.

CHAPTER 19

"**W**hat do you mean you want to drop all the charges?" a flabbergasted Judge Durazio looked at Sarah's motion while Connie remained silent. Once again, they were in the judge's chambers.

Sarah had a pleading look in her eyes. "Your Honor, please. Connie has agreed. My understanding is that when both parties agree, a hearing to dismiss all charges will be a mere formality."

"Nothing is a mere formality in my court, Ms. Cornell," Judge Durazio said. "Mr. Baker has insulted this Court. While you are technically correct from a legal point of view, I see little reason to give you any latitude on this motion."

The fact of the matter was that Judge Durazio had to agree to set Kwame free. That was the law. If the prosecutor drops all charges, the suspect has to go free. It was that simple.

But Judge Durazio was still livid over the abuse and disrespect Kwame had heaped upon her. She relished her power, and she enjoyed the thought of him spending years in jail for defying her. She wished she lived in medieval times and could put him in the Iron Maiden. And now these two women expected her to release him? She could deny the motion, but Sarah would simply appeal and win.

But there would be a problem with this scenario from Sarah's point of view. The judges, regardless of their judicial philosophy, were members of an exclusive club, and like doctors, they offered each other professional courtesy. All Judge Durazio had to do was pick up the phone, speak to the appellate judge, and describe the indignities to which Kwame had subjected her. That judge could then delay hearing the motion for weeks, if not months, while

Kwame languished in jail. This meant that Sarah could not live up to the agreement she had made with the voice that emanated from the triangular speakerphone. It meant that her $10,000,000 was gone. Thus, she had only one recourse. She had to lay her cards on the table and beg like a dog.

Sarah recounted the recent events in her office: the videos, the loss of her money, and the utter arrogance of the voices that emanated from the triangular speakerphone. Judge Durazio listened in horror.

"There is no other way you can get your money back?" the judge asked.

"We called the SEC. The money is gone—a stream of untraceable electrons somewhere in cyberspace."

"It would seem to me that E-Trade should reimburse you," the judge said.

"No, Your Honor. E-Trade is only on the hook for $250,000. I signed an electronic document when I set up the account acknowledging that they are only liable for security breaches of their system. It specifically states that if someone obtains my password, they are held harmless. Even obtaining the $250,000 will be problematic—let alone $10,000,000."

"What do you have to say about this, Connie?" Judge Durazio looked to the defense attorney. "Obviously, you would like your client to be freed. But do you think I should cave to such extortion?"

"Sarah and I have been friends for years. We joust in the courtroom, but she is the best prosecutor the State has. She could get a job on Wall Street for five times her present salary with a simple phone call. I agree that the Court should not normally capitulate to extortion, but this is an extenuating circumstance. I would beg the Court to grant this motion."

Judge Durazio pondered this for what seemed like an eternity, according to Sarah's watch anyway. Then she said, "I will grant this motion under two conditions. First, I don't ever want to see Baker in my courtroom again. If he appears, I will order the death penalty—even if he was caught jaywalking. Second, we are going to find out who is behind this. And when we do, there will be no mercy. Sarah, you will see to it that the perpetrators are put into my Court, and trust me, justice will be served, and they will learn respect for this Court and for our judicial system."

She signed the order, making Kwame Baker a free man.

"Thank you, Your Honor," Sarah said. "And I promise you, I *will* find out who did this, and I *will* bring them to your Court."

━━━◦((�))◦━━━

Connie sat in the room for released prisoners with Kwame.

"I knew you'd come through. You the best." A huge smile crossed his face.

Connie did not return the smile. "Kwame, you listen to me, and you listen very carefully. Some very powerful people have made you their cause célèbre."

"Cause célèbre? Is that the same as modus operandi?"

"I'm serious, Kwame."

"You got to speak English. I ain't no celebrity. You don't see me on the cover of *People*."

"What I mean, Kwame, is that someone out there likes you. And without going into the details, I assure you that I had very little to do with getting you freed. Now here is what's going to happen. Officer Fletcher is going to come here and apologize for hitting you. You must graciously accept his apology. No smart-ass comments. Do you understand?"

"He's gonna apologize to me?" Kwame's eyes lit up in disbelief. Even the bad one. "Boy, I'm gonna enjoy that. Maybe he'll shine my shoes while he's at it."

"Kwame, I'm serious!" Connie yelled. "I'm a lawyer, and I'm a damn good lawyer. And my job is to protect you. Just do what I say!"

"You serious, aren't you?" It was starting to register into Kwame's head that this apology really was about to take place. "How 'bout that dyke who was with him? She apologizing, too?"

"That wasn't part of the deal."

"Makes sense. She didn't like it when he whacked me. I should be apologizing to her. That was out of pocket."

"When Officer Fletcher is done apologizing, you simply say 'I accept your apology, Officer.' Now say it." Connie had to be sure Kwame was going to play along, not that this was any type of guarantee.

"Say what?"

"I accept your apology, Officer."

Kwame smiled and repeated, "I accept your apology, Officer."

"Not with the shit-eating grin on your face, Kwame. You have to be polite."

"To the man who punched me in the face and lied about it?"

"Please, Kwame." He was really starting to get under Connie's skin. "You're driving me to drink. Just do what I say. Now say it again."

"I accept your apology, Officer."

"Much better. Now, this apology is going to be videotaped."

"Why?"

"You don't need to know. Just do what I said. After that, Officer Fletcher is going to drive you to see Dr. Trybus. She's going to check your eye. Officer Fletcher was also rude to Dr. Trybus, so he will apologize to her as well. After that, you are on your own, and please, don't ever get arrested again. I won't be able to help you." All Connie could think about was if poor Kwame ever ended up in front of the "dyke" judge again. But knowing that was a promise the poor guy couldn't keep, she simply got up and exited the room.

Fletcher and McMahon were standing outside, dour expressions on their face. The three reentered the room together, and McMahon took out his iPhone and put it into video mode.

Fletcher shuffled his feet and looked at the floor in front of Kwame. He couldn't bring himself to make eye contact. "Mr. Baker, I apologize for hitting you."

There was a pause. Connie glared at Kwame, daring him to deviate from his rehearsed lines.

Finally, Kwame said, "I accept your apology, Officer."

177

McMahon watched the video. He then forwarded it to the e-mail address that had appeared in his personal e-mail. From there, it was time for phase two.

Connie rode in the backseat of the patrol car with Kwame while they traveled across town to Teresa's office. It was a madhouse, with so many patients waiting that it was standing room only. Connie spoke discreetly with the secretary, and within thirty seconds, they were in one of Teresa's examination rooms.

McMahon aimed the iPhone at her. Fletcher approached and said, "I apologize for my rudeness, Doctor."

Teresa responded. "You're very kind. Your apology is accepted, and I really do appreciate your getting rid of that difficult patient."

Fletcher couldn't help but smile. "Don't mention it, Doc."

McMahon replayed the video and then forwarded that one as well.

The two cops quickly vanished, while Connie remained with Kwame and Teresa.

"I gotta be the luckiest nigga alive," Kwame said with a long grin on his face. "Cops apologizing and two hot white women taking care' a me."

Connie just shook her head while Teresa let out a laugh. "We love taking care of you, Mr. Baker. Have a seat over there in the big brown chair," Teresa pointed.

"Speak for yourself, Teresa. He has been a total pain in the ass," Connie said.

The swelling in Kwame's right eye had decreased and was now partially open. The bright red blood in the white part of the eye had faded to a reddish-yellow.

Teresa was pleased as he rattled off the 20/20 line with each eye covered. She asked him to follow her finger with his eyes, noting that the previously injured right eye moved freely in all directions.

"Looks like the muscle is no longer entrapped."

"What's that?" Kwame asked.

"Let me check one more thing," Teresa said without even acknowledging Kwame's question. She wanted to be 100 percent certain before she answered him.

She found an apparatus with two triangular mirrors that slid along a ruler. She brought it up to Kwame's eyes, inspecting whether the injured eye was beginning to recede or bulge. It did not.

"It means no operation, at least for now. I'll check you in a month just to be sure."

She looked at Connie. "I'll give you a call. We'll grab dinner at Barcelona's. The only place I can drink Cardinal Mendoza; but I have to get back to work. As you can see, the office is a zoo."

——◦((◦))◦——

Sarah turned on her computer. The past few days had been the worst days of her life. Her family would disown her if they found out she had lost her inheritance. Her father had told her to keep the money with Pendergast and Sons, the financial firm that had invested in her family's wealth for generations.

But she told her father she could invest it better on her own and not pay the outrageous 3 percent management fee. Which was true. For the past several years, she had outperformed her father's portfolio simply by buying low-maintenance-cost index funds while her father's prestigious firm, replete with young Ivy League wizards, had lost a bundle in REITs and Internet start-ups. But now it may all be gone.

She typed in her password, yaZ1979.

It seemed like an eternity, but then the number appeared at the bottom of her screen. $10,346,834.04. There were no changes in any of her positions. She noticed she had slightly more cash though. She quickly calculated in her head that the increase was due to the LIBOR rate. She changed her password to random letters and numbers and added a few characters. It was just a precaution. The entire portfolio would be safely in the hands of Pendergast and Sons within a day. And she would gladly pay the 3 percent.

But the relief quickly turned to outrage, now that she had her money back, of course. It's a little difficult to express such anger to the fullest when someone has your entire life savings in their possession. She would find out who did this, and she would use all the power of her office—and Judge Durazio's—to make his life—or hers—a living hell.

"Kwame Baker has been released."

Cord was smoking a Partagas in his attic while watching a television miniseries. He held the untraceable disposable cellphone to his ear.

Joe's voice continued. "Our heroes graciously apologized to Kwame Baker, personally escorted him to his eye doctor's office, and apologized to her also. The prosecutor has dropped all charges, and he is a free man. In fact, I think if anyone ever arrests him again, they may be afraid to prosecute him" . . . with the exception of Judge Durazio, unbeknownst to Joe.

"What did you do?"

"Remember what I said? No questions. You need plausible deniability."

"I understand that, but I would hope that no one was seriously injured or killed. I'm still angry, but, remember, all I want is an apology."

"So far, so good."

"Were you also correct about the cameras for racial profiling?"

"Cord, same answer. It's better that you don't know. In fact, the less we talk, the better. Remember, there is a reasonable chance you will be arrested. Just say you have no idea what anyone is talking about. There will not be any evidence linking you to any of the events. Don't even let your lawyer in on any of the events we've arranged. Take care."

The internal components of the phone disintegrated as he closed it.

CHAPTER 20

S arah spent little time determining her next course of action. She knew exactly who to ask for help. This was why she was now on the front porch of Pierre Appollon's modest three-bedroom house.

"Sarah, you sounded so upset when we spoke. And such secrecy. Please, come in." Pierre stepped to the side to allow Sarah to enter.

Sarah did not respond. Instead, she handed Pierre a piece of paper in which the following was written: *"The walls may have ears. Can we go out to your backyard?"*

He ushered her through the house, through their Florida Room, and to a patio behind the house. It was a pleasant Connecticut summer day; high seventies with a slight breeze from the Sound. A cardinal was singing in a dogwood tree. Several turkey vultures hovered lazily directly above them. Pierre gestured for her to sit on one of the chairs, but she shook her head. She grabbed two chairs and walked to the middle of the yard. Pierre followed and the two sat down.

Finally, she spoke. "Pierre, when I explain what is happening, you will understand my paranoia."

Pierre was a legend. He had arrived from Haiti at the age of six after his parents were killed by the Tonton Macoutes, the secret police of the Duvalier government. Raised by his aunt and uncle in Queens, he worked his way through community college and landed a job as a police officer in Bridgeport, where he quickly distinguished himself as a prodigy in crime solving and rapidly rose to the rank of chief detective. After thirty years of distinguished service, he retired but was quickly tapped by the Homeland Security people as a consultant, specializing in database analysis and criminal profiling.

He smiled warmly as his wife, Louisa, brought out two Rum punches made from Haiti's famed Barbancourt five-star rum.

"You two look like you're going to have a serious discussion. This should help." Louisa handed them each a punch.

"Thanks, honey." Pierre smiled at his wife with every bit of admiration in his eyes for her.

Pierre had the high cheekbones characteristic of Caribbean blacks. His close-cropped hair had been invaded by a few gray hairs, but his overall appearance still made him look ten years younger than his age of sixty. Sarah noticed he had developed a slight paunch.

Louisa, who knew when a conversation was going to become tense, bid goodbye to their guest.

Pierre took a sip of the rum punch. A smile crossed his face. "Nice and sweet, just like I prefer. So what's going on here?" He looked at Sarah and waited for her to enlighten him on her paranoia. Her words, not his.

She responded. "Are you aware of the Kwame Baker situation?"

"Yes. Not our finest moment, if I am reading in between the lines correctly."

"You are. But are you aware that I dropped all charges against him? It was done discreetly; no fanfare, no press."

Pierre cocked his head. "I did not know that."

"That's because it just happened."

"I see. Was it because of the video of the two officers who were engaged sexually? That was quite embarrassing. I could not watch it."

"But did you see the beginning, where the narrator links this video as retribution for the Kwame Baker situation?"

"I did."

"Didn't that alarm you?"

"Not really." And it showed in his nonchalant tone. "Retribution of this nature is quite common with the advanced technology available these days. I assumed that one of Baker's friends broke into that lady cop's apartment. I really didn't have much sympathy for either of them. You know my opinion on infidelity."

Sarah sipped her rum punch while keeping her eye on Pierre's face. "It's worse than that, Pierre. Much worse. That's so why I need your help. The officers involved assumed the same thing and further abused Baker in order to determine the culprits. But I don't think Baker had anything to do with it."

Sarah went on to explain how there were also videotapes of the two police officers abusing Fletcher's wife and harassing Teresa. She mentioned how they needed FBI experts to find similar video equipment in her office and Judge Durazio's. She culminated with how threats were relayed via a triangular speakerphone, how her money had been stolen, and how she had been blackmailed into dropping all charges against Kwame.

"It was just a matter of time until this happened," Pierre said, still nonchalant and seemingly more captivated by the rum punch versus the conversation at hand. "Our police officers continue to take the law into their own hands, and the judges—don't take this wrong, Sarah—and prosecutors, like you, look the other way. I started out as a patrol cop, and I was amazed at the disrespect and attitude the general public has toward authority in this country. But that does not give us the right to beat handcuffed suspects."

"Pierre, these cops behaved like thugs. And I have been assured they will be disciplined internally. But this cannot be allowed. I need your help. We have to get to the bottom of this."

Pierre stroked his chin. "You are right, of course. The citizens must not be allowed to extract revenge on even errant cops with impunity. They must use our legal and political system, as imperfect as it is. How can I help you?"

Jeez, Sarah thought she'd never get him to lean toward her concern. "You're an expert on criminal profiling. Can you give me an idea who's behind this?"

Pierre smiled for a quick second. This is what he lived for:

puzzles. Who would do this and why? Whether he agreed with Sarah or not, he wouldn't pass up a chance to put the pieces to this one together. He took another sip of the rum punch and said, "Well, with a little luck, I can point you in the right direction. How many people know about the Kwame Baker situation? Did you speak to his family, friends, and associates?"

"We have made some preliminary inquiries with no substantial leads. But the level of sophistication required to launch such a vendetta seems beyond the capabilities of anyone Baker knows."

"You are probably correct unless he has people in his family with a military or paramilitary background."

"Paramilitary?"

"CIA, FBI, Special Forces, Navy SEALs, Delta Force. Those types."

"I don't think so. Kwame Baker is the son of a single mother who died of a cocaine overdose. His father was never identified. He was raised by his grandmother. He was actually a fairly good student but fell in with the wrong crowd and became a drug addict. He has been in and out of jail at least a half dozen times."

"But he could have a large extended family. He could have friends who have piles of cash from dealing drugs. Has that been investigated?"

"I hate to tell you this, Pierre, but the cops who abused him abused him again and asked him the same questions. He denied any knowledge of this. And I believe him. Also, I am good friends with the public defender who represents him. She has represented him a dozen times and knows him quite well. She feels it is next to impossible for Baker to plan and finance such a plan. Furthermore, she knows of no one in his family and limited social circle who could launch such an attack." Sarah wanted to add, "Why do you think I'm here?" but felt he could still be on the fence a tad and such a comment could push him over to the other side.

Little did she know, Pierre was now in his element. That meant he'd already jumped the fence and had landed right next to her. "Okay. Let's assume that no one in Baker's life—family, friends, and the like—has the sophistication to launch this vendetta. We are dealing with individuals who know how to break into houses and office buildings, plant expensive and sophisticated surveillance equipment, and not leave a trace. They have access to software that changes their voice, and they can embed keylogging software into a computer."

"Keylogging software?" Sarah raised an eyebrow, deciding to sip some of her own rum punch. This could take a while, especially if she had to keep interrupting to get explanations.

"How do you think they got the password for your account? Whoever is behind this placed software on your computer that records every keystroke you make and sends it into cyberspace to an untraceable dedicated server."

"But I never download anything into my computer. How could that happen? Whoever spoke to us on the triangular speakerphone said they had tried various combinations to determine my password."

"You could be right. But the bottom line is that somehow, they got your password. By the way, don't ever use that computer again."

"I already bought a new computer and moved the money to a brokerage firm my family uses."

"Who do you use?"

"Pendergast."

"You may want to make sure that Pendergast can't be hacked too. It's scary, but few systems are safe now."

"Pendergast has insurance if the money is stolen, unlike E-Trade."

"Good. But getting back to my point . . . What we are dealing with here are mercenaries, military and intelligence experts who were hired."

"But we have already determined that it is unlikely. Baker does not have the money or connections to do this."

Pierre smiled. "I concur. Someone is making a statement here. Someone heard about this case, was outraged, and launched this vendetta. And this person never met Kwame Baker before in their life."

"I don't buy it, Pierre." Sarah shook her head. With so many cases of police brutality being videotaped and cops still getting off scot-free, why now? Why for some low-life crackhead? What about the ones that had actually died and not just got their eye popped out of their socket? "Why would anyone do that? And if it is true, it would be impossible to find the culprit."

"That is where you are wrong, Sarah," Pierre said, as his grin increased to the point that it looked like it might keep going beyond the confines of his face. "Let's go to my computer."

Sarah went to stand up but then had a sudden thought. "Your house could be bugged."

"Highly unlikely, but I will get my laptop, just to be sure." He looked down at her half-empty glass. "Can I freshen up your rum punch?"

"I'm fine."

"Too sweet for non-Haitians," Pierre said and then headed into his home.

He returned a minute later with his laptop and a glass of Pinot Grigio. He handed her the glass. "This should be better."

He sat down and flipped open his laptop. "With my consulting work, I have access to all the data accumulated by the Homeland Security people. It's scary, but it's necessary. You would not believe how many terrorist plots we discover that never hit the newspapers. I was just involved in a case where we prevented the suicide bombing of a synagogue in Cincinnati."

He pecked away at the keyboard while Sarah took a sip of the wine. Finally, he said, "Okay. We're all set."

Pierre was now logged into a software program benignly named, Babydanielle3, presumably the name of one of the lead programmer's young daughters. It was not benign. This program could access every conceivable database and cross-reference with other databases. It had information on anyone who had an Arabic-sounding name, anyone who married an Arab, any Arab who entered the country, and anyone who visited an Arabic country. It also included Iranians and other non-Arab Moslems.

Babydanielle3 created a large portion of the Terrorist Watch List used at airports for screening passengers. But the government had taken it a step further. This software was programmed to troll Facebook, Twitter, LinkedIn, Tumblr, and all the lesser-known social media sites, constantly creating gigabyte after gigabyte of data that was perused with complex algorithms capable of predicting the probability that an individual would engage in terrorist activity or other criminal activity. It could access police records, hospital records, legal filings, college disciplinary hearings, chemical purchases; any conceivable event that could be theoretically associated with a potential terrorist action.

"Do you think this could be terrorists?" Pierre said.

"I seriously doubt it. Their tone was sarcastic. They did not make any abstract political statements—U.S. out of the Mideast, Death to Israel, etc. Besides, what terrorist group would return my money?"

"I agree completely. I just wanted your opinion. Now let's think. What type of person would launch this vendetta?"

Sarah pondered this and said, "It would have to be someone who is wealthy."

"I agree," Pierre said, "but how wealthy?" He looked at Sarah. "What do you think the net worth of this person would be?"

"At least ten million, probably more."

He entered this information into the program. "Where would this person live?"

"Baker's situation was known to only a few people. There was a blurb about his arrest in the *Connecticut Post*, but we managed to keep all subsequent events out of the media and even out of the blogosphere and social media."

"So it is fair to assume that this vendetta was launched by someone who is upset about the way Baker was treated. I would take it a step further. This is someone who is upset about police brutality."

Pierre Googled "*Connecticut Post*" and "Kwame Baker." Several results popped up. He clicked the third one and read the report several times. "The report suggests that Baker was beaten, but it doesn't prove it. It would seem to me that to launch this kind of vendetta would require more evidence."

He clicked out of the article and returned to BabyDanielle3. He typed in "Subscribers to the *Connecticut Post*" and then the icon that read "CR," meaning cross-reference. In front him he had the 269 individuals who both had a net worth of over ten million and had *Connecticut Post* subscriptions.

He scrolled down the list and laughed. "You're a suspect, Sarah," as he pointed to her name.

He named the list Baker1 and continued. "The problem is that anyone can read the *Connecticut Post*. It doesn't necessarily have to be a subscriber. Furthermore, someone could have heard about the police abuse of Baker from another source."

"It is a long shot," Sarah said. "And it could be anyone. Someone who wanted to launch a vendetta against the police could live any-where. They could just Google police abuse and randomly pick Baker's case."

"You're right. Let's think about this differently. Rather than look at newspaper readers, let's come up with the type of person who would do this. We already agreed he would have to be rich."

"It could be a she."

Pierre laughed. "Unlikely. Women are too civilized to behave in this manner."

He looked at Sarah. "What is the most interesting fact about this event?"

"What do you mean?"

"The man who paid these mercenaries. What did he want?"

"An apology."

"Don't you find that odd? How did this man make you apolo-gize? Did he kill anyone? Did he hurt anyone? Did he even threaten to hurt anyone? With his resources, he could easily have done that. But he didn't."

"So?"

"So what kind of man would do that?"

"You're the expert on criminal profiling. That's why I came here." There. Sarah had finally said what she'd been thinking all along. Pierre had asked her a zillion questions it seemed; yet, she was the one there to ask the questions and get the answers.

Pierre nodded. He appreciated the compliment. Clearly the hint of sarcasm in her tone had gone unnoticed. "Think about it. How did this man get you to apologize?"

"You're losing me, Pierre." Sarah was getting a tad agitated, but she answered anyway. "He did it by recording compromising videos and threatening to take my money."

Pierre spread his hands while balancing the laptop on his knees. "He humiliated you. He made you feel powerless. And why? Because you—and by that, I mean the police and legal system—humiliated him and made him feel powerless. We are looking for someone who was arrested and treated unfairly and feels he was treated unfairly, not because of what he did, but because of who he is."

He paused for emphasis and stared directly at Sarah. "We are looking for a black man. A *rich* black man."

"Pierre, you are being ridiculous. Even you can't conjure that up. Everyone is unhappy with the cops and the legal system. Every legal confrontation has at least one loser. Usually, they both lose when the winner sees the bill."

Pierre touched his nose. "I can smell it. Trust me. Not only is it a rich black man, but it is a professional man, well-educated. Not someone who came into his money due to some talent that is in an absurdly high demand, like the ability to dunk a basketball. We are looking for an inventor, a Wall Street guy, or an entrepreneur. We are looking for someone who had the savvy to contact a mercenary group and leave no fingerprints."

"No offense, Pierre, but I think you are returning to your Haitian roots and using Voodoo."

Pierre smiled. This actually was an offensive comment. Although he never had practiced Voodoo, it was a legitimate religion and was part of his culture. To insult Voodoo was to insult him. But he had long ago concluded that if he became upset at the insensitive re-marks white Americans routinely tossed at him, he would be in a state of perpetual outrage. Plus, he liked Sarah.

"When black people speak among themselves, we say things that white people never hear. We complain that eyes linger on us when we are shopping," Pierre said. "I always save the receipt when I buy something so I can prove I didn't steal it. I learned this the hard way as a teenager. I am not complaining. I would much rather live under white people than Haitian butchers any day. But being constantly humiliated and feeling powerless is part of the black experience. We are looking for a man who wants some members of the power structure of this country to feel like he does."

Sarah nodded while Pierre continued. "Humor me. Give me a minute."

He turned his attention to Babydanielle3. He typed in "net worth over $10,000,000 and black." He named the database Baker2. He then created Baker3, a database that consisted of everyone arrested in Connecticut since the date of Kwame's arrest. He cross-referenced Baker2 and Baker3. No matches appeared on the screen.

"I'm not finding anything."

"Try New York," Sarah suggested. She was warming to Pierre's theory now.

He correlated all the arrests in the state of New York with blacks with a net worth of at least ten million. Four names came up.

"I got something here." He clicked on all four names. Two were athletes who got into bar fights and the other two were rap stars arrested for illegal gun possession. He shook his head. "They don't fit the profile."

"Can you find the names of people who were just pulled over by a police officer? Does your database do that?"

"I can, but it would be more tedious."

"If your theory is correct, it's possible that the police may have just given the guy a parking ticket, a speeding ticket, or a warning. I've dealt with this situation on several occasions. The cops pull over a black professional who becomes belligerent, usually because he is doing nothing wrong. They calm the guy down, and no arrest is made. But there is a record of the encounter."

"There is no statewide database for that. I have to go town by town. Where's the *Connecticut Post* mostly read?"

Sarah responded. "Bridgeport, Milford, Stratford, Trumbull, Fairfield. Darien, Westport, and New Canaan—although I think the *Norwalk Hour* may have greater penetration there."

It took Pierre ten minutes to compile Baker4, the database of all documented police encounters in the towns Sarah mentioned since Kwame had been arrested. He then called up the database Baker2 and clicked the icon CR. Immediately, one name popped up on the screen.

CORD CAMPBELL

A huge grin encompassed Pierre's face. "Got him. I know who this man is. He fits the profile perfectly."

Sarah pulled her chair beside Pierre's. "I know of him too. He keeps a very low profile, but he's a very wealthy man. Hedge fund guy, if I recall. But this is very sketchy. What was he pulled over for?"

Pierre found the police report of Cord's encounter with the Westport police.

"He was pulled over for speeding," Pierre said.

Sarah started reading the report also. "Why are you always right? He certainly would have found this encounter humiliating. Look. There's no mention of any radar gun information. I've seen this dozens of times. DWB, Driving While Black."

"You are convinced now?" An *I-told-you-so* smile was resting on Pierre's lips.

She pointed to the author of the police report and said his name. "Officer Jack Fletcher—the same guy who punched Baker. Fletcher is an arrogant and nasty guy." Sarah had another request for Pierre.

"Can you run the program again with the same parameters but make it for everybody, not just an African-American."

He complied. Twelve names popped up. Pierre took about two minutes to determine the reason these people had encountered the police. Finally, he said, "They are all unlikely. Five parking tickets. Six speeding tickets and a DUI. It would be uncharacteristic that one of these incidents would outrage someone to the point of launching this vendetta."

"So what do you think the probability is that the culprit is Cord Campbell?"

"At least 85 percent. Let me check something else."

He typed on the keyboard. "He does not have a Facebook account although his hedge fund does."

He played the keyboard again. "Let me check something else." Pierre's eyes went left from right as he read the results of his recent input. "He's done two hundred Google searches in the past month."

"How do you know he did over two hundred Google searches?"

Pierre laughed. "There's no privacy anymore. I have access to the Homeland Security database that scans everybody's search history."

"But how does it work?" Sarah asked with a concerned tone in her voice.

"It would take me an hour to answer that question, but everyone who uses e-mail, Facebook, Google, Twitter, Tumblr and the less popular social media sites leaves an electronic trail that can be traced."

He read each of Cord's past searches. "Mostly financial stuff and some vacation information. Not one search for mercenaries or surveillance equipment."

"That doesn't help our case."

"Actually it does. He was told not to do any searches of this nature. I bet our friend went to Yale or some school with a military tradition. The CIA recruits a lot from Yale."

He found Cord's bio on the Hegemon Hedge fund Web site. "I was close. MIT. The CIA also heavily recruits there."

He played the keyboard again. Soon, he had the entire MIT yearbook from Cord's senior year. He found the senior picture of Cord and executed a facial recognition search of the entire yearbook. A dozen pictures showed up, most with him standing in group shots of various clubs. Pierre clicked through them and came upon a picture of a youthful, bare-chested Cord with his arm around a bare-chested white guy with dark hair and Mediterranean features, each hoisting a mug of beer in the air. The caption below said, "The Brothers. Roommates for four years. Joe and Cord celebrating with fluid and electrolytes."

He zeroed in on the white guy's face and executed another facial recognition search of the yearbook. He soon located his senior picture and noted the name, Joseph Montalbano.

He then entered Joe's name into another database. After about thirty seconds he looked at Sarah. "Remember when I said the probability was 85 percent?"

She nodded.

"Make it 99 percent. His roommate is in the CIA and his clearance is so high, I can't even access more information on him."

Sarah pulled out her iPhone. "Give me a second."

She scrolled down her contact list and made a call. "Gwen, I'm sorry to bother you on a Saturday, but I have quite a mess here. Are you aware of an incident where a man named Cord Campbell was pulled over by two of your officers?"

Pierre could not hear the response, but he could tell from the look on Sarah's face that his suspicions were being confirmed.

"What are you going to do?" Pierre said after Sarah severed the connection.

"We're not sure yet."

"You are not going to arrest him, are you? You must have evidence. We still have a Constitution in this country."

Sarah Cornell just took another sip of her wine.

CHAPTER 21

Chief Driscoll entered Gwen Trudeau's office. Without looking up from her desk where she was writing down some information she said, "Sit down."

She was attired in a flowing teal-blue dress that matched her earrings. Chief Driscoll never understood how such an attractive woman could have such a nasty personality. Women like her could get whatever they wanted just by smiling. Maybe it was just genetic.

She continued writing for almost a minute and again, without looking up, said, "Do you think he knows?"

"Who knows?"

"Don't be coy with me, Chief Driscoll," she said while looking him directly in the eyes. "Without my input, you arranged to kowtow to this low-life Baker. Not only did Officers Fletcher and McMahon apologize to this lowlife, they actually escorted him to a doctor's office."

"We were blackmailed. We had no choice."

"I know all about what happened. Sarah Cornell and I discussed it at length. And for your information, I agree with the decision to apologize. Given the alternative, there was no choice. But I return to my initial question. Do you think he knows?"

"Who?"

"Oh, Chief, you always impressed me as someone who is a little smarter than you look, which, in your case, is not difficult. Who do you think arranged for the events that we have just witnessed? Who hired a team of mercenaries with the ability to plant sophisticated video equipment in Officer Fletcher's house? A team that knew how to access Sarah Cornell's personal wealth and steal it with impunity. A team that broke into Sarah Cornell's office—not leaving a trace—and placed a speakerphone in her desk. A team of highly competent professionals."

Chief Driscoll shrugged his shoulders.

"You have been a police officer for thirty years. You have a wealth of experience. Surely you deduced who was behind this."

"I have some thoughts."

"Please enlighten me with your perspicuity."

Chief Driscoll ignored the obvious sarcasm and responded. "There is a possibility that it may be the individual Fletcher and McMahon pulled over recently, that Campbell guy. We discussed the incident previously."

"A *possibility* you say? Well, Sarah Cornell thinks it is a probability, a very *high* probability. In fact, she spoke to one of your colleagues, Pierre Appollon. I'm sure you know him."

"Pierre and I have been friends for years."

"You may not know this, but Pierre has access to a variety of databases in his position as a consultant for Homeland Security. Apparently, there are sophisticated databases and algorithms that enable experts like Pierre to solve crimes of this nature. He and Sarah are quite confident that Campbell paid mercenaries to extract revenge for his perceived humiliation. The fact that most of the retribution was aimed at Officer Fletcher makes this highly probable in their opinion."

She paused for emphasis and then continued. "Thus, I return to my original question, Chief Driscoll. Do you think he knows? And let me be more explicit. Do you think Campbell knows about the system we created to keep the wrong people out of that neighborhood?"

Chief Driscoll thought about this for a second then responded, "No. I don't think he knows. I assume he believes he was pulled over for being black, but I doubt he suspects it was due to hidden cameras. He probably thinks our cops spotted him or some neighbor called in a suspicious vehicle."

Trudeau rubbed her chin. "You assume so?"

"Yes," said Chief Driscoll forcefully, trying to mask his insecurity.

"'ASSUME' makes an ass out of you and me." A quizzical look crossed Chief Driscoll's face. Trudeau grabbed a scrap of paper and jotted something. "Perhaps this will enable you to visualize what I am saying."

She shoved the paper at Chief Driscoll, who grabbed it and saw the following words written:

ASSUME = ASS + U + ME

After looking at the paper for several seconds, Chief Driscoll understood what she meant, but he said nothing. Trudeau continued. "We are not in the *assuming* business here."

He thought about this for a second. "But I did what you said. I removed those cameras immediately. In the dead of night. Nobody saw me. Why would he suspect such a system? Even if he did, how could he prove it?"

Trudeau considered politics to be a constant chess game, and the best players were not only those who could see several moves ahead, but who anticipated the unexpected. Her job was to protect her town. In this she took immense pride. She was not about to take the chance of Cord unleashing a scandal that would make Westport synonymous with racism. She had no compunctions about portraying Chief Driscoll, Fletcher, and McMahon as rogue, racist cops, but it was not the smart move. Her town would still be incriminated. And she could be too.

When she initially launched her plan to keep undesirables out of that neighborhood, she had the foresight not to send any traceable e-mails. But she did not think to limit her Google searches, the searches that eventually allowed her to discover and indirectly hire Cozy Bed Security. She had figured out how to delete her Google searches, but technology, being what it is, she was afraid there could still be a digital path leading to her door.

"Let's put ourselves in Mr. Campbell's place. He is angry and humiliated. He is also arrogant and has unlimited resources. He has hired a team of tech-savvy wizards. Appollon thinks they are CIA trained. Don't you think that it has dawned on these people that cameras were posted?"

"What's your point?" Chief Driscoll, trying to put an assertive tone in his voice. "The cameras are gone."

Trudeau peered at him over her reading glasses. "My point, Chief Driscoll, is that he certainly knows about those cameras, or at least the people he hired do. So the question we have to ask ourselves is this."

She took off her glasses and continued. "Is Mr. Campbell going to be content with his retribution against Officer Fletcher, or does he have something else planned? Is he going to have his lawyer go to the media? Is he going to put a camera in *your* bedroom or *my* bedroom?"

Chief Driscoll hoped that Trudeau did not notice the slight leer that enveloped his lips.

But she was on a roll. "We must see to it that Mr. Campbell understands that there are consequences to his behavior. He cannot peer into the bedrooms of our police officers. He cannot raid the accounts of public officials, and he certainly cannot have any of his minions publicly allege that this town is engaging in racial profiling."

Chief Driscoll now realized where this was going. "I hope you do not expect my department to discipline Campbell."

"That is exactly what I expect, and that is what you will do. You are to instruct Officers Fletcher and McMahon to pull over Campbell for erratic driving. They will then administer a breathalyzer test, which will confirm that he was driving under the influence. They will then bring him to the county jail in Bridgeport, where he will have, shall we say, some *unpleasant* experiences."

Chief Driscoll, who usually deferred to any inane suggestion made by local politicians, could not believe what he was hearing.

"Ms. Trudeau, there are several problems with this scenario. What if he is not driving erratically?"

"Don't be ridiculous. Everybody drives erratically. Use your imagination. He was weaving in traffic. He came too close to the curb." She shot off a couple of examples.

"But what if he is not drinking?"

Trudeau just stared at him.

Finally, Chief Driscoll spoke. "You're not serious?"

"I'm *deadly* serious."

"You expect us to manufacture false evidence?"

Trudeau couldn't understand what the big deal was now, considering the history of how the man standing before her had operated in the past. "You've done it before. You can do it again."

"But don't you understand. It's not as easy as it was fifteen years ago. The breathalyzers are practically tamperproof."

"No, Chief Driscoll. It is you who does not understand. Before being released, Kwame Baker called Judge Durazio a dyke. He called Sarah Cornell a whore. And because of Campbell's blackmail, he was released. Such insolence cannot be tolerated. Campbell needs to discover his freedom is in our hands, no matter how much money he has."

"It was your idea to racially profile in that neighborhood, not mine. Why should my staff and I take all the risk here?"

Trudeau sat back in the high-backed leather chair. She gazed the sweating, red-faced blob in front of her and sipped on a rectangular bottle filled with blue juice. It was time to put this peon in his place.

"Present value and compounding interest. Do you know what those concepts mean?"

Chief Driscoll knew this was coming. Trudeau was playing her trump card. "What does that have to do with arresting Campbell?"

"I asked you a question. 'Present value and compounding interest.' Do you know what those concepts mean?"

"It has something to do with the value of money over time."

"Very good. Very good. Now, if memory serves, you are fifty-eight years old."

"Just turned fifty-eight."

"Happy birthday," Trudeau said, not necessarily in the tone someone wishing another good cheer would have.

"Thank you."

"Now, you are also familiar with actuarial tables?"

"It has to do with how long people live."

Trudeau smiled broadly. "Chief Driscoll, you are on a roll, and you are correct. One thing about being first selectman is that you are forced to learn a great deal about actuarial tables, present value, and compounding interest. In fact, that is the main issue in the endless budget talks I have with the finance committee."

She paused while holding eye contact with Chief Driscoll and then continued. "Do you know why this is?"

Chief Driscoll, who had been involved in numerous pension negotiations for decades, knew exactly why. An obsequious smile crossed his face. "It's so that you can provide us with decent pensions and health insurance."

"Decent? Did I hear you say 'decent'?"

Chief Driscoll continued to smile obsequiously while fantasizing about rearranging Trudeau's perfect face with a wicked right hook.

Trudeau shook her head and frowned. "The finance board would not concur with your assessment. They did not use the word 'decent.' They used words like 'lavish, extravagant, unaffordable, and confiscatory.'"

Trudeau grabbed a piece of paper from her desk and put on her reading glasses. A puzzled look crossed her face. "You have been working very diligently lately, a lot of overtime, I see."

"I do my best to serve the people of Westport." Chief Driscoll wore a proud smile as he looped his thumbs through his belt buckle loops.

"Yes. You certainly do. Any you have done a remarkable job as chief over the past ten years. But I do notice that it wasn't until recently that you saw fit to work these extra hours. One of the members of the finance board pointed out to me that with overtime, you will earn $223,000 this year."

Chief Driscoll felt his face flush, but he held his obsequious smile. The heck with smashing her face. He wanted to wrap his fingers around her perfect neck and squeeze the ever-loving life out of her. He was just doing what every policeman did the year prior to retiring. Westport, like most towns in Connecticut, determined the pensions of its police officers as 80 percent of the salary of the final year. Padding it with overtime was an unwritten rule. To bring this up was a violation of etiquette. For the past thirty-five years, he had kept this town safe and protected the powerful. He had looked the other way while the children of influential people drove shit-faced, smoked pot, and gang-raped drunken girls. He had covered up domestic abuse when cocaine-aroused executives had bloodied their wives' faces for refusing to have sex. He had smashed the faces of mouthy minorities when they refused to "move along." But he just continued to smile. "With the increased state mandates, I have to spend a lot more time doing paperwork."

Trudeau nodded. "Paperwork, paperwork. I can sure empathize with that."

She shuffled through some papers on her desk. "Here is an interesting piece of paper that was produced by a finance board member. She is retired from GE Capital and is quite versed in the concepts we were discussing: actuarial tables, compounding interest, and present value. Makes for interesting reading. For example, did you know that a fifty-eight-year-old male has a 50 percent probability of living to eighty-three years old and—this is interesting—a 23 percent chance of living to be ninety? The wonders of medical science, I guess." She took off her reading glasses and smiled at Chief Driscoll. "She creates the theoretical scenario of this individual retiring with a pension of $184,000 at age fifty-eight."

Left unsaid was that this number was 80 percent of $223,000. Chief Driscoll's anticipated first-year pension. Trudeau continued. "Then she assumes that the pension will increase by 3 percent a year because—as I am sure you know—these pensions increase every year according to inflation. Thus, we come to one of the concepts we previously discussed, compounding interest."

She put on her reading glasses again and looked at the report. "After one year of retirement, this individual will make about $189,500, an increase of $5,500."

She slid the glasses down her nose and peered at Chief Driscoll. "Now, Chief Driscoll, let's see if you really understand what compounding interest is." She cleared her throat, suggesting she was now really getting to the point. "When this individual enters his second year of retirement, will he or she have another $5,500 added to the annual pension?"

Boy, how he hated her. What would it be like to handcuff her and stand behind her with a knife like one of those ISIS guys? He wished he could use her head as a bocce ball. But he just smiled and responded, "Not exactly."

"What do you mean by 'Not exactly'?"

"It will be a little more than $5,500."

"Very good, and, of course, you are correct. Do you know why it will be more?"

"Because you multiple the 3 percent by the most recent pension."

"Exactly right. The 3 percent will be multiplied by $189,500, not the original pension of $184,000 to calculate the next year's pension; and this process will continue and continue. This is why it is called compounding."

She sat back in her chair and continued. "Now, Chief Driscoll, I want to ask you another question to test your knowledge of these financial concepts." She looked dead at him and said, "How large will this pension be if this individual lives to be eighty-three years old, as expected from our actuarial charts?"

"I dunno, around $250,000?"

"You're a little off. A little off. I'm surprised. You were doing so well. The actual amount is $350,000."

Chief Driscoll just nodded but thought to himself, *This bitch is the one who's off. It's actually $385,000.* Of course, he had done the math. He'd been doing the math for the past couple of years, once he could really see the light at the end of the tunnel.

"If he lives to be ninety, it is over $400,000."

$473,000 to be exact, Chief Driscoll thought to himself.

Trudeau continued. "Now we come to the concept of present value. So far, you have an A-. But you can bring it up to an A. How would present value apply to this pension?"

Yes, her head would make an excellent bocce ball. "It would be the amount of money needed right now to pay for an annuity to provide the pension," Chief Driscoll said.

"You are so smart, Chief." She applauded with several hand claps. "In fact, this report has the actual formula and calculation. Would you care to speculate as to how much the good people of Westport have to pay to provide this 'decent' pension, as you call it?"

He shrugged his shoulders. "Around $5,000,000."

Trudeau raised her eyebrows in mock surprise. "Chief Driscoll, you may go to the head of the class. You are exactly right."

She continued. "Do you think that that we have $5,000,000 saved to provide this pension?"

"I hear the pensions are not entirely funded."

"That's a polite way to put it. In fact, the finance committee estimates that we have to raise taxes 12 percent a year for the next ten years to do so. Not politically possible. But there is good news. By the time the bill comes due, I won't be here." She took off her reading glasses. "Now, do Officer Fletcher and Officer McMahon have the same financial acumen as you do?"

"I dunno."

"You don't know. You seem to like that expression."

She continued. "You and your union did an excellent job of pushing our generous legislature to defining your job as 'hazardous duty' so that you can retire after only twenty years of work. You almost convinced them to give you disability for post-traumatic stress disorder if you see a murder victim. Maybe the doctors can get disability if they see a sick person. Perhaps the firemen should get disability if they witness a burning building."

Chief Driscoll remained stone-faced, determined to not respond to her taunting while she continued.

"Fletcher and McMahon were both hired at the age of twenty-three, meaning that at the age of forty-three, they can move down South and work on lowering their handicaps. I'm sure that during their final year with our fair town, there will be some extra 'paperwork' for them also. I would bet that they both receive pensions in the $120,000 range. Since this is fifteen years earlier than your retirement, what do you think the present value of their pensions will be?"

"Probably the same, around $5,000,000."

"Actually, it is less; around $4,500,000, but when we include health insurance, it is closer to $6,000,000."

She continued. "So, basically, if these two officers retire at age forty-three—as appears to be their intention—the taxpayers of Westport will give them a lump sum of $6,000,000. Do you know of any other job that pays that well? Do you know of any other job that gives you a forty-five-year vacation for the rest of your life?"

Trudeau leaned forward and glared at Chief Driscoll, her face flushing. "Nobody makes that kind of money except for athletes, elite entertainers, and a few Wall Street guys. My husband's doctor and lawyer friends can barely afford to live in this town after retirement, and I assure you, very few of them have $6,000,000 in the bank by their early forties. Crime doesn't pay, but fighting crime certainly does."

She took another sip of the blue elixir. "This is nonnegotiable. I will not allow these people to mock us. I will not allow Campbell to believe he can continue this vendetta with impunity. This stops *now*."

"But how does arresting Campbell help either of us? What makes you so sure he won't seek more revenge?"

"Because when he is jailed, he's going to have, shall we say, some *unpleasant* experiences . . . And it is *your* job to arrange these unpleasant experiences. And after he has these unpleasant experiences, he will not dare to mention to anyone his suspicions on racial profiling."

"I can't do that." Chief Driscoll was adamant.

"Chief Driscoll, please. Do not insult my intelligence. You cops always figure out ways to handle disrespectful thugs. I'm sure between you, Fletcher, and McMahon, you can speak to the prison guards and have him placed in a cell with individuals of a violent nature who have, what we call, pent-up sexual frustration."

"This is crazy. It's way too risky. Besides, he'll be out on bail in no time."

"No, he won't."

"He'll be a first-time offender for DWI. The bail will be minimal."

"You leave that to me. I assure you, Mr. Campbell will not see the light of day until he understands that this vendetta stops, and stops now." Trudeau saw no need to mention to Chief Driscoll that Sarah and Judge Durazio had assured her that Cord would remain a guest of the criminal justice system for a long time.

It didn't matter what she did or didn't mention to him, his mind was made up on the matter. "I'm not doing it."

Trudeau paused just long enough for the chief to reconsider, which he didn't. "Perhaps I'm not making myself clear. I can survive a scandal on racial profiling. I don't need this job. I do it as a public service because this is my town."

Raw fury was now in her voice. "You, on the other hand need this pension, and I assure you, if you do not do what I say, I will *not* protect you."

"You can't touch my pension. You wouldn't dare."

"I'm not the problem here, Chief Driscoll. Should this become a public scandal, I will be the least of your problems. It will be the media, the blogosphere, the African-American politicians, and then, finally, the courts. And when that happens, do you know what you and Fletcher and McMahon can say to your pensions?"

She sat back in her chair, smiled, and waved her hand. "Ta-ta, adios, arrivederci."

He had been on autopilot. Six months. A lousy six months, that's all he had left! And then he and his beloved wife of thirty-five years would be at Hilton Head. Parishioners at St. Francis by the Sea. Members of Hilton Head Irish American Club. He had already contacted the realtors and figured out that he could buy a five-bedroom condo overlooking the ocean for cash after selling their Westport house. Plenty of room for family and friends to visit. He would join a health club, drop thirty pounds, and get off all his medications. And he would enjoy his fat pension, because he had earned every penny of it—and more. But Trudeau was right. He may not survive the political fallout of a racial-profiling scandal.

Chief Driscoll's face lost its subservient demeanor. His eyes narrowed as he glared at Trudeau. He was going to leave this meeting with a shred of dignity. Pointing directly at her face, he said, "I will fulfill my end of the bargain; you had better fulfill yours."

With that, he walked out of the room without another word, slamming the door.

CHAPTER 22

Fletcher was going to enjoy this. Whoever said that "Revenge is a dish best served cold" was dead wrong. He wanted to get even, and he wanted to get even *now*.

Cord Campbell had made his life miserable. Fletcher had heard the expression, "the video went viral," but he never understood the implications. At last count, there were over 1,200,000 YouTube views in 57 different countries of his tryst with Sharon Kline. He had even received several calls asking him to endorse herbal aphrodisiacs.

He was the laughingstock of the police department and his neighborhood. His in-laws despised him. His daughters would not speak to him. His wife, in spite of his threats, was planning to divorce him. Officer Kline wanted nothing to do with him and had formally requested that they not be assigned together. Having been kicked out of his house, he had moved into an apartment, although he had to bully the landlord to get a month-to-month rent.

His main fear was that he would lose his job. But the union lawyer assured him that would not be the case. The recent update of the Diagnostic and Statistical Method of Mental Disorders, the bible of psychiatrists, had defined a narcissistic personality disorder to include the inability to maintain intimate relationships. And the latest union contract stated that any diagnosis from this manual was defined as a disability, meaning that any attempt by the powers-that-be to fire him could result in his getting a fat disability check for the rest of his life. His promiscuous behavior was now a disability. Is this a great country or what?

The union lawyer—with a flirtatious twinkle in her eye—even

encouraged him to continue his extramarital behavior for the foreseeable future in case it was necessary to bolster his case. Obviously, she had enjoyed the video, too.

Chief Driscoll informed him that due to Pierre's wizardry in criminal profiling, the entire political structure and criminal justice system were convinced that Cord was behind his humiliation. This meant they had his back. Thus, he agreed to speak to some of his buddies who were prison guards. These guys knew how to handle disrespect. They had developed systems for handling mouthy prisoners—looking the other way while they were beaten and raped. Even the so-called tough guys, the self-proclaimed alpha dogs, could not handle the coordinated actions of prison guards who decided to make their lives miserable.

He and McMahon sat in their cruiser waiting as the parade of luxury cars zoomed by. They had picked a spot on a side street that Cord would pass between 5:30 and 6:30 in the evening.

"The chief didn't like this idea," McMahon said.

"Yeah, but I bet he's just following orders. The political people are pissed. Driscoll doesn't have the juice for what I think is going down here."

"What do you mean?"

"Faking the breathalyzer with the old model, taking him to Bridgeport County, even telling us what guards to deal with when we arrive. Driscoll wouldn't arrange this unless he knew his butt was covered by the powers-that-be. They don't give a shit that Campbell screwed me, but when they cleaned out that Cornell bitch's account, that means they can do it to anybody. It's always about the money."

They sat in silence for several minutes until spotting a silver Lexus with the license plate number WWF-454. "You would think someone that rich would hire a driver or at least have a vanity plate," Fletcher said.

McMahon aimed the radar. "We don't have to accuse him of erratic driving. He's going thirty-eight and the limit's thirty-five."

Fletcher put the car in gear and turned on the flashers.

McMahon said, "Remember what the chief said. Assume the car is bugged and that we are being videotaped. Be polite—no matter how rude he is. We don't have to fabricate a resisting arrest charge here. I know this guy screwed you, but we don't want any problems."

"I'm in control. If what they have in store for him is what I suspect they have in store for him, he's about to learn the price of fucking with us."

The Lexus pulled over, and both men exited the cruiser. Cord quickly texted Barry. He placed his iPhone in his jacket pocket, lowered his window and placed both hands firmly on the top of the steering wheel.

Fletcher and McMahon both approached the driver's side.

"License and registration please." Fletcher stood with his hands on his waist and waited.

Cord complied. There was not a hint on his face that he recognized the two officers.

"Sir, have you been drinking?"

"No, sir." Cord shook his head.

"Can you please step out of the car?"

Cord complied.

McMahon produced a black apparatus with a tube protruding from it. "Please blow into this, sir."

Cord did as he was told.

McMahon and Fletcher looked at the breathalyzer. The number 0.00 appeared. An identical model was in the glove compartment with the number 0.12 already registered—well above the legal limit. Because Fletcher was such a big man, he had to consume eight Samuel Adams until he was able to generate the 0.12 on this breathalyzer last night.

Fletcher stepped toward Cord. "Sir, you are under arrest for driving under the influence." He continued with the Miranda warning culminating with the sentence, "Do you understand the rights I have just read to you?"

"Yes, sir." Cord was nothing like the erratic, mouthy black man they'd encountered right before their lives had gone to hell.

"With these rights in mind, do you wish to speak to me?"

"No, sir." Cord had anticipated and prepared for this moment.

This was not going as planned. Both Fletcher and McMahon had expected Cord to be outraged at what was an obvious frame. Their discomfort was further confirmed as Cord meekly assumed the position as instructed and was then frisked and cuffed without incident or comment. He asked no questions about the disposition of his car or about contacting his lawyer.

As they drove to Bridgeport, Cord remained stone-faced and silent. Traffic was heavy, even after exiting off the Merritt Parkway to 25 South. Toward the end of the ride, Fletcher said, "Do you remember us?"

Cord remained silent.

Shortly off the exit, they arrived at an ugly drab yellow building with coils of barbed wire overhanging a perimeter. Cord was ushered in by McMahon and asked to sit on a hard, plastic chair.

McMahon handled the booking process, pecking away on a computer for at least a half hour. Cord was then placed in a room where his mugshot was taken. A polite Hispanic man then asked him to remove his clothes. He was asked to bend over and spread the cheeks of his buttocks while the man searched his anus with a flashlight. He was given an orange prison outfit that was several sizes too large. He was asked to sign a form that inventoried all his possessions. He noticed that his wedding ring was not listed on the form and this mistake was promptly corrected.

During the process, the staff tried to make polite conversation with him. He said nothing until the very end when he asked if he could call his lawyer. It was at this point that McMahon looked at him with an ominous smile and said, "We have twenty-four hours to honor your request."

He looked at one of the prison guards and said: "Take him to the Animal House."

There were various holding cells throughout the jail and prisoners were assigned to each one based on their perceived potential for violence. The most dangerous one was called Animal House.

The guard, with the same ominous smile, looked at Cord and said, "Follow me, sir."

They walked down a gray corridor until arriving at a 20-by-20 holding cell. The guard opened the door, looked at Cord, and said, "Meet your new friends."

Some things cannot be explained; they must be experienced. Joe had warned him about prisons, but Cord figured he could handle the situation. However, as soon as he looked at the faces and physiques of his new "friends," he realized that he had stepped back in time—to when dominance and social status were not determined by intelligence, but by physical prowess.

This assessment was quickly confirmed when a huge white guy with a sculptured torso and shaved head walked up to him and placed his face two inches from Cord's. Several scars traversed the man's cheeks, one of them intersecting with his upper lip. His body was covered in tattoos, the most conspicuous being a black skeleton with red blood dripping from its teeth.

He smiled. "I'm having trouble seeing."

The other prisoners circled around, laughing, enjoying the spectacle. One of them yelled out, "Maybe you need glasses."

He stared directly in Cord's eyes. They were the same height. Cord could smell his rancid breath, but he didn't flinch. "Yes. I think I need glasses. Can I try yours?"

"They would not be the proper prescription," Cord stammered.

The guy stepped back laughing and then with a menacing smile mocked, "They would not be the proper prescription."

Cord looked around. He noticed several muscular black guys, hoping that out of racial loyalty, they would come to his rescue. But they were laughing and enjoying his terror just as much as the white guys.

"What the fuck. The only way to tell if they are the proper prescription is if I try them on."

He reached for Cord's glasses and Cord reflexively blocked his hands with his wrists.

The smiling face quickly turned to outrage. He grabbed Cord's neck and squeezed. "Don't you ever, *ever* raise your fuckin' hands to me again or I will smash your goddamn face. Do you understand, you fuckin' worthless pussy?"

Cord, who could barely breathe, nodded in assent. The thug released his neck and slowly took the glasses off his face. Cord did not budge. The man placed the glasses on his own face. They were oblong camel-colored Swarovski's; specifically chosen by an optician with an artistic flair to go with Cord's skin color and the intellectual image he wanted to project.

"You look good, Repo! Makes you look like a fuckin' genius," one of the prisoners said.

"Nothin' could make Repo look like a fuckin' genius," another guy said.

Everybody laughed and a small smile crossed Cord's lips. Cord was right. The glasses were not the proper prescription. But unfortunately, not so inaccurate that Repo could not see this smile.

"What are you laughin' at, asshole?" Repo said. "Do you find this fuckin' funny?"

One of the black guys yelled, "Boy, you is one dumb nigger."

Repo looked at the black guy. "The dumb shit's right."

Even in the hellhole of prison, political correctness reigned. The black guys could call Cord a "dumb nigger," but Repo would not dream of repeating the same expression.

Repo continued, "They are not the proper prescription. I can't see shit."

He flung the glasses to the ground and stomped on them, destroying the frame. The lenses popped out, one shattering but the other intact.

Without his glasses, Cord had what his ophthalmologist called "Big E vision." Even this was an exaggeration, because he could only see the big E without glasses if he squinted. He was now essentially blind, barely able to make out the sea of laughing faces.

He heard the prison guard's voice. "Are you making trouble already?"

Without his glasses, Cord could not determine whom the guard was addressing. He pointed to himself.

"Yes. I mean you."

"He's having trouble assimilating," one of the prisoners yelled. The other prisoners started laughing. Apparently, every prisoner knew the word "assimilating" because it was repeated over and over by the prison staff in their attempts to educate the prisoners on how to avoid confrontation.

Cord fell to his knees, grabbing his now useless eyeglass frame. He groped around and picked up one of the lenses. He brought it to his eye just in time to see the prison guard walking away. Repo gave him a kick to the abdomen. Cord started to gasp as he lost his breath.

"Who gave you permission to use my glasses?" Repo said.

Cord struggled to get to his knees. As he tried to catch his breath, the sharp pain from his bruised ribs brought tears to his eyes. Repo pushed his foot into Cord's buttocks, flattening him onto the cold, concrete floor.

But by now, even the other prisoners were feeling sorry for the pathetic Cord, especially since a wet stain was spreading from his crotch.

One of the black guys said, "Leave him alone."

Cord had the sense not to thank the guy. He just held the lens over his right eye so that he could remember what he looked like.

"Just what I expected," Joe said.

Both he and Trip were reviewing the video feed and audio from Cord's arrest. The GPS tracker on the cruiser had indicated that Cord was now at the Bridgeport Prison.

"His welcome there is going to be less than cordial," Joe said, feeling concern for his friend, whom he had warned several times of how this thing may pan out.

"Look on the bright side," Trip said. "If anyone touches him, maybe you'll let me bust a few heads instead of all this pussy surveillance shit."

"That hundred grand we used to bribe one of the guards has paid off. We know the name of the guy who is supposed to beat up Cord—Danny Cochran—also known as Repo."

"If he does, Repo will soon be learning how to walk with a cane."

CHAPTER 23

Barry arrived at the prison as quickly as he could. He had received Cord's text, and thanks to the efficiency of the prison system's Website, he rapidly determined when and where Cord had been booked.

He marched into the prison and addressed a listless clerk. "My client, Cord Campbell, is here. I need to see him immediately."

"Your name, sir?"

"Barry Hoffman."

She typed into the keyboard and then responded, "There is nothing here to indicate you are his lawyer. I'm sorry, you can't see him."

"That's not possible. Did you give him the opportunity to call me?"

"I don't know. All I know is the computer says he has no lawyer. That usually means he will have a public defender."

"I assure you, Mr. Campbell will not be represented by a public defender. Get me your supervisor now."

The woman picked up the phone, after a minute of conversation she said, "He'll be out in twenty minutes."

"I want to see him now!"

"He's on break. He'll be out in twenty minutes." Her tone was dry, as if Barry was nothing more than a fly bugging her.

Barry stewed. Thank God for iPhones. At least he could read the *New York Times* and *Wall Street Journal* while he waited. After a half hour, a graying man with hanging jowls appeared. Barry smiled at the man. He had long ago learned that bullying bureaucrats rarely worked. These people lived to have their asses kissed.

Both men exchanged pleasantries, and the man introduced

himself as Herb. Barry got to the point. "My client, Cord Campbell, has been arrested for DWI. Business is a little slow for me now, and I really need this case. College tuitions are out of control. Can you help me out here?"

The man smiled. "I hear you. I'm paying twenty grand a year to send my daughter to Central, and that's supposed to be a state school."

He spoke to the clerk and then turned to Barry afterward. "The problem is that you are not identified as his lawyer."

"Sir, I am sure he is in a holding cell. If you would be so kind to find him and ask him, I'll owe you a beer."

"Yuengling?"

"You got it."

Herb hurried off and ten minutes later he returned. "I'm sorry for the inconvenience. Follow me please."

Herb escorted him to a room reserved for lawyers and clients. Cord raised his manacled hands and peered through a lens as Barry entered. Barry immediately smelled the stench of urine, a common experience for any criminal attorney.

Barry sat down in a hard, wooden chair. "Before you say anything, I want you to listen to me very carefully and then choose your words judiciously."

Cord nodded.

"First of all, are you okay?"

"I'll live."

"You don't look good. What happened to your glasses?"

"I had an altercation with some of my newfound colleagues."

Barry was glad to see that Cord still had a sense of humor, but he was afraid it would not last. He knew how things went in those places. It wasn't pretty.

"Any other injuries?" He didn't want to mention that Cord had obviously urinated on himself, probably as a result of something a little more drastic than simply having his glasses broken.

"My colleague kicked me in the ribs. Painful." He rubbed his ribs and winced.

Barry shook his head. This was one of the worst parts of being a lawyer; feeling powerless to help a client, even in the face of egregious injustice.

"Cord, I have received cryptic phone calls from the Westport Police Chief Ray Driscoll. As you recall, I spoke to him before regarding the incident that upset you."

Cord remained stone-faced.

"Cord, there is a quiet consensus emerging among our political, legal, and criminal justice system that you are behind the disruption of the fabric of our system—the Rule of Law. I will remain agnostic on this point. I will represent you to the best of my ability. But if you admit that you have disrupted our system, then we will have to acknowledge this and plan our legal strategy accordingly."

Cord began to open his mouth but Barry raised his hand. "Don't speak. Please. Let me continue." He put his hand back down. "The only reason you were arrested was for DWI. You were stopped for breaking the speed limit. Now I am going to ask you a series of questions. Answer them as tersely and honestly as you can, please."

Cord nodded. He was definitely going to follow the instructions of those who could navigate getting him of there. He couldn't mess things up and risk staying in jail any longer than need be.

"According to the police report filed, you were pulled over for speeding. The officers involved were the exact same officers who upset you recently, Jack Fletcher and Kevin McMahon. Were you in any way rude or disrespectful to these officers?"

"No."

"Did any of the officers ask if you recognized them?"

"Yes."

"What did you say?"

"I said nothing."

"Meaning you did not respond to the question?"

"Yes."

"Unlike the last time, they used a radar gun. You were recorded as going thirty-eight miles per hour in a zone where the speed limit is thirty-five. Do you think this is correct?"

"Yes."

"How do you know?"

"When I saw the cops' lights flashing behind me, I looked at the speedometer. At that time, I was going forty-two. It is highly likely that I exceeded the 35-mile-per-hour speed limit."

Barry continued his line of questioning as if Cord was on the witness stand. "According to the report, you had an alcohol level of 0.12, well over the legal limit."

"That's not possible."

"These levels can vary appreciably depending on your metabolism, when you drank, how much you drank, etc. When was the last time you had a drink?"

"I had one glass of wine with dinner last night."

"A full glass? Half full? Do you remember?"

"It wasn't even half full."

"You had nothing else to drink, the rest of the evening—no port, Cognac, scotch, gin?"

"Nothing."

Barry smiled. "Not even a touch of Cognac with a cigar? I know you, Cord."

Cord smiled back. "Put it like this, I don't get lucky if I have a cigar and Cognac, if you know what I mean."

"Yes, I do. How about during the day? Did you have a pop with some clients: a martini, a drink from the bar in your office?"

"Nothing."

"Are you absolutely sure?"

"I had nothing to drink, Barry."

Barry tightened his lips. "This does not make any sense, Cord."

"Why?"

"Because you knew you were being framed and you were not outraged. You are the first client I have ever had where this has happened. From this, I must deduce that you expected to be pulled over by these two officers."

"Why? Maybe the breathalyzer was inaccurate. Besides, losing one's temper with the police is generally not a wise move. I learned that the hard way, remember?"

Barry gave his client a bewildered look. "You are the guy who wanted me to launch a legal war against these cops. Now you passively accept this treatment? Bull."

"Like I said, I've learned my lesson for getting hot under the collar, at my mother's expense, no less. The minister's sermon this week was about forgiveness. I'm doing my best to become a better person."

Barry leaned in and in a harsh whisper said, "Cord, don't bullshit me. I'm not buying this for a second. A leopard does not change his spots overnight. As a matter of fact, a leopard *never* changes its spots; only its location, and right now, I'm sure you're not in a location you want to be in."

Cord sat there and did not respond.

Barry exhaled and leaned back. He gathered his composure. It really didn't matter what he thought about Cord as far as being behind the whole justice system shakedown. He was his client—had been for years—and he needed to defend him at all cost. Especially with the machine behind the gavel that he knew would come down on Cord harder than ever. "Do you remember what the breathalyzer looked like?"

"It was black, that's all I know."

"How big was it?"

Cord brought his manacled hands forward and spread them. "About twenty centimeters."

"English, Cord. Please."

"Eight inches."

Barry brought his hand to his chin. "I knew it."

"What?"

"They used an old model."

"Meaning that it does not record the time the test was taken?" Cord said.

"How can such a smart client get into so much trouble? You are right, of course. Westport has used the new models for at least a decade. They had to go into the basement to find those ones, I bet."

"So you think I was framed?"

"You know it and I know it, which is why we must get to the point of this conversation."

Barry stared at his client. He had never seen him before without glasses. "Are you aware of a video featuring Officer Fletcher that shows him copulating with another officer who is not his wife?"

"No."

"Then you are the only person in Connecticut who is unaware of this, Cord."

"A lot of complex trading has been going on lately. Sometimes I get behind in the news."

"Well, let me catch you up."

He told his client about the Fletcher-Kline video and how it had destroyed Fletcher's life. He went on to state that a man by the name of Kwame Baker had been released from prison after being beaten by Fletcher because further compromising videos had been released and that the prosecutor, Sarah Cornell, had her E-Trade account drained of over $10,000,000. He also explained how Kwame had taunted Sarah and a judge by the name of Rita Durazio, but because Sarah dropped all the charges, he had to be released.

Cord just looked at him with a poker face. "This is all news to me."

"Let me explain something to you, Cord. There is no privacy anymore. Your life—all of our lives—are an open book."

He went on to explain how Sarah Cornell met with Detective Pierre Appollon who determined that only a very wealthy man could launch a vendetta of this nature. And the overwhelming consensus of the local power structure was that the man who did this was Cord Campbell.

"I don't have the slightest idea what you are talking about," Cord said. He was following Joe's advice to the tee; he wasn't even going to share what he'd done with his attorney.

"Really? Do you know who Joe Montalbano is?"

Cord just shrugged his shoulders. "He's an old friend from college."

"Have you seen him lately?"

"Sure. He was over for dinner a few weeks ago."

"Do you know what he does?"

"He works for the government, but he's not allowed to talk about it."

Cord was a better liar than most clients. "So you are telling me categorically that you did not arrange for any mercenaries to harass the cops who harassed you and Kwame Baker?"

"Like I told you, Barry, I don't have the slightest idea what you are talking about."

"Well, let me explain something to you. It is well-known that you were livid when the cops harassed you and your mother. You spoke to me, and I spoke to the chief of the Westport police about this incident. You also took the time to explain your outrage to Senator Daniels."

"But, Daniels wouldn't do anything for me, and he certainly wouldn't accuse me of anything."

"He's a politician, Cord. You can trust him as far as you can throw a piano. The local power structure—including Daniels, Cornell, Durazio, and Driscoll—has concluded you are behind this. That's why you were pulled over on a bullshit speeding ticket and framed."

Barry looked at Cord's eyes but did not see a hint of guilt. He continued nonetheless. "Like you, I believe you were initially pulled over because there was some sort of system of racial profiling. But there is no evidence as to how this was done, although there are rumors that cameras linked to face recognition software were used. Those in the know say these cameras were removed, but they are afraid someone has evidence of their existence. And that some- one is you. Racial issues are tearing this country apart, and nobody wants it to become public that these cameras existed."

"You and I discussed that possibility, but I know nothing about it."

"Cord, if you could assure me that this evidence will never see the light of day, I can have you out of here tomorrow."

"Barry, how many times do I have to tell you? I don't have the slightest idea what you're talking about."

Barry gave his client an exasperated look. "Cord, I am not going to be able to get you out of here."

"Come on. I can post bail."

"There is not going to be any bail."

Cord knew his lawyer was right, but challenged him anyway. "For DWI? Come on, Barry. You're a good lawyer."

"What happened to your glasses?"

"I would rather not say. I'll deal with it."

"You have to tell me."

Reluctantly, Cord recounted the incident with a thug named Repo.

Barry listened intently and responded. "Cord, did you touch this Repo guy?"

"No. He's nothing but muscle, and he's half my age. Why would I confront him?"

"Cord, answer my question. Did you touch this guy? Did you push him? Did you try to block a punch? Anything?"

Cord thought for a moment. "The first time he went for my glasses, I blocked him. It was a reflex."

Barry slammed his fist on the table. "Goddamn it. They planned this right."

"What do you mean?"

"You will be charged with assault."

"I wouldn't last ten seconds with that animal. He put his hand around my throat. How can they charge me with assault? It was just a reflex."

"I will not bore you with the legal definition of assault, but trust me, they can, and they will."

"So you don't think you will be able to get me out?" Cord asked the question he already knew the answer to.

"You will be arraigned tomorrow. I'll do my best. But—wrongly or not—you have pissed off some powerful people, and they are going to make your life very miserable."

221

"I guess we will see what happens. Don't forget to send me your bill."

Barry looked at Cord. There was no doubt in his mind that his client was behind the vendetta. He was afraid for his client. But he was afraid for the people who crossed Cord even more. He remembered how outraged Cord had been. Now he had the quiet confidence that he would soon be avenged.

CHAPTER 24

"**C**an I have a word with you, Sarah?"

Barry Hoffman could tell by the stern look on her face that this was not going to go well. "There's not much to discuss, Barry."

The two had a cordial relationship. Both were considered among the elite in their respective bailiwicks, Sarah being a cracker-jack prosecutor and Barry well-versed in obtaining the best possible results for his criminal clients . . .who were almost always guilty. Barry's financial security and ethical standards meant that he never prolonged proceedings with endless billable legal maneuvers, such as making ridiculous discovery requests or by deposing everybody in sight. His hungrier colleagues did not give their clients the same courtesy. Thus, he and Sarah often came to a plea bargain agreement, saving the court's time, and more importantly, their own.

But Sarah was not in a bargaining mode. "Your client was speeding, driving under the influence, and assaulted a fellow inmate."

Barry motioned Sarah to a corner of the hallway of the third floor of the Bridgeport Courthouse. "Sarah, we both know what's going down here. My client categorically denies having anything to do with any videos or the looting of your account, which, if I understand correctly, was replaced with interest."

"Do you believe him?"

"Sarah, you know lawyers never ask that question of each other."

"Do you believe him?" She was stern in her tone and willing Barry to tell the truth with her eyes.

"Sarah. Come on. Be reasonable."

"Reasonable? Your client is attacking everything you and I are sworn to uphold. You are the one who is not being reasonable."

"Do you have one scintilla of evidence that he did so? If so, why isn't he being charged?"

"I have evidence that he was speeding, driving while intoxicated, and he assaulted another inmate. That's all I need for now."

"I assume that the inmate he assaulted is the one you just allowed to walk out even though he threw his live-in girlfriend down the stairs?"

"You are not his lawyer, Barry. You know I can't comment on that case."

"This is not going to end well, Sarah."

"And what do you mean by that? Are you threatening me too?"

"Don't be ridiculous."

"Barry, there are unwritten rules here, and one of them is that nobody can threaten, intimidate, or abuse police officers, prosecutors or judges. We'll let the judge decide."

The two strode into the courtroom. Barry took a seat by himself at the defendant's table while Sarah joined her underling—a short gentleman with a bowtie, wearing gingham suit—at the prosecutor's table.

Barry turned around, and to his horror, saw his client being practically carried to the table by the bailiff. Cord winced in agony as the bailiff wrapped his arms around the bruised ribs in his torso—courtesy of Repo's kick—to ease him into the chair. He had not realized how badly his client had been injured. Thank God, he had convinced Cord's wife not to come to the arraignment. She had no idea of the forces that her husband had unleashed.

He gave his client a pair of old glasses he had gotten from Cord's wife. Cord placed them on his face. He looked at Barry, the glasses tilted because of the facial swelling.

"Maybe I can get on the cover of *GQ*. *Ebony* is a bit too picky."

Barry couldn't believe his client was displaying a sense of humor at a time like this. "I do not find any humor in this."

"I don't either, but look on the bright side, I haven't been raped yet."

Cord had no idea how accurate he was when it came to his choice of words—*yet*. "We have to get you out of here." His tone revealed his urgency.

"I'm sure you'll do your best."

Judge Durazio strode into the courtroom while the bailiff proclaimed, "All rise," along with the usual formalities.

Cord struggled to his feet but was unable to stand up straight. Judge Durazio glared at him and then at Barry. "Mr. Hoffman, please instruct your client to have a modicum of respect for this Court and stand up properly."

Barry quickly moved behind Cord and gently placed each of his arms under his client's armpits. He hoisted him while Cord, although in considerable pain, refused to show any emotion in his face.

"Sorry, Your Honor." Barry apologized on his client's behalf.

He eased his client back into the chair after Judge Durazio sat down.

"Docket number BRG-CV-11-5045976-S, Cord Campbell versus the State of Connecticut. Speeding, driving under the influence, and assault," the bailiff intoned.

The judge motioned with her right hand, palm up. Barry rose to his feet. "Not guilty to all charges, Your Honor."

The judge's left hand motioned toward Sarah.

"We request no bail be permitted. Mr. Cord has engaged in behavior that endangers the community and has demonstrated to be of a violent nature. He has a passport, travels frequently, has access to a private jet, and is a significant flight risk."

Normally, Barry would be flabbergasted by a request of this nature; but given the bizarre recent events, this was anticipated.

"Your Honor, my client is a stellar member of the community. He is married and has three children, one in medical school and two in college. His contributions to charities to help inner-city youth, to fight cancer, and to encourage fellowship among religions are well-known around our state and our country. He is a communicant at the Trinity Episcopalian Church. He has no criminal record. Furthermore, he is in need of medical attention. He is not a flight risk. The charges against him are without basis, and we ask that he be released on his own recognizance."

Sarah replied, "Your Honor, Mr. Campbell was speeding while intoxicated in an area where young children walk to school. Such irresponsible behavior cannot be tolerated. The reason he needs medical attention is because his violent nature was manifested by his assault of another inmate."

Barry reached into his briefcase as pulled out an 8-by-10-inch glossy mug shot and held it up before Judge Durazio. "Here is a picture of the inmate that Ms. Cornell alleges that my client 'assaulted.' His name is Danny Cochran, also known as Repo. If he looks familiar to Your Honor, it is because he has been in front of the Court on multiple occasions on charges of assault, battery, resisting arrest, possession of illegal firearms, and other crimes that I will not bore the Court with. He has been imprisoned three times and—"

"Your Honor, why is this relevant? This is an arraignment, not a trial," Sarah interrupted.

"It is relevant because Ms. Cornell dropped all charges against Mr. Cochran in return for his affidavit alleging that he was assaulted by my client, even though he was arrested for throwing his live-in girlfriend down a flight of stairs, breaking her arm in two places."

"Your Honor, such give-and-take arrangements are part of the judicial process. Mr. Hoffman and I have engaged in similar arrangements multiple times."

Judge Durazio nodded. "Offering leniency in return for information is part of our system, Mr. Hoffman."

"But it is not part of our system for prosecutors to launch personal vendettas and present evidence to the Court that has been manufactured in order to pursue those vendettas."

Sarah came from behind her desk and marched directly in front of the judge. She pointed her finger directly at Barry. "Your

Honor, I demand an apology from Mr. Hoffman and request that he be censured for questioning my integrity and the integrity of my office."

Judge Durazio glared at Barry. "You cannot attack an Officer of the Court with such bombastic rhetoric without strong evidence. You have presented none."

In his decades of practice, Barry had learned that being pleasant and agreeable to a judge —no matter how egregious the miscarriage of justice—was in the best interests of his client. But Judge Durazio was testing this axiom.

"Your Honor, I beg the Court's indulgence. Why would my client—who has never stepped foot in a prison—pick a fight with another inmate?"

"A rhetorical question is not evidence, Your Honor. As stated in the affidavit, Mr. Cochran was merely adjusting Mr. Campbell's glasses, when Mr. Campbell violently responded."

Barry looked down at his client to make sure he didn't react unpredictably to such obvious mendacity. But Cord stared blankly at his manacled hands, folded together gently on the table.

"If Ms. Cornell wants evidence, why don't we examine the fraudulent breathalyzer test she has entered into evidence."

"Two respected police officers administered the test and found Mr. Campbell to be well above the legal limit," Sarah said in her defense. "Is Defense now going to accuse me of falsifying results I never even administered?" She rolled her eyes and let out a tsk-tsk.

"Your Honor, the test is a fraud."

"We can produce the breathalyzer at trial or anytime the Court wishes."

"Your Honor, my client did not have a drink the day he failed that test. The police officers manufactured evidence."

"These are outrageous allegations!" Sarah expressed her annoyance with Barry.

"What model of breathalyzer was used?" Barry asked.

A perplexed Judge Durazio and Sarah both stared at Barry. He continued. "The police officers deliberately used an old model that does not record the time the test was taken. My client was deliberately framed."

"In my chambers *now*," Judge Durazio said.

CHAPTER 25

J udge Durazio plopped into her chair as the two lawyers entered her office. They took a seat in front of her.

"Nobody told you to take a seat, Mr. Hoffman," the judge said.

"Sorry, Your Honor," Barry said as he rose. Sarah remained seated.

"Ms. Cornell, Mr. Hoffman has accused you of presenting fraudulent evidence. What is your response?"

Sarah knew that Barry would not make that allegation without basis. "Your Honor, if the police officers presented fraudulent information but I was unaware of it, I cannot be accused of complicity."

"What are you saying? Are you telling me that Mr. Hoffman is correct?" Judge Durazio raised an eyebrow.

Sarah wasn't sure exactly what the raised eyebrow meant. Was it the judge pretending to be none the wiser, or was it the judge signaling for Sarah to be dishonest?

"May I respond, Your Honor?" Barry asked, uncertain if permission would be granted considering permission wasn't granted for him to take a seat.

"Please enlighten me. And you may have a seat now. Me and my herniated cervical discs are tired of looking up at you." The judge clinched her back for effect.

"Thank you, Your Honor." Barry sat down and continued. "What she is saying is that she knew that the evidence against my client had the potential to be bogus, but she presented it anyway. Now she is attempting to claim ignorance to cover up the shoddy job the police officers performed in framing my client."

Sarah rotated in her chair and looked up at Barry. "Barry, I would never deliberately present fraudulent evidence to the Court. You know that."

"Then you are simply incompetent. Take your pick. Show the Court your evidence and let her decide."

"This is not the proper venue for presenting this evidence, Your Honor," Sarah faced the judge and said.

"I will decide what the proper venue is," Judge Durazio said. "What evidence is there?"

"We have the breathalyzer. But not physically here. We will present it at trial," Sarah said.

Barry responded. "The police officers have gotten in the habit of taking a picture of breathalyzer results with their iPhones. Surely Ms. Cornell has that picture."

Judge Durazio turned her attention toward Sarah. "Where's the picture?"

"Your Honor, I would prefer to present the picture at trial."

"Well, I would prefer to see the picture now. Do you have it with you?"

Sarah reached into her briefcase while Barry prayed to himself that Cord's recollection was correct. She sheepishly handed the photograph to the judge.

Judge Durazio looked at the picture for several seconds. "I don't see what the problem is here. The breathalyzer clearly shows a reading of 0.12. How can this be fraudulent?"

"May I see the picture, Your Honor?" Barry asked.

Judge Durazio set the picture on the front of her desk.

"May I?"

Judge Durazio nodded while Barry rose, picked up the picture, and returned to his seat. He bit his lip to prevent a triumphant smirk from crossing his face. "Your Honor, this model has not been used for at least a decade and Ms. Cornell knows it."

"Are the old models inaccurate?" Judge Durazio asked.

"They can be, but that's not the point. Ms. Cornell and I skirmished at least a dozen times when she began her job as prosecutor over the use of this model. It does not record the time the alcohol level was checked."

"I'm not following you?" Judge Durazio tightened her eyes in confusion.

Sarah moved nervously in her chair while Barry continued. "Police officers used to be able to frame someone for DWI by having an inebriated person breathe into this model and then stating that the driver blew into it. The newer models record the exact time so this is no longer possible. Every police department in Connecticut, including Westport, uses the newer model. My client categorically denies having a drink, let alone drinking enough alcohol to raise the level to 0.12. The police officers knew if they used a model that recorded the time, it would show zero. They also know if they used the same model to frame my client, the time signature of the reading would be different from the time of the arrest."

Judge Durazio looked to Sarah for an explanation. "Sarah, speak to me. She was really annoyed now. Sarah was supposed to prepare an airtight case so that she could keep Cord in prison. Now she would have to fudge the law to issue her predetermined "no bail" ruling.

"Your Honor, I noticed that this was the older model, but I assumed that budget cuts may have resulted in the police being unable to purchase more breathalyzers."

"Budget cuts!" Barry interjected. "In Westport? A town that budgets $120,000 a year for a teacher to give a high school seminar on Impressionist painters? A town where a major problem is DWI? And Ms. Cornell expects this Court to believe they would equip their police officers with outdated breathalyzers? Especially, when it is well-known that the modern breathalyzers are used routinely?"

"Your Honor, there are numerous explanations. Perhaps they ran out of batteries. Perhaps all the newer breathalyzers were in use."

"Ran out of batteries? Your Honor, Ms. Cornell is being ridiculous. First of all, the old models ran on Double A batteries. These are rarely used today. Second, the modern breathalyzers are powered by coin cell batteries, specifically the CR3202 model. These are the same batteries used to power key fobs to start cars. The police department buys them by the bushels. Finally, breathalyzers are dirt-cheap, about $30 each. Ms. Cornell is desperately trying to justify what she knows is the obvious framing of my client."

"Your Honor," Sarah said, "if the police officers wanted to frame Mr. Campbell, they could have used two modern breathalyzers and had one of the cops blow into one of them."

"Again, Ms. Cornell is being ridiculous, Your Honor. I had a case exactly like that two years ago and the police officers learned in brutal but effective fashion that they cannot get away with the scenario Ms. Cornell has just described."

"Refresh my memory," Judge Durazio said, leaning in.

"The police attempted to frame my client in the manner Ms. Cornell just described. But my innocent client smelled the alcohol on the breath of one of the cops while he was being carted off to jail."

"That wouldn't prove anything," Judge Durazio said.

"No, it didn't. But when we discovered that the police officer did Google searches on how to hide alcohol on his breathe, he mistakenly purchased vodka under the assumption it could not be smelled. When I further discovered that my client had a vicious argument with another police officer in the department over a disputed call at a Little League game, the charges were dropped."

Sarah responded. "Your Honor, all of Mr. Hoffman's arguments are speculation. He is accusing two respected police officers of manufacturing evidence."

This was the second time Sarah had referred to Fletcher as a respected officer. It was the second time Barry had to let it go without begging to differ. *Respected?* An officer who was caught on video about to assault a handcuffed perp? An officer having extramarital relationships with a fellow officer in violation of department policy?

Sarah continued. "This is not the venue to make this decision. The question before this Court is whether Mr. Campbell is a significant flight risk."

"I am inclined to agree," said Judge Durazio.

"Your Honor, then allow bail to discourage my client from fleeing if you are so concerned," Barry said.

"Your Honor, if you set bail at $5,000,000, Mr. Campbell is going to say, 'Cash or check.' The State requests no bail." She tried to appear pensive, even though she was certain Durazio would rule in her favor.

Judge Durazio sat back in her chair as if to ponder this dilemma. But Barry knew it was all show. "Bail is denied."

"Your Honor, my client is in need of medical attention."

"That will be arranged at the prison, Your Honor," Sarah said as if she herself were going to escort him to the infirmary.

Barry hung his head. He was not going to lose his temper. "Your Honor, I have been in practice for over thirty years. I've never seen bail denied to a first-time offender for DWI."

"And assault," Sarah added.

"If you are going to frame my client, at least do it competently, Sarah."

"I will treat that remark with the silence it deserves," she said, folding her arms and turning her nose up. But the angry glance Durazio shot at her made her realize that Barry was right.

Several minutes later, Sarah and Barry reentered the courtroom. During their recess, Cord had managed to cajole the friendly court reporter into giving him her newspaper and thus was in the midst of doing the crossword puzzle. He was able to rise on his own accord when Judge Durazio entered the room this time, the pain becoming more tolerable. He had resumed working the puzzle when Barry nudged him.

"We're not getting bail."

Cord nodded.

Judge Durazio opened her mouth to speak and then stared at Cord who was engrossed in the puzzle.

"Mr. Campbell, are you enjoying our hospitality?"

Cord looked up but did not reply.

"Your Honor, if you don't mind, I shall speak for my client," Barry said.

"I do mind. I would like your client to answer my question."

Cord looked down at the puzzle.

"Mr. Campbell, I'm speaking to you."

Finally, Cord looked up at the judge, looked at the puzzle again, and then again looked up at the judge. He then said, "Famous attack."

A quizzical look crossed Judge Durazio's face. "I beg your pardon."

"Famous attack. Four letter word. The third letter is an 'a.'"

Judge Durazio's jaw dropped. "You have no respect for this Court," she shrieked.

"Your Honor, I apologize for my client's—" Barry started.

"Don't waste your breath. Bail is denied." She gave Cord a vicious smile. "You will be our guest for the foreseeable future."

Cord just looked at her and said, "Got it. It's D-Day."

Danny Cochran was walking to the second-floor bathroom of his small cape. A social worker from the battered woman's shelter where his former live-in girlfriend was housed wanted him to come there for counseling. He couldn't see the point. If she didn't want to put out on demand, what was the sense in tolerating her presence?

Thus, he was confused when he saw a figure in the hallway. It couldn't be his former girlfriend. Besides, the figure was too big. Instinctively, grasping that a potential confrontation was on the immediate horizon, he squared his shoulders and narrowed his eyes. His intuition was justified. The figure was wearing a ski mask.

The figure blew him a kiss. "Hey, pretty boy. I understand you're quite the tough guy, throwing women down the stairs and beating up middle-aged men with thick glasses."

"What the fuck are you doing in my house?" he growled.

"You have a foul mouth. Perhaps I should wash it out with soap. Unfortunately, I don't have any. Wait a minute, let me check."

Trip started patting his pockets. "Hold on a minute. What have we here?"

He pulled out a bar of soap and showed it to Cochran. He held the soap in front of him. "Please wash your mouth out with soap."

"Are you out of your fucking mind? Get outta my house."

"We are not making any progress here. You insist on using foul language. Perhaps I am not explaining myself properly."

Trip's torso turned sideways, his right leg whipping behind his back with the sole of his shoe impacting directly on Cochran's knee. The kneecap immediately shattered into numerous fragments. The piece of tissue known as the anterior cruciate ligament, which connects the longest bone in the human body, the femur, to the second-longest bone in the body, the tibia, snapped like an old rubber band. Cochran fell to the ground in agony, cradling his knee.

Trip's gloved hands grabbed his collar and dragged him into the bathroom. Cochran attempted to pull on Trip's arms. It was like trying to displace steel beams. He never felt such raw power.

"What a pleasant surprise. I don't have to lift the toilet seat. You see in my house, I always put the toilet seat down, or my wife gets upset. Of course, given your previous behavior, you may not be familiar with such nuances in etiquette in dealing with the fairer sex."

He grabbed Cochran's head and submerged it in the toilet bowl. After several seconds, he pulled it out. Cochran started coughing uncontrollably. Finally, he said, "What the fuck do you want?"

"Such foul language. I hate slow learners." Trip then resubmerged his head into the commode. This time, Cochran had the sense to hold his breath. When Trip pulled his head out, Cochran said, "Please, what do you want?"

"You're learning how to speak in polite society. We are making progress."

He held up the bar of soap. "But I think such good behavior needs to be reinforced. Please wash your mouth out with soap."

"I don't care if you kill me, I am not doing it."

"You do not have a conceptual grasp of the fragility of your situation. Death would be too kind." Trip could be well-spoken when so inclined. He had majored in English. "You see, either you are going to wash your mouth out with soap, or I will. The problem with my doing so is that your teeth will get in the way, so I must remove them first."

He grabbed Cochran's head and with great velocity rammed it into the edge of the toilet bowl. Cochran saw a flash of light and started coughing on the bloody enamel fragments that were invading his throat.

Once the coughing stopped, Trip rotated his head. "Smile for the camera, Tough Guy."

He then submerged his head in the toilet bowl again.

Removing his head, he now looked at Cochran's terror-filled eyes. The guy was actually tougher than he thought. "I see you have finally grasped the fragility of your situation."

He held up the bar of soap. Cochran tepidly took it in his hand while Trip gave him a vicious smile.

"Go on."

Cochran moved the soap in and out of his mouth. Pain radiated through his head as the soap touched his newly exposed dental nerves.

"You do that well with that motion. Must have had a lot of practice. You're not a faggot, are you?"

He grabbed Cochran's wrist. "Good boy. Now, here is all you have to do. In about fifteen minutes, the police will be here with an ambulance. When they ask what happened, you merely tell them the truth. And you tell them that this is what happens to anybody who lays a hand on Cord Campbell."

"Cord who?"

"Cord Campbell. The name of the gentleman you assaulted in prison. Say the name please."

"Cord Campbell." He spoke as clearly as he could with missing teeth, blood pouring from his mouth, and porcelain stuck in his throat.

"Say it again."

"Cord Campbell."

"Good boy."

Trip then held his head in the commode for about twenty seconds and left the gasping Cochran on the bathroom floor.

"Don't forget to do the physical therapy exercises after the doctor repairs your knee. Should be as good as new in about a year. The teeth will be more of a problem unless you have really good dental insurance."

CHAPTER 26

"**C**ome on, Joe, let me do at least one of them."
"Trip, you can't be trusted. You had fun whacking around that Repo guy, now relax."
"I promise to behave."
"Let me see how the first two go, and then we'll see."
Both men were sitting in a warehouse in Derby, Connecticut. In front of Joe were two laptops and a joystick with three buttons on the handle.
He moved the joystick forward.
"What are you doing?" Trip asked.
"I want to see what species of bird that is."
He looked at the laptop displaying a panorama of water, espying a shorebird with a black head and a white belly.
"Just as I thought. American Oystercatcher. You can tell by the orange bill."
He pulled back on the joystick, and the azure sky filled the screen.

⇒)((())(⇐

Judge Durazio was making a turn onto the street that housed her summer cottage. It was hump day, but since her Friday schedule was limited, she only had one more day of real work. She had succeeded in her life's ambition to become a judge, but it wasn't all that it was cracked up to be. While she loved the power and majesty of her office, there was always one case on her docket that made her queasy.

She had put Cord Campbell in his place. He would not dare continue his supposed threats. Not after what he had experienced. Raw judicial power. But the arrogance. The look on his face. It unsettled her. She flicked off her CD player, ending the recitation of one of her favorite books, *With Charity Toward None*, by Florence King.

She put Cord out of her mind. She put all her cases out of her mind. Her latest lover, Rebecca, would be home soon. They would have a quiet dinner of barbecued fresh salmon, a beet-and-goat-cheese salad, and the latest *New York Times*-approved Chardonnay.

She pulled into her driveway and pushed the garage-door opener. In the corner of her field of vision, she saw a model airplane. Her brother loved flying them when he was a teenager. But when she stared at it, it looked different. It was too big. The sound was different. Suddenly, a red streak emanated from the plane. It shot into her house, which now exploded with a booming sound. The roof beams flew into the air like matchsticks. One of the beams spun toward her, smashing the front window of her car. Glass flew into her face as she screamed, using her forearm to protect herself. The next thing she knew, a man was tugging on her car door.

"Are you all right? Are you all right?"

She couldn't see. She was blind. But then she realized that her face was covered in blood. She wiped it away, and her vision returned.

"Are you all right? Are you all right?"

She turned and saw her neighbor.

"Rita, unlock the door."

She groped around, randomly pushing buttons on the armrest until suddenly, the door flew open and her neighbor helped her out.

A retired doctor, he quickly felt her pulse. "Nice and strong," he said. "Let's get you an ambulance." She turned and looked at her house which was now ablaze.

Gwen Trudeau held up the measuring cup and looked at the meniscus formed by the Ketel One Vodka, exactly 6.5 ounces. Jiggers were too inaccurate for this level of precision. She poured it into her monogrammed cocktail shaker that contained exactly five ice cubes. She then poured 7.5 ounces of Tropicana cranberry juice—nothing else would do—into the measuring cup. This was added to the cocktail shaker. She filled a small measuring cup with exactly 30 milliliters of Orange Cointreau and added it to the shaker. Finally, she squeezed half a 2-inch diameter lime into the shaker.

She placed the lid on the shaker, looked at the second hand on the wall clock, and shook the drink for exactly 75 seconds. Reaching into the freezer, she retrieved two martini glasses, both covered with frost. She poured the drinks. She inserted sectioned limes on the edge of the glasses and walked out onto the flagstone patio.

Hank, her husband of twenty-five years, took one of the glasses and held it up to the fading sunlight.

"Perfecto," he said. "Best Cosmo on the planet."

They clinked glasses and took a sip. "Made it just like I prefer, not quite 50 percent vodka." Gwen preferred more vodka, but such was the compromise of marriage. Both relaxed into their Adirondack chairs.

Emanating from the patio was a sparkling pool, fifty yards in length. Hank had specialized in the butterfly at Princeton and still practiced this difficult stroke as part of his exercise regimen when weather permitted.

Two stately oaks commanded the far corners of the pool. In between them was a stone cottage that doubled as both a guesthouse and a storage shed.

"No meetings tonight?" Hank asked.

"There are always meetings. The finance board wants to give the firemen a $200 deductible on their health insurance, and they are in riot mode. Parks and Rec are still arguing over how to repair

the wharf after Sandy, even though we got the environmental people to sign off and the town committee wanted an update of the
budget."

"They really want to know if you're going to run again. You already made up your mind to do so. Why don't you just tell them?"

"Because I am not quite there yet. I want to spend my time with
my hot husband." She took a sip of her drink, making eyes at him
over the rim of her glass.

He grabbed her hand and kissed it. "And I want to spend more
time with my gorgeous bride."

She sat back, admiring the reflection one of the oaks made
in the pool. Suddenly, a red streak flashed across the water. She
looked up as a hole appeared in the stucco shingles of the gate
house. Time dilated, with seconds becoming what seemed to be
minutes. Silenced reigned . . .and then a fireball rose through the
roof.

Instinctively, she brought her hands to her face, and the instinct
paid off. Shards of glass embedded in her arms but went no further.
A chunk of stone wall was propelled into the pool, resulting in a
miniature tidal wave that enveloped both her and her husband.

Her husband screamed and then yelled, "We're being bombed!
It's a terrorist attack!"

But Gwen Trudeau knew better. In fact, she had the presence of
mind to quickly decide that she would *not* run for reelection.

⸺⸻◈⸻⸺

"Come on, Joe, you gotta let me do the last one."

"You'll screw it up."

"I swear to God, I won't kill anybody. Come on, Joe," Trip pleaded. "You used to let me do it in Afghanistan all the time."

"Precision wasn't required in Afghanistan. The more towel
heads we killed, the better."

"Pretty please. Pretty please! The next time you come to the house, I'll cook those filet mignons again."

Joe paused and then looked at Trip. "And make sure they're rare?"

"Of course. Anything. Just let me do the last one."

Joe reluctantly gave up his seat and allowed Trip to sit down.

Drone technology was constantly evolving. Most drones used for military applications were huge, anywhere from fifty to one hundred feet long and equipped with Hellfire missiles capable of blowing up a city block. While using such a drone to help Cord was theoretically possible, for all practical purposes, having one of these huge objects fly over residential neighborhoods and blow up houses was not feasible. They harbored missiles that were too destructive, were easily picked up by radar, and had a higher chance of being videoed, which was something Joe hoped could be avoided.

Fortunately, the Israelis had developed a five-foot drone equipped with small missiles containing slightly more explosive power than a hand grenade. Ironically, the Israelis developed this drone out of altruism. Assassinating the leaders of Hamas and Hezbollah with aerial bombs had resulted in international condemnation as there had been considerable collateral damage, the polite term for the death of civilians. Thus, the Judith was created. It was named after the Jewish beauty who ingratiated herself with enemy General Holofernes, and then decapitated him after he fell asleep in a drunken stupor. It was Trip's favorite Bible story.

The Judith, like the woman herself, was fickle. Because of its small size, slight breezes could make it difficult to maneuver, let alone fire a missile accurately. This was especially problematic in coastal Fairfield County, where unpredictable zephyrs blew off the Sound.

"There she is."

Both men looked at the screen, espying Sarah Cornell and her latest beau finishing dinner on the upper veranda of the Greenwich Yacht Club restaurant.

"Don't think you're going to get lucky tonight, pal," Joe said.

"They shouldn't be fornicating anyway. We're doing them a favor."

Trip moved the joystick, allowing the Judith to circle above the moored yachts. Like the other two targets, the coordinates were already programmed; it was simply a matter of aiming the drone at the proper angle so that the green circle surrounded the target, and then pushing the firing button.

"You're doing fine,"Joe said. "Bring her around."

Trip looked at the camera view on the laptop. The yachts came into view.

"Now bring her down."

Trip pushed the handle forward.

"There she is."

The Cornell family's sleek Azimut Flybridge came into view. A green circle surrounded it, and Trip pushed the firing button. The missile entered the cabin—a flaming red streak. Large pieces of fiberglass rose into the air as the boat exploded, raining down on the neighboring boats.

"Nice shot."

"O ye of little faith," Trip said. "No applause, just throw money. It's a shame to destroy such a beautiful boat though."

"Don't worry. I'm sure it's insured, but you're right; that boat was a work of art."

CHAPTER 27

"**A**re you convinced now, Barry?"

Sarah tilted her head as she fixated on Barry.

"There is not a shred of evidence that my client had anything to do with these incidents. But speaking from a theoretical point of view, I could see how my client could be pushed to this behavior due to the unmitigated arrogance, abuse of power, blatant lying, and manipulation of the criminal justice system that you and others in this room have rained upon him to cover up your illegal racial profiling."

"How dare you!" screamed Judge Durazio. Her face had several abrasions along with some sutures, the work of a competent but irritated plastic surgeon whose surprise visit from his daughter was interrupted by Judge Durazio's rather urgent medical needs.

Senator Bentley put his hand up. He was a compact athletic man: bald, bespectacled, and well-groomed. His inherited wealth and patrician upbringing had given him the liberty and confidence to be the rare politician who solved problems rather than one who engaged in ideological divisiveness. "Please, let's keep the discussion on a rational level."

The Senator had interrupted his vacation in Nantucket to meet with all parties in his Stamford office. The local newspapers were clamoring for more information. The official party line was that gas leaks had caused Judge Durazio's house to explode along with Trudeau's gate house. The problem was that neither house was heated with gas, plus the fact that it was summer and no gas heat was necessary. Now, the press could smell a cover-up. This was further compounded by the destruction of the Cornell family's yacht.

The press had yet to connect the dots, but there was rumored to be a YouTube video of a drone buzzing around the Greenwich Yacht Club.

Senator Bentley had quickly assembled everyone involved in what was now called The Campbell Situation: Westport First Selectman Gwen Trudeau, Westport Police Chief Ray Driscoll, Sarah Cornell, Judge Durazio, and Barry Hoffman. Senator Bentley also insisted that Pierre Appollon attend along with Reverend Jeremiah Daniels. They were seated around a large oak table in an airy glass-enclosed room that gave a panoramic view of the Stamford skyline. In the center of the table was a triangular speakerphone the senator had personally carried into the meeting. The table was otherwise empty except for the senator's laptop, crystal glasses, napkins, and several pitchers of ice water flavored with sliced lemons.

"They will be contacting us momentarily," Senator Bentley said. The triangular speakerphone had magically appeared at the apartment of his chief of staff, along with instructions to arrange this meeting.

Senator Bentley looked at Pierre. "Pierre, you determined that Campbell was the culprit here. Can you please expand on your reasoning?"

"I never said with absolute certainty that Campbell was behind this. I have yet to see any evidence that he had anything to do with any of these incidents. All I said was that given the nature of the events, he was likely to be the financier."

"But you do think he is behind this?" the senator questioned.

"In all likelihood, yes. He fits the profile perfectly. When Ms. Cornell asked my advice on the case, I deduced that only skilled intelligence operatives could have arranged the embarrassing videos, along with the seizure and return of Ms. Cornell's assets. I concluded that these events were financed by a wealthy black man who had been treated poorly by the police and knew about the alleged beating of Kwame Baker. Only one person fit that profile—Mr. Campbell. Furthermore, I got lucky. When I checked his college yearbook, I discovered that his roommate of four years had joined the CIA. His clearance level is so high that I could not determine the exact nature of his work, but I strongly suspect that this man planned and executed Mr. Campbell's wish for revenge."

Senator Bentley, who sat on the Intelligence Committee said, "What was his name?"

"Joseph Montalbano."

"I will check it out, but believe it or not, sometimes even I cannot get access to the names of high-level operatives, especially those involved in Full Black Operations. The CIA is practically a shadow government, as Trump has learned the hard way."

"But it is my understanding that incidents of this nature are becoming more common," Pierre said.

Senator Bentley took a sip of water. "I have been following this situation since its inception. You should be aware that I totally agree with your analysis that Campbell is behind all that has happened. The drone bombings of the three individuals who are directly responsible for his incarceration cannot be coincidence, in spite of Mr. Hoffman's protestations that there is no direct evidence."

"But why is this happening?" asked Sarah.

Senator Bentley responded. "Over the past generation, a profound disrespect and distrust has developed in the American people with regard to our institutions, especially our police, the judiciary, the IRS, and our bureaucratic enforcement agencies—the SEC, who oversees our financial laws, and the EPA, which oversees our environmental mandates. It is the reason for the Trump phenomenon. These institutions are almost impossible to fight legislatively or legally; thus, we are seeing frustrated individuals resorting to violence. When these individuals are of limited means, then they can be caught and punished without repercussions. The problem is that a significant number of these individuals are quite wealthy and have untraceable financial reserves in foreign banks. This, coupled with advanced technology, has enabled them to launch vendettas against the authorities and avoid prosecution. Mr. Campbell is such an individual."

"But certainly he knows about the details," said Sarah.

"No, he doesn't. The mercenaries he hired did not reveal their plans to him, giving him what is referred to as 'plausible deniability.' In other words, Campbell probably arranged for these people to receive a large lump sum of money. After that, he has no input or idea of what is being done. All he knows is that these people will attack those who have angered him and those who are attempting to discipline him. He may not know the names of anyone doing his bidding. An accurate lie detector test—if there were such a thing—would be useless."

"But can't he be fought? Can't we keep him incarcerated until he agrees to call off the wolves?" Judge Durazio asked.

"It's very risky. Haven't you already seen what these people are capable of? Are you going to go into hiding for the rest of your life? Even then, these people will find you. In my capacity as a member of the Intelligence Committee, we have witnessed a dozen similar situations and seen a variety of responses. One judge used your exact approach, Rita, and was shot in the leg with an expanding bullet. The leg had to be amputated."

For the first time during the discussion, Judge Durazio's face bore the look of fear.

Senator Bentley continued. "The subsequent judge, fearing a similar fate, released the individual suspected of paying for the assault."

"Why was this man arrested?" Pierre said.

"He had cut down a tree on his ranch that was the potential nesting site of an endangered species."

"But surely there was no serious penalty for that crime."

"Not true, Mr. Appollon. He was looking at ten years in prison."

Pierre just shook his head.

Senator Bentley took another sip of water. "We had another instance where the local cops arranged for an 'accident.' A software entrepreneur worth millions was vacationing in rural Wyoming. He was arrested for getting into a bar fight with the son of a local policeman. Even though it was obvious that the policeman's son was at fault, the entrepreneur was placed in jail, beaten, and bond was not permitted. He arranged to have the policeman threatened. The police responded by arranging to have him shot and killed while supposedly trying to escape. One week later, both the policeman and his son were dead, killed by a remote-control bomb placed in their car. It was later discovered that a video camera was placed outside the policeman's house, thus enabling the murderer to detonate the bomb at the appropriate time. I could go on. IRS agents, trial lawyers, even FBI agents have been maimed and killed by untraceable shadow mercenaries."

"But why did they kill the cop and his son after the software engineer was dead?" Sarah asked.

"To send a message. These mercenaries are killing machines, if necessary."

"Senator, couldn't these assaults be stopped with better security?" Chief Driscoll asked.

"This has been tried. The problem is that with advancing technology, even the best of security can fail. In that Wyoming case, there was twenty-four-hour surveillance of the police officer's house. This decreases the chance of actual physical assaults—for example by a paid assassin. But a remote-controlled bomb can be detonated by an assassin in Singapore using a video camera or a private spy satellite. But you are correct, Chief Driscoll. New technology now enables us to jam signals from videos and also signals to detonate these bombs. But something else—what has been our worst fear—has now happened."

"Drones,"Pierre said.

"Exactly, Pierre." Senator Bentley now felt he could address him by his first name.

"But I thought drones with military applications were tightly controlled, like nuclear weapons and Stinger missiles," Chief Driscoll said.

Senator Bentley shook his head. "We're trying. Years ago, we armed the Taliban with Stinger missiles and stopped the Russian invasion of Afghanistan. But when the Taliban became our enemy, our operatives had a hell of a time locating and destroying those weapons; but they managed to do so—at least we hope. One man with a Stinger missile near a major airport could bring the world economy to a halt."

Senator Bentley took another sip of water. "As you know, we are using drones to fight terrorism in the Middle East. What you do not know is that when ISIS, the self-proclaimed Islamic state, took over Mosul, an Iraqi city that we captured during the Iraqi War, they were able to get their hands on five Judiths."

"Judiths?" Sarah said.

"These are drones developed by the Israelis. They are small with only five-foot wingspans but are equipped with missiles that have the power of two hand grenades. As ISIS needed hard currency fast, our intelligence sources believe that at least two Judiths were sold to international arms merchants. It is my opinion that the assaults carried out yesterday were done by one of these Judiths."

"What does that mean?"Trudeau asked.

"It means that the mercenaries Campbell hired have the power to kill anyone in this room at any time, and we can't stop them. It means that when they contact us, we will have to accede to any reasonable demands."

CHAPTER 28

S enator Bentley could tell by the ashen faces and pinched lips that he had convinced everyone in the room of their power- less position. It was then that Joe spoke from the speaker- phone, using the software-generated voice of Robin Williams.

"Greetings and salutations to all, and thank you to Senator Bentley for arranging this meeting with such august company."

"Can you please identify yourself, sir?" said Senator Bentley.

"Senator, we have been through this before during our cor- dial and fruitful discussion with our contrite Officers Fletcher and McMahon, and the lovely Ms. Cornell. But we do not wish to be ill-mannered. I'm Robin Williams, and my friend here is Arnold. Like you, he is a politician and was once the governor of the great state of California. Say hello, Arnold."

"Hello Arnold," came Trip's voice in the guise of the software- generated voice of Arnold Schwarzenegger.

"Everybody's a comedian," said the Robin William's voice. "But just for your information, we represent an organization that search- es for cases of the abuse of power by those in authority, and at- tempt to discourage this type of behavior. We helped Mr. Kwame Baker in the past, and we are now coming to the aid of a Mr. Cord Campbell. You should be aware that neither of these individuals have anything to do with our activity."

"Just for the record. What you are doing is a threat to the fabric of our society. Rule of Law separates society from barbarism. It is the Rule of Law that has created a country that is the beacon of the world. It is the Rule of Law that—"

"Senator, please. Save your mindless clichés for your speeches.

We have work to do. But since you brought up Rule of Law, what do you think about pulling someone over because they have the wrong skin color? Please point to the law that gives you the right to do that."

"I would never countenance such behavior."

"Ah, yes. You are a true beacon of rectitude. But we cannot say the same for your colleague Ms. Trudeau. She seems to believe that she can implement such a policy."

Trudeau sat forward and looked at the speakerphone as if it were an actual person. "You have absolutely no proof of such a policy."

"Ms. Trudeau, for such an accomplished politician, you are a lousy liar. Have you ever heard of Cozy Bed Security?"

"I have not," she said emphatically. Her red cheeks and trembling hands stated otherwise.

"See, there you go again. One of the biggest mistakes liars make is to raise their voice and respond quickly when lying. People who are telling the truth actually think before speaking to make sure they are telling the truth, then respond."

"I have no recollection of Cozy Bed Security." Trudeau spoke in a much calmer tone this time.

"Better. Much better. Now you can claim you have early Alzheimer's. Senator, would you be so kind as to enter your private e-mail and click the e-mail titled Cozy Bed Security."

"You can't possibly have access to my account," Senator Bentley said.

"Humor me, please, Senator."

Senator Bentley moved the mouse and typed in several passwords that led to his encrypted supposedly secure personal e-mail. An irritated look crossed his face. "How did you do that?"

"Please, Senator . . . Just click the link."

Immediately several pages of what looked to be random data appeared.

"What you have in front of you is an abbreviated report of Ms. Trudeau's Google searches from the past year. Notice the searches for facial recognition software. Then you will see that Ms. Trudeau spent exactly a total of forty-three minutes on four different occasions reading the Web site of Cozy Bed Security. Next, you will see numerous cellphone calls and transcripts of texts made by Ms. Trudeau to a Mr. Byron Talbott. Mr. Talbott, along with several members of his neighborhood, pressured Ms. Trudeau to keep blacks out of their neighborhood after a black drug dealer delivered heroin to his daughter. Scrolling down the page, you will see the wire transfer of funds by Mr. Talbott to Cozy Bed Security. If you are still unconvinced, please click on the provided links. There, we have the actual videos taken by the cameras, photographs of the holes in the stone pillars where the cameras were mounted, and records of electronic signals sent to the police car of Officers McMahon and Fletcher that correlate nicely with the video feeds that depict black and Hispanic individuals. So I must ask you, Senator, who is violating the Rule of Law here?"

Senator Bentley, Pierre, and Reverend Daniels glared at Trudeau. Then the senator said, "Our system is not perfect."

"Agreed! But one way to make an improvement it is to hold our public officials accountable when they refuse to hold themselves accountable. Yet, what we are seeing here is the opposite. When Mr. Campbell had the audacity to complain about his treatment by the police, the police responded by framing Mr. Campbell, jailing him, and arranging for him to be assaulted by a career criminal."

"That's totally ridiculous," said Senator Bentley.

"*Really*, Senator? You don't have to believe me. Ask the accomplished lawyer, Mr. Barry Hoffman."

"I have no comment on this accusation," said Barry, who had yet to utter a word. He'd learned in his years of being a defense attorney that it never paid to add his two cents unless the collection plate was right under his nose.

"Perhaps I can refresh your memory, Mr. Hoffman. You accused the police and Ms. Cornell of framing Mr. Campbell for DWI. You further accused them of arranging for a career criminal by the name of Danny Cochran to assault Mr. Campbell while in prison.

You then accused Ms. Cornell of allowing Mr. Cochran to be released by having him sign an affidavit in return for accusing his Mr. Campbell of assault. Judge Durazio then used these charges to deny Mr. Campbell bail. Are you having trouble remembering these events, Mr. Hoffman?"

Barry wanted to spring up in his chair, point an accusing finger at Sarah, Chief Driscoll, and Judge Durazio and state, "*I told you so. I told you this would end badly. But you morons would not listen.*" But his job was to protect his client. And at this point, there was not a shred of objective evidence that Cord had anything to do with recent events. Such a statement could not only implicate his client further, but could, theoretically, implicate him for concealing a crime. Thus he simply said, "I have no comment."

"Well, perhaps we need to refresh your memory."

After several seconds, Barry heard his voice emanating from the speakerphone. He soon realized that he was listening to a recording of his discussion with Sarah and Judge Durazio while in Judge Durazio's chambers.

Judge Durazio grabbed the speakerphone yelling, "You have no right! You have no right!"

Senator Bentley grabbed Judge Durazio's wrists. "Put that down. I want to hear this."

"That recording is illegal and out of context," Judge Durazio said. "Connecticut law forbids the recording of conversations without consent."

The recording stopped and the Robin Williams's voice returned. "Your Honor, we did not mean to upset you. But as long as we are talking about breaking the law, let's show you a fascinating video, shall we?"

Senator Bentley's laptop dinged, the sign of another e-mail arriving. "Senator, please click onto the e-mail that says 'An altercation with the toilet bowl' and show it to Her Honor."

Senator Bentley, who was now livid at Judge Durazio and Sarah, did as instructed.

"This is against the law too, Your Honor," said the speakerphone.

To the concealed horror of all, they saw a pair of gloved hands push Cochran's face into the edge of a toilet bowl. They then saw the gloved hands hold his face for the camera, blood dripping from the area previously occupied by his front teeth. The gloved hands then submerged his head into the commode.

"You see," said the speakerphone, "we are not really concerned with laws here, Your Honor. None of us. Mr. Cochran saw fit to attack Mr. Campbell and smash his glasses. This was arranged by a prison guard who was a colleague of our hero, Chief Driscoll. Ms. Cornell then arranged for Mr. Cochran to accuse Mr. Campbell of assault in return for a plea deal. Thus, Mr. Cochran got what he deserved . . . as will you if you don't do what we say."

Senator Bentley had heard enough and decided to cut to the chase. "What do you want?"

"First of all, I want your opinion, Senator. What do you think about Ms. Cornell's behavior? What do you think about Judge Durazio's behavior? What do you think should be done? You who are all wise and munificent. Better yet, I want to hear Senator-Reverend Daniel's opinion. What does *he* think about the treatment of Mr. Campbell?"

Reverend Daniels responded. "None of this disturbs me. I have long acquiesced to the reality that my tribe lives in a world run by the likes of Ms. Trudeau, Judge Durazio, and Ms. Cornell. Even having a black president changed nothing. My concern is providing affordable housing, health care, and safe streets to my constituency. Trying to change the innate racism of the white race is a waste of time."

"Spoken like a true politician. It is because of gutless leaders like you that your race is always being pushed around. You exchange security for pride."

Pierre now spoke. "Sir, you are a coward. Show yourself."

"Monsieur Appollon, you Haitians did the opposite. The only successful slave revolt in history. Your country has pride but no economic security. You have my admiration."

"Will you get to the point," said Senator Bentley impatiently.

"I will, but I am also trying to get to the truth. You were the one expounding on the Rule of Law. How can we have Rule of Law without getting to the truth?" the speakerphone said.

Senator Bentley responded. "You know, it never ceases to amaze me how many people believe that the law is a search for the truth. It is not. It is a system of resolving conflict in such a fashion so that political turmoil and violence are minimized. Which is exactly what we are trying to do here. Just tell us what you want."

"Very well. What we want is very simple. We want Cord Campbell released from prison immediately, and we want apologies from all the offending parties. Nothing more."

"It's not that simple," Senator Bentley said.

"Au contraire, au contraire. It's quite simple. Ms. Cornell and Her Honor, Judge Durazio, know the drill."

Sarah now spoke. "I'll write the motion up today, give it to the judge, and he'll be out by tonight."

"Now we're talking, but we would like to see Mr. Campbell released with him present while he is in open court."

"Why is this necessary?" said Judge Durazio.

"So that you and Ms. Cornell can publicly express your sincere apologies to Mr. Campbell for conniving to imprison him."

"That's not happening," Judge Durazio yelled. Enough was enough. She'd bent enough. She would not grovel. Let the chips fall where they may.

The voice of Arnold Schwarzenegger now emanated from the speakerphone. "I told you, Robin. We should have waited until the bitch was in her house and then blown it up."

"Arnold, please. Why do you have to be so confrontational? Judge Durazio is a reasonable person. I'm sure she does not want to spend the rest of her life in fear that her house or car will be bombed at our discretion. Or having her face smashed into a toilet bowl. Or having her spine severed with a baseball bat. Those adult Depend diapers are expensive."

"What kind of animals are you?" Senator Bentley said. "Threatening to maim a sitting judge."

The Robin Williams voice replied. "A sitting judge who conspired with Ms. Trudeau and Ms. Cornell to imprison Mr. Campbell on falsified evidence. A sitting judge who smirked at Mr. Campbell's pain after he was assaulted by a thug."

Arnold's voice interjected. "He won't be doing any more assaulting for a while though."

"Arnold, please. Don't interrupt!"

"Why do we have to reason with these people? Let's just waste them," Arnold said.

"You know, Arnold, I am starting to agree with you. Here is what you people are going to do. Ms. Cornell will present the motion in open court. She will apologize to Mr. Campbell. She does not have to admit that she helped frame him and ruin her career. She must simply apologize. Judge Durazio will then grant this motion with sincere apologies from her personally. If you do not agree to this, you will be either maimed or killed, depending upon our mood. Is that agreed?"

"We agree," yelled Sarah. She made it a point to speak on behalf of both her and the judge. With the way Judge Durazio was flipping off at the mouth, their heads would be severed before they even left the meeting.

"I want to hear it from the judge."

Sarah exhaled, closed her eyes, and hoped the judge would come to her senses. This was a battle they could not win.

Judge Durazio, literally feeling all eyeballs glaring at her, said with clenched teeth, "I agree."

"Good. Once Mr. Campbell is released, we would like Officer Fletcher, Officer McMahon and Ms. Trudeau to visit the Campbell residence. You will receive e-mails as to the exact time along with other instructions. Officer Fletcher will present Mr. Campbell's mother with a bouquet of a dozen red roses and both officers will humbly apologize to the entire family. Ms. Trudeau, you will bake one of your famous carrot cakes and present it. You will apologize also. Then you will all have drinks with the Campbell family. In return, you will have our assurances that there will be no violence against you. There will be no further vengeance. There will be no release to the media of our overwhelming evidence that you engaged in racial profiling. There will be no legal filings. The incident will be forgotten as if it never happened. Am I making myself clear?"

"If we agree to your terms, what assurances do we have that this will never happen again?" Senator Bentley said.

"You have our word. But if we hear of your profiling innocent individuals, beating handcuffed suspects, and in any way, abusing the public trust . . . tell them, Arnold."

"I'll be back," said Arnold's voice.

The speakerphone went dead.

CHAPTER 29

ord Campbell walked to the line to get breakfast. He was getting used to the orange prison garb. He found it to be more
comfortable than the jacket and tie he wore to work daily,
especially with his bruised ribs. He really liked the loose collar of his
shirt and comfortable baggy pants. Like most highly successful people, he preferred comfort to style. Dressing well was for the vain,
the insecure, and the incompetent.

He had quickly learned in prison that making eye contact was
perceived as an act of disrespect. Look down. Speak quietly and
only when spoken to. The pecking order was established in primi-
tive terms. Physical size and youth were paramount unless you
were favored by the guards. There was no celebration of diversity.
Blacks stuck together. Hispanics stuck together, and whites stuck
together. And among each race, there was a strict hierarchy. He
hadn't quite figured it out; but he had deduced it had something to
do with tattoos.

So he was surprised when everyone was smiling at him. These
were not the threatening sarcastic smiles he had encountered in
the holding pen his first day, when he had been assaulted by that
Repo character. They were full-faced smiles, smiles of admiration,
smiles of respect.

But why?

He shuffled into the cafeteria holding a tray of inedible food. All
the servers addressed him as Mr. Campbell and piled extra portions
on his tray. He was heading toward a table in the corner, populated
by blacks who committed the least prestigious crimes: just domestic violence, DWI, and nonpayment of child support. Even there, he

had to ask permission to sit.

Suddenly, Peat Moss stood up. "Mr. Campbell . . . Please join us. Have a seat."

Peat Moss was the alpha male of the black gang. At six foot six, he was a tower of sinews and tattoos, topped with an iridescent bald head that literally reflected the overhead lighting. Nobody knew why he was called Peat Moss. Nobody dared to ask.

Peat Moss extended his hand in a welcoming manner. His table occupied the most prestigious portion of the cafeteria, near to the serving line but far enough so that nobody could walk around his table to get to another table. This is how Peat Moss liked it.

"Are you sure, sir?" Cord said.

Another black man with a sculptured torso, two gold front teeth, and sporting a Mohawk said, "My man, it would be a fuckin' honor to have you at our table."

Cord sat down in a slow, deliberate manner, his eyes moving rapidly at the half-dozen smiling black faces at the table—murderers, drug dealers, con men—men who would rather die than be disrespected.

A large, intimidating Hispanic man with a huge tattoo of the Virgin Mary on his right arm approached Peat Moss. "Can I have his autograph?"

"What are you going to give me?" Peat Moss asked.

"Whatever you want. I had to kiss the guard's ass for five minutes just to get this pen." He displayed the pen he held in his hands. "Please, I gotta have his autograph."

Peat Moss nodded, and the Hispanic man approached Cord. "Can I have your autograph, Mr. Campbell?"

Cord looked at the Hispanic man in bewilderment, but then finally said, "To whom should I address it?"

The man with the gold teeth laughed. "*To whom should I address it?* Our main man, Cord, knows how to speak proper English, not like the other dumb fucks at this table."

Everyone laughed while Cord forced a smile. The Hispanic man said, "Make it out to Maria."

Cord did as he was asked. The Hispanic man held the paper with his autograph in the air while another table cheered wildly.

Suddenly, Peat Moss put his fist in the air—the Black Power salute—and started chanting "Campbell, Campbell, Campbell."

Soon the entire room was on its feet. "Campbell, Campbell, Campbell."

Cord was used to being admired. His whole life had been a litany of academic awards, praise for his financial acumen, and applause for his generosity. But there is one thing he never was: popular. He was never the high school quarterback, the handsomest guy in the room, or the Big Man on Campus. But here he was, among the so-called dregs of society, people he had tried to avoid all his life—and he was popular! Yesterday, they terrified him. Now, he felt a kinship with them. Like him, they were outsiders.

Several guards poured in the room, sticks drawn. Cord smiled at the guards, stood up, and held up his hand. The cheering stopped.

"No more racket," one of the guards yelled.

"No problem, sir," Cord said. But he was still confused.

The man with the gold teeth reached over and shook his hand. "My name is Maurice. It is an honor to meet you. At first, I thought you should have killed that bitch Durazio, but now I understand. You're scarin' the fuckin' shit out of that lyin' dyke. You're scarin' all those muthafuckas. Those lyin' pigs and corrupt judges. Man, I'm wantin' to be a fly on the wall while they be shittin' themselves."

"What do you mean?" Cord said.

"You firebombed her fuckin' house. That's what I like. Put that muthafucka her place."

"I don't know what you're talking about." Unlike his conversation with his attorney, in this case, Cord truly was oblivious to everything Maurice was saying. Judge Durazio? A bomb?

"Who the hell else did it?"

Peat Moss looked at Maurice. "You are the dumbest muthafucker on the planet. You had to have learned to be so fuckin' stupid 'cause no one is born that dumb."

He put his arm around Cord. It felt like it weighed a ton. "You think my man, Cord, is stupid enough to admit he bombed that bitch's house? You know nothing 'bout that shit, right, Cord?"

"No, I don't," Cord said.

The table erupted with laughter. A small wiry guy at the end of the table said, "Just like you know nothin' about bombing that whore Coronel's yacht, the rich slut."

"It's Cornell, not Coronel, you stupid fuck," Maurice said. "Like the fuckin' university."

"I got a right to thank the man who put that bitch in her place," the wiry guy said. "Fuckin' pigs planted marijuana in my car, cuffed me, beat the shit out me, and that bitch lies out her fuckin' teeth, and I'm stuck here listenin' to your shit. *Like the university.* What the fuck do you know about a university? You can't even read a comic book."

The entire table laughed along with Maurice. "Normally, I'd go down there an' whoop your puny ass, but I'm in too good a mood. I'm with my main man, Cord." Maurice turned and smiled at Cord.

Cord couldn't help but smile himself. This was all news to him. It looked like Joe had given him his money's worth.

The wiry man looked at Cord. "Tell us how you helped our brother, Kwame."

Peat Moss looked at the man. "You not listenin'. You be gettin' Cord in trouble. He's got to know nothin', deny every thin'. You think he uses those dumb-ass hippie public defenders we're stuck with? He's hiring those smart Jew lawyers that be chargin' him $1,000 an hour. They tellin' Cord to say nothin'."

"But I hears the pigs been apologizing to Kwame. That true?" Maurice said.

"You fuckin' serious? Cops be apologizing to that junkie Kwame? Man, it don't get no finer than that," the wiry guy said.

"Not only that, pigs drivin' him to his doctor," Peat Moss said.

"Damn right," Maurice said. "Those pigs don't apologize, one of Cord's airplanes be bombing those muthafuckas."

"Cord don't use airplanes," Peat Moss said. "He usin' the same things Obama used to keep those sand niggers in their place over in Arabia. Drones."

"Drones?" Maurice said.

Peat Moss smiled as he showed off his knowledge. "You fly them by remote control. Guy flyin' it could be in fuckin' China. No way to get caught. Cord's too smart to get caught."

He wrapped his arm so tightly around Cord that he was afraid of getting a rotator cuff injury.

"Cord gettin' those fuckin' pigs to apologize to him too?" Maurice said.

Peat Moss said, "Damn right. Cord knows how to scare lyin' scum. Pigs dissin' us, what do we do? We burn down our own fuckin' hood. Like those dumb niggas in Ferguson and Baltimore. We should be burnin' down the hood where those pigs and judges live."

"You try to burn down those hoods and those pigs and crackers be usin' your black ass for target practice," Maurice said.

"But our main man, Cord, just be bombin' their fuckin' houses. He's payin' guys. Can't touch him. Cord's one mean muthafucka," Peat Moss said with a huge smile.

Cord stifled a laugh. He was enjoying this immensely.

Maurice said, "How'd you make so much money, Mr. Campbell?"

"I'm an investor."

"Cord makes big money like a white boy," Peat Moss said. "None of this bouncin' the ball, rapin', or Hollywood shit. Cord be turnin' on the computer, talkin' on the phone, and rakin' in the dough."

The alpha male from the white gang appeared. Peat Moss took his arm off Cord and turned to look at him. While both men were hardened criminals, each had become skilled politicians and were quite adept at resolving conflicts between their constituencies.

"Lester, what can I do you for?" Peat Moss said.

"Everyone wants Mr. Campbell's autograph," Lester replied.

"You aren't pissed about what happened to Repo?"

"Cocksucker got what he deserved picking on Mr. Campbell."

Cord put on his best poker face. He hoped that Repo was still alive.

"Cord, do you mind signing a few autographs?" Peat Moss said.

"It will be my pleasure."

Lester waved his hand. Soon, a line formed in front of Cord's seat. He meticulously signed the autographs, writing his full name and taking pains to make sure everyone's name was spelled correctly. The guys at his table beamed with pride.

One of the guards walked up to Cord. "Mr. Campbell, your lawyer, Mr. Hoffman, is here."

"Please inform Mr. Hoffman that I will be there at my earliest convenience," Cord said like a true rock star, showing his fans nothing but the loyalty they deserved.

The table roared with approval. Peat Moss said, "Our main man Cord be makin' his lawyer wait at his *'earliest fuckin' convenience.'* I be rememberin' that line. At my earliest convenience. You gotta love it! You gotta fuckin' love it!" He shook his head and smiled a wide, proud grin.

Maurice added, "You guards should be gettin' some coffee for Mr. Campbell's lawyer at your earliest convenience."

The table roared with laughter. Cord continued to sign the autographs for the next fifteen minutes. He loved being popular. When finished, he excused himself and spoke to one of the guards who then escorted him to a room where an obviously annoyed Barry was sitting. In front of him was a white plastic cup with coffee.

"Thank you for gracing me with your presence," Barry said. "Can I have your autograph too?" Evidently the guard had also informed Barry the purpose behind his wait.

"To whom should I make it out?" Cord asked, the corner of his mouth raising into a smirk.

"Cord, this isn't funny. Did it ever occur to you that signing autographs could be construed as an admission of guilt?"

"Guilt for what?"

"Cord, you know what I am talking about. Drone attacks on prosecutors, judges, and politicians. Do you have any idea of the terror you have unleashed?"

"I have no idea what you are talking about."

Barry leaned back, exasperated. His mouth said nothing, but his facial expression read: *"So we're back to this again, huh?"* For the next ten minutes, Barry recounted all the events that transpired, including the meeting with Senator Bentley and the demands for an apology.

When he finished, Cord repeated, "I have no idea what you are taking about."

"Well, whoever advised you and set this up knew what they were doing. You obviously plan to deny everything, even to your lawyer, but I *know* you're behind this. You can't bullshit me."

"I have no idea what you are talking about," Cord said while looking directly into his attorney's eyes.

"You know how I know? Because these people you hired are doing exactly what you wanted me to do the first time we spoke. They are not asking for money. They are not asking for publicity. They are not destroying anybody's career. All they have asked for is an apology."

"And you construe this as proof?" Cord leaned in and said.

"Yes, I do."

He paused, then leaned back into his chair. "I have no idea what you are talking about."

"Fine," an exasperated Barry said. "But you don't have to live with me. You have to live with Clara, and she is *not* pleased. Not pleased at all. And your parents are trying to convince themselves that you had nothing to do with this."

"You were at my house?" Now Barry had Cord's attention.

"Of course I was at your house. Twice. Your family is worried sick. Thank God, you've only been here for three days. I really didn't want your wife to see you like this."

Cord looked down at the table while Barry continued. "Here is what is going to happen . . . thanks to these mercenaries that you deny hiring."

For the next few minutes, Barry explained how Cord was going to receive an apology from both Sarah and Judge Durazio in open court. It took all of Cord's self-control not to smile at this news. Barry further described how Cord's mother would be receiving a dozen roses and an apology from the officers involved, and that the politician who ordered the racial profiling system was going to bring him some homemade carrot cake.

At this Cord could not help himself. A huge smile enveloped his ebony face. "Thank you for representing me, Barry."

"Cord, even though this is wrong, I have to admire you. But the fact that these mercenaries insisted that the cops bring your mother a dozen roses is beyond coincidence. It *proves* that you hired these mercenaries, and they fulfilled your wishes."

Cord continued to smile and said, "I have no idea what you are talking about."

CHAPTER 30

Cord was not yet accustomed to his celebrity status. What he had achieved was the dream of everyone who had ever felt maltreated by the criminal justice system. That is why the story of his vendetta had spread so widely among his fellow inmates. But now, word was filtering out to the press. There were rumors on various blogs and Internet sites about a high-tech vendetta against the police and rumors of drone attacks on public officials. There were even Twitter hashtags titled #dontmesswithcampbell and #copsbegrovelin.

Cord waited patiently in the courthouse holding room, surrounded by three prison guards, all addressing him as Mr. Campbell and asking him frequently if they could get him some coffee, which he was finding annoying. He had on a fresh orange prison uniform and was uncuffed this time.

The other prisoners in the room, even the white ones, kept giving him the upraised fist Black Power salute. He just politely nodded and said nothing. Several reporters were milling around, but the guards would not let them speak to him. After about twenty minutes, one of the bailiffs, an attractive Hispanic woman, escorted him into the courtroom where he was seated beside his attorney.

"How does it feel to be a rock star?" Barry asked. "I was practically mobbed by reporters. Thank God Durazio closed the courtroom. If all goes well, we're going to walk out of here. Just keep your mouth shut."

Judge Durazio entered with the usual formalities. The bruise on her forehead was fading in color but extended down to her right eyelid. A careful inspection of her left upper brow revealed several dark-colored nylon sutures. Cord rose respectfully and remained standing until instructed to sit.

"Is there a motion before the Court?" Judge Durazio said. Her lips were tight, as if they were trying their darnest to keep other words at bay.

Sarah rose. As usual, she was elegantly dressed, this time in a black Chanel suit; although she decided pearls would not be appropriate. "Your Honor, the State wishes to drop all charges against Mr. Cord Campbell. It has come to the attention of the State that these charges were filed in error and we—including myself personally—extend our deepest apologies to Mr. Campbell. I hope Mr. Campbell will accept our collective apology and my personal apology."

Cord looked at Sarah and nodded politely.

Judge Durazio looked at the papers in front of her. "All appears to be in order. Do you accept this agreement, Mr. Campbell?"

Barry rose. "We appreciate the State's withdrawal of the charges and have nothing further to say."

Judge Durazio looked at Cord. "The motion is accepted. Mr. Campbell, you are free to go."

Cord stared at her intently. Judge Durazio hesitated, then she said, "Mr. Campbell, it has come to this Court's attention that you were unfairly detained because you are African American. This Court apologizes to you and will do all in its power to prevent further incidents of this nature."

Cord thought to himself since he was about to walk free, *Why rock the boat?* But then emotion overtook logic. "Excuse me, Your Honor." It was as if the spirit of Kwame Baker was in the courtroom. Cord just couldn't keep quiet.

Barry literally put his hand over his client's mouth. "Your Honor, my client has slept poorly and is not thinking clearly. We appreciate the Court's ruling."

Cord remained calm but as soon as Barry removed his hand, he continued. "The slave labor of my ancestors built this country. My great-grandfather was a cook for the army in World War I because he was not allowed to fight. My grandfather was in the D-Day invasion and took a bullet to his leg. Two of my uncles were killed in Viet Nam. My niece had her leg blown off in Iraq by a landmine. We are not African Americans. We are Americans. So please don't patronize me."

He then stared blankly at the table, willing to accept any change in his fate. Barry was about to apologize for his client's behavior, but then he realized he would just make the situation worse.

Judge Durazio stared at Cord, searching his face. Such insolence. Such insubordination. She could cite him for contempt, but then she remembered Cochran's toothless bloody face. She remembered her house ablaze. What other terror could this man unleash on her? And all this happened while he was imprisoned. The wheels of revenge were in motion. She was helpless. So she simply said, "This Court is adjourned."

Barry sighed with relief. A black bailiff gave Cord the thumbs-up sign.

Together, Barry and Cord walked out of the courtroom. Cord said, "I'm sorry I didn't listen to you, but I couldn't let her get away with that."

"Don't worry, Cord. But wait until you see my bill."

Cord just laughed.

—◦《◉》◦—

Cord's homecoming was uneventful until he had to tangle with his wife. Clara was aware of all the controversy surrounding him and asked him repeatedly if any of the rumors were true. Seeing Cord had failed to even make a single call to her, she could only assume his silence was a sign of guilt. That maybe he didn't want to involve her in any way, shape, or form.

Finally, he said, "Honey, what you don't know won't hurt you."

"Cord, we've been married twenty-seven years, and after those cops in Westport pulled you over, you haven't been the same. I have a right to know. You can't just think about yourself and your big ego.

What about me? What about the kids? You could have been locked up for the rest of your life . . . or even worse."

"There's enough money saved that you and the kids will always be comfortable."

"Cord, that means nothing if you're in jail or you're dead. Look at you. You're limping and you look like you aged five years in three days. Why do men have to be so stupid? Everyone's saying you bombed the judge's house because she refused to give you bail. They're saying you bombed the prosecutor's boat, and that you bombed some politician's house."

"I was in jail. How could I do any of that?"

"What were you and Joe talking about when he visited? You two are as thick as thieves."

"We just caught up. Joe can't talk about his work. You know that."

"You were back to the same old Cord when Joe left. I knew you were up to something. He planned all this. He went to bat for his old friend just like he used to do in college. He loves you like a brother."

Cord remained silent.

"Cord, just tell me the truth and promise me this won't happen again."

"Honey, I'll tell you what. Give me some time. We'll take a nice vacation, and if things are stable, we can discuss this in greater detail."

"Is it over?"

"Almost."

"Almost?"

"Some people will be coming to the house to apologize in the next few days."

"Some people? Like who? Don't tell me those cops are coming?"

Cord did not respond.

"Cord?" Clara was at her wits' end. What people were saying had to be true.

"Clara, these men practically molested Mom as they searched her and accused her of carrying drugs. They grabbed her iPhone.

They lied. They framed me. Actions have consequences. Joe's right. We blacks are gutless. I refuse to have my mother treated like that. And guess what? I won."

He gave his wife a defiant look. "Those cops and the politician who set up the policy of racial profiling will visit us. I expect you to be at my side. You are my wife. We will be polite and civil, and we will accept their apologies."

"And you think humiliating these people is helpful?"

"Yes. It puts them in *their* place."

"Do you really think so?"

"Yes. I do."

"Good. Then you can explain it to your mother. She has been reading about all your adventures on the Internet, and she is *not* pleased. Not pleased at all."

Cord was afraid of this. Heaping on Christian guilt was his mother's specialty.

"I'll speak to my parents now. Are they upstairs?"

"We're not done here."

"Honey, please. There isn't much else to discuss."

Clara relented. Cord had to come to bed sometime and engage in pillow talk. He'd be lucky if she didn't smother him with it. "They're upstairs."

Cord climbed the stairs to the second floor, where he had set up a separate apartment for them. His parents had over 1,500 square feet of living space that included a kitchen, family room, and two bathrooms. He even had an extra bedroom in case help needed to sleep over, although that had not been necessary so far.

His mother was reading the Bible while his dad was watching a baseball game.

Mrs. Campbell set her worn Bible on her lap and glared at him. "Please tell me that what I have been hearing is *not* true."

His father muted the game and turned toward his wife. "Betsy, we discussed this. We don't know if any of this is true, and if it is, Cord did what he had to do."

"Cord, you were raised better that this. Someone could have

been killed," his mother scolded.

"Betsy, please," his father said. "There is nothing to be gained by this discussion. Cord is a good son. He is protecting his family, and he is protecting our race."

Mrs. Campbell held her Bible in the air. "Vengeance is mine; I will repay, says the Lord."

"It also says a wife should obey her husband."

"Not in the case of overwhelming stupidity."

Cord did his best to suppress a laugh. His father walked into this line at least once a year.

"This isn't funny, Cord." His mother shot him a glare.

"Betsy! Enough!"

Mrs. Campbell stared at Cord, then opened her Bible and resumed reading. Herman quickly unmuted the television before she could say another word.

"How they doing?" Cord asked.

"Up four to two. Bottom of the seventh," his father answered, his attention focused back on the television.

One legacy of Cord's friendship with Joe was that he was a hardcore Yankee fan. His father had followed suit.

Cord sat down beside his father. They made strained small talk for several minutes. Finally, he excused himself and gave his mother a kiss. She smiled at him but said nothing.

He went up to his palatial attic and immediately poured himself a huge glass of Louis XIII and fired up an Espléndido. Opening his safe, he pulled out one of the encrypted disposable cellphones Joe had given him.

He sat down in one of the high-backed leather chairs. After the cigar was half-finished, he dialed.

Joe answered immediately. "You okay?"

"Everything's fine. Thanks, Joe."

"Sorry it got a little ugly for you in the jail there."

"You warned me, but I wasn't prepared for it. Even still, it could have been worse."

"Heard you became quite a hero when word got out."

"First time in my life I was ever popular. Felt so good I almost wanted to stay for a few more days to relish in it."

"Are you serious?"

"Joe, I did exactly what you said. Denied everything. But nobody believed me. It was like you said; they came up with a profile, and they knew it was me. And somehow, the prisoners found out too."

"And that made you popular?"

"Popular? I was sitting at the head table in the cafeteria with the meanest guys I've ever seen, signing autographs."

"Are you serious?" Joe chuckled through the phone.

"Swear to God. They lined up while my lawyer waited for me to finish."

"So where do we go from here?" Joe said.

"You take three million."

"Cord, that's ridiculous. I can't take that much."

"All right. Make it four."

"Cord, I have a reasonable salary and a good pension and health insurance for life. And I've stashed away a few bucks. You don't have to do this."

"I'm getting the better end of the deal here. Let's leave it at that three and make sure your sidekick gets at least a million, although I wish he hadn't smashed that guy's teeth out. Was that really necessary?"

"I thought about that . . . Maybe not. But actually, I think the video of it scared the piss out of those people. Quite frankly, I'm amazed we were able to pull this off with so little violence."

"Make sure all that guy's medical bills are paid."

"Will do. Listen. We took about $50,000,000 from your account. The drone cost $20,000,000. Don't ask me what I went through to get that. Greased a lot of palms. A *lot* of palms. You have around $25,000,000 left. To get it back to you will not be easy. They will be watching you very closely. Even if you set up another account, putting the money in there will be a problem."

"Do you think they'll come after me?"

"Cord, here's what I would recommend. If you don't need the

money, let me keep it sheltered. The way it is now, it will be impossible to find it. Besides, I may need a few more bucks."

"But what about the drone?"

"The drone is long gone. It's being shipped out of the country and I've arranged to have it discovered by our military in Syria."

"You mean that it's going back into enemy hands and then found by our military? How are you going to pull that off?"

"Don't ask. Suffice it to say I may need some of the money still in your account."

"But what about you? Won't they suspect you?"

"We have to be careful. That detective Pierre Appollon is a damn genius."

"Who's Appollon?"

"The detective who did the criminal profiling and figured out you were the main suspect. He tried to find out about me. He was unsuccessful, but he is damn suspicious, and he gave my name to Senator Bentley."

"Will they go after you?"

"I doubt it. Too many people owe me favors. Besides, there is no proof of anything."

"How did he figure it out?"

"You know MIT. Everything has to be online, including our yearbooks. He searched ours from Senior Year and saw the picture of you and I shit-faced, celebrating our graduation. He knows I'm in the CIA. He just put two and two together."

"You're right. They can't prove a damn thing. But I'm still worried about you." The concerns Cord had about Joe's involvement in the beginning had now resurfaced in the end.

Joe laughed. "Don't worry, buddy."

"What do you mean 'Don't worry'? You brought a drone into this country and bombed the property of a judge, a prosecutor, and a politician."

"Cord, things like this happen more often than you think. Don't worry. I'll be fine."

"Will we ever be able to see each other again?"

"Not at this point. We'll get together in a couple of years. Until then, never e-mail me. Never refer to this episode to anyone. Not even Clara."

"She knows you're behind it, but she still loves you anyway. She is really pissed at me, though."

"Cord, it had to be done. We had to put the people in power on notice. You have rights. We have rights. Those cops will think twice before they whack another suspect, and word will spread. Those politicians will think twice before they harass law-abiding citizens with silly laws. You've done the country a great service. I'll be in touch when things calm down. Until then, take care, my friend."

"Take care," Cord said. He closed the phone, and it immediately disintegrated. He sipped on his Cognac and took a long draw on the Espléndido. Tears were rolling down his face.

CHAPTER 31

First Selectman Trudeau arrived first. She gazed at the massive Tudor, noting the exquisitely manicured lawn, freshly laid mulch, and wraparound porch. The tulips had just bloomed.

Her husband was still having nightmares. He would wake up in a cold sweat, reliving the miniature tidal wave created when the stone façade of their guest house plunged into their pool. But she was much tougher. Politics had given her a thick skin. He had insisted on coming, but she said no. The e-mail was very explicit. She was to come alone, wear a pantsuit, and make her trademark carrot cake.

Before she could ring the doorbell, the door opened. A handsome black woman in her fifties, also attired in a pantsuit, smiled at her. "You must be Mrs. Trudeau. My name is Clara. Please come in."

Trudeau gave a weak smile and presented her cake.

"Oh, you didn't have to do that."

Clara took the cake. "Cord, Mrs. Trudeau is here," she called out over her shoulder.

Cord walked into the foyer. He was attired in chinos, a collarless white button-down shirt, and a blue blazer. He had not yet gotten a chance to replace his glasses so he was still wearing his old pair.

He extended his hand and gave her a friendly smile. In fact, he had practiced this smile in the mirror. He did not want to smirk. "My name is Cord Campbell. It is a pleasure to meet you."

He looked at the cake. "Carrot cake. One of my favorites. Clara makes a mean carrot cake."

"But it's getting harder to find good buttermilk," Clara said.

"I know," said Trudeau. "The low-fat buttermilk you find in the supermarkets detracts from the flavor. I go to Wades in Bridgeport."

"So do I," said Clara smiling. "Please, make yourself comfortable."

Trudeau was ushered into the family room, filled with comfortable unostentatious furniture and a large flat-screen television. Three large oil paintings depicted a young woman and two young men, all well-groomed and seated in leather chairs holding books.

"Your children?" Trudeau said.

"Yes," Clara replied. "Darryl is in medical school at Tufts. Carol and Robert are still at college."

"They must be good students."

"Carol is," said Cord. "The boys can be lazy at times."

"The same with my boys," Trudeau said.

At this point, Cord's parents walked into the room. Herman was dressed similar to his son, with chinos and a blue blazer, except he wore a collared beige shirt. Mrs. Campbell was attired in a gray skirt that extended to the middle of her calves, along with an orange blouse with white flowers.

The doorbell rang. Cord excused himself and opened the door. There in front of him were Officers Jack Fletcher and Kevin McMahon, both dressed in civilian clothing. Fletcher was holding a bouquet of a dozen roses.

Cord had thought long and hard about how he would handle this moment. He had concluded that false courtesy would send the wrong message and quite frankly, they didn't deserve it. He looked at both men sternly. They gazed back at him, their jaws clenched.

"Come in," Cord said dryly.

He did not offer them his hand. The outrage was gone, but the anger persisted. "You will be presenting those flowers to my mother."

The three men walked into the family room. Trudeau looked at the two officers, tight-lipped.

"I believe you know Ms. Trudeau," Cord said. "That's my wife, Clara." He pointed to Clara.

"Welcome to our home," she said.

"You may recall meeting my parents, Mr. and Mrs. Campbell,"

Cord said. He stared directly into Fletcher's eyes.

Fletcher stepped forward and presented the flowers to Mrs. Campbell. At first, he had told Chief Driscoll he would never apologize; he would rather die. The chief did not respond to Fletcher's statement, but rather he just showed Fletcher the video of Repo having his teeth knocked out and his head dunked in the filthy commode. He then pointed out that Cord had the power to bomb his house at any time. This ended the discussion.

Fletcher said, "I hope you like roses, Mrs. Campbell. My partner and I would like to apologize to you, your husband, and your son for the way we treated you."

Cord had told his mother that the officers were going to visit and apologize, but the whole idea seemed so ridiculous to her that it took several seconds for her to comprehend what was happening. Finally, she said, "Your apology is accepted, but I think you were just doing your job."

McMahon now spoke. "I would also like to offer an apology to you, your husband, and your son."

"Thank you, Officer."

Trudeau stood up and walked over to the elderly black couple. "These men were acting on my orders. It is I who truly owe you an apology, and also to you, Mr. Campbell." She nodded toward Cord.

The elder Mr. Campbell looked at Trudeau. "You and the officers have a difficult job. I've been around a long time, and it isn't easy getting people to live together in peace. I think my son is at fault here too."

Cord raised an eyebrow but gave his father his moment. He deserved it.

Mrs. Campbell now spoke. "Cord looks mild-mannered, but he has always had a vindictive streak. Now that I'm in the house, he is reading the Bible again, every day, like he's supposed to. If people would just follow the Ten Commandments, we wouldn't have any trouble. Right, Cord?"

"Right, Mother."

"Now you nice people sit down," Mrs. Campbell said. "I made

you a Charleston specialty, Huguenot Torte."

"My ancestors were Huguenots," said Trudeau.

"Well, I hope you like it. It's Cord's favorite."

She left the room and quickly returned with a pan of a delightful-smelling concoction of pecans and apples. It invaded Cord's nostrils and spread to his brain, mellowing his personality. He could feel the hate leaving him. He could feel the vindictiveness and ruthlessness leave him. He started to feel guilty. "Mom, could you please say a prayer?"

His mother set the Huguenot Torte on the coffee table and put her hands together. "Lord, we are not perfect. We are sinners. But with your divine love and guidance, we can learn to live together in peace. Thank you for this wonderful food, this wonderful life, and our new friends. Amen."

Cord now smiled warmly at Fletcher and McMahon. "This goes very well with Cognac."

"Cord thinks Lucky Charms go well with Cognac," Clara added.

The two police officers laughed. McMahon said, "I've never had Cognac before, sir."

"Well, you're in for a treat." Cord placed Riedel Vinum glasses in front of the two men and started to pour. Trudeau espied the oblong bottle with the characteristic medallion. "That's Louis XIII."

"Would you like some too, Ms. Trudeau?" Cord offered.

"If you don't mind."

"You just made a friend," Clara said to her. "He can never get me to drink it."

"My lovely bride is a white wine girl," Cord said.

Clara and Mrs. Campbell passed out the Huguenot Torte on Waterford crystal plates.

Trudeau tasted it. "Mrs. Campbell, you must give me the recipe. But it's not really a torte."

"It isn't Huguenot either," Cord said. "It's basically pecan pie without the crust. The Huguenots came to Charleston in 1680 at the behest of Charles II, for whom the city is named. The recipe was modified by a woman who worked in a restaurant called the

Huguenot Tavern, thus, the name. But the original recipe came from the Ozarks."

"There goes Cord, showing off his memory again," his father said.

"Got it from you, Dad."

Fletcher dove into the dessert, demolishing it in several bites. He savored the Cognac. He looked up at Cord's mother. "Mrs. Campbell, may I have another piece?"

She smiled at Officer Fletcher. "It will be my pleasure."

CPSIA information can be obtained
at www.ICGtesting.com
Printed in the USA
BVHW071325291118
534270BV00002B/3/P